Darkwater Echoes

PSI Sentinels: Darkwater Guardians

A PSI Sentinel Novel

Pamela Moran

PSI Sentinels: Guardians of the Psychic Realm
Extraordinary senses in a world full of danger.

Protectors and hunters, PSI agents lay their
abilities, sometimes their lives, on the line. They
defend and shield unwary victims against the
twisted underside of a psychic society bent on
exploiting an unsuspecting, mundane world.

Acknowledgements

M.A. Taylor, Stephanee Ryle, and Janelle Denison

Thank you for your help, your support, but mostly for your friendship.

Ladies, you're the best!

✧ ✧ ✧

Danielle Peterson and Kyle Clark

Danielle, between sunglasses, a persistent pup, wine, and good friends, what a great time we had!

Kyle, with and without weapons, our photo shoot was a blast – looking forward to another project!

Thank you both for making Darkwater's cover so gorgeous.

Dedication

Jim and Shari, extraordinary friends.

Thank you both for exposing me to the beauty of Key Largo and the BVI. Jim, my fellow wordsmith, for the guided tour of the islands, for keeping life fun, for being you. Shari, Jim's a lucky man, but we're also lucky to have you in our lives. Love you both.

As always, Warren. I love you.

Chapter One

FOOTSTEPS POUNDED ACROSS THE deck above. Trent Sawyer, awake at the first thud, rolled from his berth and snatched his gun from under his pillow.

Barefoot and wearing only a black pair of shorts, he ignored the dull throb in his head to shove his senses outward in an attempt to psychically test the boundaries of the boat. Of the structure. Of the space within.

Pain stabbed from inside his skull. Black dots swirled at the perimeter of his sight.

Fuck.

His free hand braced on the wall, he sucked in several quick breaths.

No damn answers. No *extra* info. Nothing but a mental brick wall an inch in front of his face.

He flicked a glance at the ceiling.

That thud hadn't been his imagination.

Psychic senses be damned, he wasn't alone on this boat.

His jaw tight, he moved silently across the dark cabin to the door. He waited several heartbeats before letting the motion of a small wave hitting the side of the sailboat cover the sound of him opening the door a small fraction.

Light from the upper galley spilled through the crack and into his room.

Voices carried down to him, voices that shouldn't have been there – much less arguing over who was going to start the effing boat's engines.

His boss' boat. Neither of those rough voices belonged to the man.

Whoever those bastards on deck were, they weren't stealing *this* boat. Not on Trent's first night. He hadn't been on the boat – or in Key Largo – more than a couple hours.

Not going to happen.

With his gun leading, and his body crouched low, he slipped into the narrow hallway. At the base of the stairwell he slid one bare foot onto the bottom stair, flinched at the soft groan of weathered wood then shifted his weight to ease his other foot up another step.

Then another.

On a deep exhale of breath, he lifted his head above the solid railing. Two men, one a blond giant and the other a squat redhead, both burly and wide through the shoulders, stood across the galley with their backs to him. Their voices lower than earlier, they seemed to be arguing over a sheaf of papers they had spread over the Captain's table.

Now's as good a time as any.

Trent straightened. He aimed his gun at Blondie's head. "What the hell are you doing on my damn boat?"

Both men whipped around, their faces slack with

shock.

A small amount of satisfaction welled in Trent's gut. Mongrels, both of them.

Their eyes brightened and their mouths widened into comical grins. They started forward.

"What the –?" Pain, sharp and sudden, splintered Trent's thoughts.

His world went black.

✧   ✧   ✧

TRENT'S RIGHT CHEEK STUNG, as if it had been cut and smacked one too many times. Both arms ached, like they'd been pulled behind his back for a long period. He tried to move his head but the intense pain rattling around inside made it difficult.

He checked the strong instinct to probe the area with his mind.

Adding to the head pain, right now, wouldn't be the smartest move.

Not that any of his moves had been smart over the last several weeks.

On a held inhale of breath, he forced his left eye open. The right one wouldn't budge. Swollen shut.

What the hell happened?

Dim light, from somewhere behind him, illuminated a faint, half circle around his body. A balmy breeze teased his skin.

Nighttime still.

Bearings. Get your bearings, Sawyer.

He lay face down on the deck of a gently rocking

boat with his left cheek pressed to the cool, damp wood. His breath stuttered in his chest. The brininess of sea water mixed with the lemony scent of whatever had been used to keep the wood conditioned. Both filled his nose.

Was this what peace smelled like? Maybe he could close his one semi-good eye and sleep off whatever nightmare held his mind captive.

"He's coming around." A roughened male voice grated close to his ear.

Guess sleeping it off isn't an option.

Trent gritted his teeth and ignored the pain in his head. He pulled his arms close to his body then pressed both hands flat against the coolness of the damp wood before pushing his upper body from the deck.

Two deep, chortling laughs scraped over him.

Right. The mongrel brigade.

A canvassed sneaker connected hard with his side, just under his rib cage. His breath whooshed out in one short blast and his arms shuddered with the effort to keep from collapsing.

Focus. To get off this boat alive, he *needed* to focus.

He sucked wet, salty air into his burning lungs. His attacker laughed again then geared up for another kick. Trent grabbed the man's burly ankle and foot. He twisted, quick and hard.

The man's scream rent the air as he struggled to pull away. Still holding the guy's ankle, Trent rolled sideways. With a grunt, the man hit the metal railing. Trent let go and kicked upward, connecting with his attacker's mid-section. A loud splash echoed as a wall of water sloshed across the deck.

One down.

Trent, with his hands, knees and feet slipping on the wet deck, pushed himself into a standing position. He kept his back to the thin rail. Every muscle ached, burned from the inside out, but he held his fists in front of him. Dizziness swamped him, those damn black dots swirled inward, but he had no time. No choice. Two other men advanced. Blondie and another that kept to the shadows. Both too tall. The squat redhead must have been the one to go over the railing.

"Who's next?" Trent's nostrils flared. With his vision blurry, he blinked several times while flexing his fists.

"You are." Moonlight glinted off Blondie's teeth as a grin stretched across his clean shaven face.

"Enough already. The night is wasting. Throw him overboard and fish that moron from the water." The other man, his face hidden in darkness as deep as the night he referred to, spun away towards the galley.

Trent nodded once. That one must be in charge. If Boss Man was inside, that just left him and Blondie.

If Trent could keep from keeling over, those were excellent odds.

The blond giant stepped forward and pivoted into a round house kick to Trent's gut. On an outward huff of breath, Trent latched onto Blondie's calf. The man spun away, but Trent held on all the way to the deck. He hit the wood with a hard thud resounding through his body, but he pulled Blondie down with him.

The man swung his fist, connected with Trent's jaw.

Trent's world went black for the second time that night.

✧ ✧ ✧

FOUR IN THE DAMN MORNING.

Jillian Rose shoved her hands through her mussed hair. With narrowed eyes, she stared hard at the front door. She should just leave her sister outside.

February in the Florida Keys. Not like Hayden would freeze to death.

Eventually her sister would stop pounding on the door.

"Jilly, please." Hayden's muffled voice ended with a furious rattle of the door knob. "Let me in."

Jillian dropped her chin to her chest. On an oath she twisted the dead bolt then stepped back to cross both arms over her chest.

The door banged open. Her sister threw a frantic look behind her before she rushed inside, slammed the door closed, and twisted the lock.

Jillian frowned.

Hayden looked wild. With the thick humidity the ends of her tousled, tawny curls stuck to her cheeks and neck. Her tilted, green cat eyes were wide with more than a hint of panic. And her lips trembled.

More drama when Jillian didn't need any theatrics. What she needed was sleep and a sister who could remember where she'd left her keys. Jillian lifted her chin and set her hands on her hips. "What's after you?"

"Nothing. No one." Hayden, her gaze on the floor a

few feet in front of her, launched herself toward the stairs. "I managed to spook myself. That's all."

"Sis –" Jillian shoved her hands through her hair. Stopped. Her sister hit the top of the stairs, flipped the upper hall light on, and banged open her bedroom door.

With every intent of heading straight to bed, Jillian followed but paused at her sister's door. A bright pink, flower-covered duffel sat on the bed. The leg portions of several pairs of Capri pants stuck out from the opening where they'd been shoved into the luggage. A pair of dark blue, canvas deck shoes sat on top of the pants.

"Where are you going?" *Calm. Stay calm. Reasonable, even.* Inside, a scream clawed at her throat.

"Away for a little bit." Hayden's chin jutted but she didn't meet Jillian's gaze. Instead she yanked a green, over-large sweatshirt from her bottom drawer and tossed it on the duffel. "Jazz is taking the Symphony out on a charter around the islands. I'm going to tag along."

One. Two. Deep breath. *Don't lose it.* Three – "*What the hell?* You can't be serious."

Hayden, her hands trembling, picked up the sweatshirt and half folded it, half wadded it around her hands. "What do you want me to say?"

"That you're joking." Jillian stared at the ceiling. Counted to three. Blinked away burning tears before she nailed her sister with a pointed stare. "That you're really not leaving me here to run Rosey's by myself. When I need you the most."

Hayden ran the tip of her tongue along her bottom lip. "I'll be back in a couple of weeks. By the end of the month at the latest."

"Don't run off, Hayden. Not right now." Jillian choked back the furious sob constricting her wind pipe. "In a week or two, we can –"

"In a week or two Jazz will have her boat in Ft. Myers." Hayden lifted her duffel and her chin. "I'll think about coming back then. Get out of my way."

"Hay –"

"Go ahead and say it, Jilly. I look the most like Dad. I *am* the most like Dad." She lifted one side of her mouth, but her green eyes lacked any evidence of humor. "Why are you so surprised I'm doing what I damn well please?"

Stunned, Jillian let her sister shove past.

"Go to bed, Jilly." Hayden snapped off her bedroom light. "You look awful."

SALTWATER, A COLD CARESS OVER TRENT'S BODY, stung through the abrasions along his jaw and the cut on his cheek. That water filled his nose, his mouth. Gagged him. He shook his head, ignored the burst of pain at his temples. Tried to clear his throat but only succeeded in sucking in more water.

Fuck.

Except for a wavering, dim light somewhere above him, all was dark.

Reflex kicked in and he clawed his way upwards. As he broke the surface he gasped air into his burning lungs.

He bobbed in the water for several moments, trying

not to breathe too fast. The blond giant's loud, harsh laughter carried over the thick air. Trent twisted towards the sound.

Those flea-bitten mongrels had dumped him into the sea. That wavering light had to be the back of his boss' sailboat as it motored away.

Trent smacked the surface of the water with the flat of his hand.

Fucking blond asshole.

Somehow, somewhere, he'd find the prick. Do something about him.

With or without his currently undependable – as in completely absent – *special* hunter skills.

He smacked the water again.

The prick would pay.

Treading water, Trent watched the boat slip further into the darkness of an endless ocean and black sky.

Time to regroup.

On a deep inhale of breath, he twisted in the water to take in his surroundings. In the opposite direction of the boat, lights glittered along a lengthy snake line of shore.

A *long* distance away.

His head ached, his jaw throbbed and the cuts on his cheek stung from saltwater in the open wounds. He glanced over his shoulder at the faint outline of the retreating boat. Then back at the lights.

Two choices. Stay here and drown. Or swim for the lights along the shore.

His own bark of humorless laughter echoed over the water. How many years later and that godforsaken SEAL training was still saving his life?

With his pace calculated and even, he set off toward the shoreline.

After what seemed a long period of time, gold rimmed the sky behind him. Dawn was finally breaking, but was he any closer to land?

The unmistakable roar of a large engine filled the air.

He sucked in a wheezy breath before glancing over his shoulder in the direction of the revving motor. In the space of a heartbeat, the bow of a charging boat loomed over him. He jack-knifed under the surface as the boat veered sharp to the right.

He hadn't gotten this far to be sliced apart by some fancy power boat.

Dark water churned and slithered around his exhausted body. He fought his way back to the surface. Gasped for air, sucked it deep into his aching lungs.

Bright light blinded him.

What the hell?

The muscles in his arms burned, but he treaded water as he angled his head away from the spotlight whoever stood on the bow of that boat aimed at him.

A loud splash sent more salty water into his nostrils and mouth.

"Grab hold." A loud voice over an outdoor speaker echoed across the water. "We'll pull you in."

Blindly reaching out, Trent's hand brushed something solid. He gripped it, pulled it closer. Some kind of flotation device.

The spotlight's glow widened, no longer tightly focused on him. He wrapped his arms around the circular device and, with blessedly little effort on his part, moved toward the bright light as they reeled him in like some big catch of the day.

Hopefully these guys were the good guys.

He'd had enough of the bad ones for a while.

At the boat, arms reached down to grab his shoulders and slip under his armpits.

"We've got you."

Trent nodded once then glanced to the side of the boat at the words on the white hull.

Marine Patrol.

About damn time something went his way.

Chapter Two

A BALMY AFTERNOON BREEZE drifted across Blackwater Sound and through the open framework of Rosey's Place. The fake thatched roof above Jillian rustled in the empty quietness. She dropped her damp rag on the wooden counter.

What she wanted to do was throw the damn rag across the room, along with anything else she could find.

Since she was the only one here, she could get away with a fit of rage.

But what good would letting go of her temper really do? She'd only have to pick up the pieces and clean up whatever mess she made.

With her sister gone and her bartender out sick, what Jillian needed to do was conserve her energy for the evening crowd. That and pray she didn't get swamped.

Even though we could sure use the money.

Movement near the entrance caught her eye. She straightened. Her easy smile faltered at the sight of the man standing there with his hands splayed at his hips. Blue jeans sat loose on those hips and a black T-shirt stretched across his broad shoulders.

Whoever he was, he wasn't local.

Dark sunglasses covered his eyes. A red, welted cut marked his right cheek and angry abrasions lined his jaw. Abrasions a stubbly five o'clock shadow in the middle of the afternoon couldn't hide.

Her mouth went dry.

Definitely not local, she would have remembered him.

Danger that had more to do with the aura surrounding him than the fact he'd been in a recent fight hung in the humid air, swirled with the languid breeze.

Although she couldn't see his eyes, the sweep of his gaze hit *every* one of her nerve endings, sparking little fires over *every* inch of her skin.

Her stomach muscles clenched. She didn't need that sudden flicker of attraction, the kind that started low in the belly and blazed at the worst possible time.

Like now.

No, this man was the kind Grandma Rosey had warned her and her sister about from the time they'd first noticed boys. And this man was no boy. He was the type she needed to run away from, as far and fast as she possibly could. That overwhelming awareness be damned.

Those abrasions along his jaw spoke volumes.

She'd had enough of men who used their fists to further their aims.

Whatever those aims might be.

She picked up her damp rag, folded it in half. "What can I get you this afternoon?"

"Whatever you have on tap." The deepness of his

voice sent quivers all along her nerves. He dropped his hands from his hips and advanced a few steps closer.

Oh, hell no. She shook her head. Him parked at her counter while she worked? She so didn't need that kind of distraction. "Grab a table and I'll bring it to you."

One side of his mouth quirked. He nodded then tilted his head slightly from side to side as if he worked out kinks that still lingered.

From under her lashes she watched him settle into a rattan chair backed against the building's one full solid wall. Even without seeing his eyes, the man was handsome. And fit. The ruggedness of his face and the tan on those muscular arms spoke of time spent outdoors.

She even liked his close-cropped, nearly black hair and that stubble along his chin and jawline.

Bad news, no matter how she looked at it. Or him.

On a resigned sigh she inched the bat she kept on the top shelf under the bar a bit closer before she pulled a chilled pilsner glass from the cold box. With practiced ease she drew his beer from the center tap, took a quick, fortifying breath and a last, longing look at her bat, then sauntered over to his table.

"Here you go." She set the glass down and dredged up a smile. "If you're hungry, our grouper sandwich is about the best on the island. Or I can get you a menu."

"The beer is enough for right now." Again, the man's voice, deep with gravel scrubbed all through it, flared those embers at the pit of her belly. One corner of his mouth lifted in a devastating half smile that creased his injured right cheek.

Not my type, remember?

Maybe not, but she bet those concealed eyes were blue. She'd like to see if they matched the rest of him, see if what lay hidden behind those dark sunglasses sparked with ice as cold as a Dakota snow storm or burned with a heat as brilliant as a Keys' winter sunset.

Positive she had better things to do than drool over the man's possible blue eyes, she gave him a quick nod and spun back towards the bar.

Get hold of yourself.

Saved by the sound of someone else entering the bar, she let her shoulders droop for a quick moment then glanced over her shoulder. "Dane."

Dane Patrick, family friend and someone different to focus on. Someone who, regardless of how good looking, didn't trip her up the way her customer did by just sitting there.

"Hey, Sugar." Dane's lopsided smile warm and safe, he jiggled the handle of his guitar case as he strolled into the room. "Mind if I play tonight? Unless you have someone else scheduled?"

"No one else all week." Although once word leaked out he was here, she had no clue how she was going to keep on top of the crowd. People enjoyed Dane's slow, rich voice and the ballads he sang with such depth. "We always love to have you play."

The extra money would be nice, too.

"I'm going to set up then." Angling himself between her and the stranger, Dane nodded once at the man before scanning the room. He set his case on a table between them. "Where's Hayden?"

From behind the bar, Jillian mentally cursed her sister's sorry ass. Dane was more than half in love with Hayden, although neither one seemed inclined to act on it.

Like she, herself, could talk.

Jillian picked up her damp rag and slid a sideways look at the stranger who sat nursing his beer and staring out over the rippling water before she answered Dane's question. "Out with Jazz."

With only a shrug, Dane pulled his guitar from its case. He spent several minutes tuning the instrument. Soft strands of music drifted in the air.

"Sugar, if you rub that any harder, you're going to scrub away the scars." A soft chuckle lined the edges of Dane's voice.

Jillian paused, realized what she'd been doing and made a face before dropping the rag on the marked surface of the wooden bar. "If that was all it took, I'd stand here all day and do my best to rub away those damnable scars."

His dark eyes clouded for a moment before he raised a brow and his enigmatic gaze searched hers. "Wouldn't we all?"

She closed her eyes as Dane began to sing. A few years older than her, he had a voice as smooth as the oldest, prime whiskey. Not anything like the underlying roughness in her only customer's voice.

Jillian snuck an under the lashes glance at the

stranger. He still sat slouched in his chair, his head angled as if he glared out at the water. But his posture seemed a bit too stiff, too alert, almost like his attention focused more on her and Dane's conversation.

With only three people in the place, though, who could blame him for eavesdropping?

Hopefully they were more entertaining than whatever had his mouth set in a hard edge to suggest he wasn't all that happy with life right at that particular moment.

Jillian understood the sentiment.

She picked up her rag, swiped it with emphasis over an imaginary spot of dust, and turned her back on the two men.

She loved Rosey's. The Unofficial Yacht Club of Blackwater Sound.

Her grandmother had built the place from nothing more than a rundown tiki-bar with a leaking thatched roof. The only thing going for it had been its location at the end of a rickety pier.

Now the place commanded the best view on the Sound and sported a section of glass topped tables each with matching glass bases inserted between the wooden planks of the floor for an open view to the water underneath. Even the manatees occasionally came out to play.

Rosey's also had an open kitchen behind the bar area, the part Jillian preferred to work, taking turns with their one cook.

A short stack of glasses behind the bar rattled.

Jillian frowned.

The glasses rattled again.

"*What?*" She kept the hiss of her voice low, hoping the two men wouldn't hear her.

Silence.

Dammit, Rosey.

How was Jillian supposed to understand what her grandmother, Lilith Rose, namesake of Rosey's Place, wanted when all she did was rattle glasses or toss silverware?

Or sometimes plates.

Jillian rubbed her forehead.

I know you're here, Rosey. I just don't know what you want.

The chug of a dingy motor cut across the soft strums of Dane's guitar. Jillian spared another glance for the now motionless glasses before turning her gaze out over the Sound, towards the long bridge connecting their part of Key Largo to the mainland of the Florida peninsula.

Oasis II. Ben Garrett's dinghy.

Ben had called the day before and left a message on the bar's answer machine. She hadn't gotten around to listening much less calling him back.

In the past, he and her grandmother had an understanding. He'd let her know when he lent the boat to one of his down and out friends so she could keep an eye on them – the friend and the sailboat – and he'd let Rosey use the boat whenever she wanted to spend an afternoon sailing.

Jillian supposed she now had the same arrangement with Ben. But who had time to lounge around on a boat for hours?

Hayden.

Jillian's lips tightened before she forced a smile at the man tying up against the end of the pier. Huge, as in body-builder huge, and so blond his hair was almost white, the man pulled himself up onto the wooden planks of the pier. He smiled back, but his frosty blue eyes remained chilly.

Okay, then.

Thank goodness for Dane's presence. Her bartender, usually here in the afternoons, had called in sick. While Jillian could take care of herself, and normally didn't let customers get to her, something about this one set the hair at the back of her neck to attention.

Then again, that might have something to do with the open cut on his chin and the swelling along his jaw. Another man who had recently been in a fight.

She glanced over her shoulder at Dane. He strummed his guitar and watched her back.

With a smile pasted to her lips, she took the few steps to the end of the bar where it abutted the railing. She braced her hands on the curved edge. "What can I get for you today?"

"A phone." The hulk of a man stood on the wood planking of the pier, at the opening into the bar area. He jerked his head towards the Sound. "My boat is having engine trouble, and the radio quit working."

"Your boat?" She cocked her head to the side. "The Oasis? Did you want me to call Ben for –"

"Son of a –" From behind her, her lone, handsome customer hurled himself across the half wall separating them from the end of the pier.

He tackled the hulk, bringing them both down on the wood planks just inside the opening. The entire structure shook. One of her blue, wooden bar stools toppled on top of the two men. The hulk, who was on top, shook himself. The stool lifted and went over the pier railing, hitting the water with huge splash.

Ah, shit. She'd actually finished painting that chair. *This needs to stop.*

Adrenalin pounding through her veins, Jillian yelled as she grabbed her baseball bat from under the bar. Both men ignored her while they struggled to stand and swing their fists at each other. Dane appeared behind her and, in one smooth move, hopped over the top of the bar. She scrambled after him.

"Guys." Dane shoved his way between them. He took a hit to his chin but caught their lone customer's offending fist in his hand. He flattened his other palm against the hulk's heaving chest. "That's enough."

"Says who?" The customer yanked his fist from Dane's grip.

"Me." Jillian's heart beat a rapid tempo that pulsed in her ears, but she gripped the wooden bat in both hands. She pressed the rounded end at the center of their customer's chest. His sunglasses gone in the scuffle, she met his deep, blue-eyed gaze. Anger, hot and bubbling, boiled just below the surface, matching the swelling almost closing his right eye.

Something even more primal than mere attraction stirred inside her, tightening into a hard knot at the center of her belly. His left eye widened a fraction, but Jillian tightened her grip on the bat's handle. "Not in my bar."

"He stole my boat." The man's nostrils flared.

Behind her, the hulk from the dinghy growled.

"The Oasis?" With her bat and a slight amount of pressure, Jillian pushed the angry, dark blue-eyed man back a foot. "She doesn't belong to either of you."

Without even glancing at the bat against his chest, her customer's lip curled. The split at the corner of his mouth oozed blood he didn't bother wiping. His hot gaze held hers. "Call the police."

"After I call Ben." She pushed him back another foot. Without lowering the bat or taking her gaze off his, she reached into the front pocket of her jeans for her cell phone.

Behind her, the hulk growled again. Dane lurched to the side, stumbling into her and knocking her off balance. The man in front, her customer, wrapped his arms around her waist and swung her away from the rail. Electricity fired along all of her nerve endings.

Dane went down, hitting the wooden planks hard. The hulk went over the side and into the dinghy.

Her customer tightened his arm around her. He twisted the bat away from her with the other hand. His gaze stayed on the dinghy making a wide turn away from the pier. "*Son of a bitch.*"

His movements slow, Dane pushed himself into a kneeling position. He stayed there for a moment then pressed his hands to his knees and rolled his head side to side. "Call the Sheriff's office, Jillian."

With the stranger's one arm around her, she grabbed at the bat but the man swung it to the other side. He turned that deep, blue-eyed gaze on her. She ignored the heat quivering in the pit of her belly and matched the man's glower.

He let go of her and rotated both his shoulders, the movement slow as if he hurt more than this little scuffle warranted. He took two steps back. "Is there another boat?"

Like she'd let this cretin take her boat.

"Guess not." He offered her the bat. She snatched it before fishing her phone from her jean's pocket.

The man shoved one hand over the top of his short hair. He offered the other hand to Dane and pulled him to his feet. Then the stranger scooped his sunglasses from the planking and shoved them over his eyes.

With the cell phone to her ear and her own eyes narrowed, Jillian moved a few feet away. The man leaned his back against the bar. Although his eyes were now covered, the heat of his gaze still scorched her skin, still coiled in a knot low in her belly.

She had her answer. His eyes were the same intense blue as the water at the deepest point of Blackwater Sound. No chilliness to speak of – just pure heat. The kind that would burn if she got too close.

On an out puff of breath, Jillian nodded at Dane who now stood on the other side of the man. She moved a few more feet away. Not that it did any good. Awareness singed her nerves.

Wrong man. Sure as hell the wrong time.

Chapter Three

"TRENT SAWYER." Trent extended his right hand to the man at his side, but kept the feisty black haired woman – Jillian, the musician had called her – in his periphery view. Probably shouldn't have given her back the damn bat, seeing how he'd ticked her off. Even with her cell phone to her ear, she looked like she still wanted to beat him with her bat.

The late afternoon breeze through the open structure of the bar played through the long length of her hair, left him with an itch to brush it away from her face. There was something in the spark of her honey brown eyes that tightened his gut, sent his mind down roads he hadn't come here to head down.

He wasn't here for sex.

"Dane Patrick."

Trent yanked his thoughts away from the woman and gripped the man's hand for a long moment. Patrick's handshake was firm. Solid. The distrust in his dark eyes almost tangible. Trent balled his other hand into a fist.

While this didn't look good, he wasn't sure he cared. He'd almost had the son of a bitch who'd stolen Ben's boat. And, despite the number of times Trent had landed his fists on the asshole's body and face, he hadn't been able to *tag* the bastard.

How the hell was he going to track the guy if he couldn't hold any sense of the prick inside his own pain laced head?

Give it time, Ben had said. Don't push.

Fuck that.

Patrick squeezed his hand once in warning then let go.

Fuck that, too. Trent splayed his hands at the waist of his borrowed, too loose, jeans.

"Shamus is out for the day and another detective is out on a call." The woman, Jillian, swiped a long, thick strand of rich, black hair away from her face. Sunlight burst from behind a cloud to momentarily spark raven blue glimmers through her hair, glimmers he'd bet hadn't come from any bottle.

Those blows to his jaw and head must have done more damage than he'd thought. Her suspicion filled eyes made mush of his mind. Along with the rest of her. That thin grey T-shirt with the wild red roses emblazoned across her chest didn't help his frame of mind or his attempt to think with any degree of rationality.

His latest mantra echoed in his head. *No sex.* Especially since she'd probably rather see him dunked back in the salt water than have anything to do with him.

"Trent Sawyer." Against all levels of better judgment, he held out his hand. "And you are?"

Her gold-flecked eyes narrowed to thin slits. She ignored his hand. "Jillian Rose. They're sending the deputy out as soon as he's freed up."

He forced a smile and kept his expression bland. "Since you don't have a boat and I can't chase the thieving bastard, I'll just wait here."

"I didn't say I didn't have a boat."

He tried to keep his gaze from following the slide of her cell phone as she slipped it into her jean's pocket. Her words registered. His gaze jerked to her shadowed gaze. "Why didn't you tell me you had a boat when I asked?"

"You're not touching my boat."

"So you may as well make yourself comfortable, Sawyer." The musician, Dane Patrick, gripped his shoulder. Squeezed. Indicated Trent should precede him to the back side of the bar. "Have a drink."

Why the hell not?

He'd been checkmated. Pure and simple. With his *hunter* skills out of commission, he couldn't track the blond asshole. And without Jillian's boat, it wasn't as if he had the means to go after him at the moment anyway.

Then there was the view of her swaying hips as she made her way to the other side of the bar. *No sex.* He had an asshole to catch. "How long do they think it will take your deputy to break free and join us?"

She shot a glance over her shoulder. "He's working a case with Shamus' trainee, so there's no telling."

"Who died?" Patrick asked from behind him. "Or should I ask who killed who?"

Trent stopped. He slipped off his borrowed sunglasses. "You called homicide about my missing boat?"

27

Patrick's hand firm in the middle of Trent's back, he gave a small shove.

Trent threw him a dirty look, but took the few steps to the end of the bar. This, too, would pass. *Keep telling yourself that, Sawyer.* He settled onto a solid-looking blue wooden stool badly in need of paint and reminiscent of a life guard chair. His movements slow and deliberate, he set his borrowed sunglasses on the darkly aged wooden counter and leaned forward on his elbows. A few feet away, at the end of the bar, Patrick did the same.

"No idea who died." Jillian slipped behind the counter. "Shamus is an old friend, but they said he's out sick. The deputy will get to the bottom of this."

"It's simple. That blond son-of-a —" Trent straightened, fisted his hands. He already had every nerve the woman had at attention, along with her smirking body guard. *Dammit.* He *hated* being hamstrung. Unable to *sense* anything, unable to move the slightest bit forward. But he had to curb his mouth. "That man stole my boat. What is there to get to the bottom of except to find the prick? And my boat."

"Ben Garrett's boat." Jillian banged her bat down on a shelf underneath the bar. "Not yours."

"That's right." He leaned against the slatted back support of his stool. "You know Garrett. Which is why I'm here."

"What do you mean?" Patrick shifted his weight forward onto his crossed arms. His dark gaze bore into Trent's.

"Garrett said to see the girls at Rosey's Place if I

needed anything. I had the sheriff's deputy drop me here after I reported the boat stolen." Trent didn't see any reason to get into the rest of the story.

"Why didn't you say so?" Jillian tilted her head to the side. Did she ever not have her eyes narrowed down to thin slits?

"I was a little busy trying to restrain the prick who stole my – Ben's boat."

"Grabbing him and trying to beat him to a pulp is what you call restraining?" Her eyes widened in mock horror.

That wasn't much better. "In this case. Yes."

Patrick chuckled. "So you are the one who did that to his face? Earlier?"

Trent rubbed his own sore jaw. Nodded.

"Ben knows his boat was stolen?" Jillian fished her cell phone back out of her pocket.

Trent pulled his gaze away from the woman's body only to meet Patrick's impassive one.

Not my fault the woman's hot. He lowered his chin, narrowed his left, not-as-swollen eye. The swelling on the right one hurt all the way down his cheek and back through the middle of his head. One side of Patrick's mouth lifted.

Trent resisted flipping the man the finger. Instead he met Jillian's suspicious gaze. "Yeah. Garrett knows."

Hadn't that been a fun conversation? It still stuck in his craw that his boss wanted him to borrow a few dollars, for a few days, from some female he didn't know. He didn't want to think about the ribbing he'd get once he made it back to DC.

"Why don't we talk to him, anyway?" Jillian punched a few numbers on her cell before tossing it to Trent.

He caught the phone and smiled even though it pulled at the cut on his lip. Then he punched the off button. A frown drew her brows down. Her nostrils flared. She opened her mouth, probably to ream him.

A loud, explosive noise ripped through the area. Trent shoved the phone in his pocket at the same time he jumped from his stool and headed to the far end of the bar with Patrick and Jillian at his heels.

Small chunks of wooden debris landed several feet from the pier, scattered and floating on top of the water. Behind a nearby spit of land, dark flames roiled and reached up against a sky darkening with smoke.

Trent shoved both hands through his short hair. "That piece of shit blew up my boat."

✧ ✧ ✧

JILLIAN STOOD TRANSFIXED between the railing and the bar, her gaze locked on the flames reflecting across the afternoon waters of the Sound.

What happened?

An explosion, fire in the same direction the blond hulk of a man had taken the Oasis dinghy such a short time ago.

Is anyone hurt?

She threw a quick glance around Rosey's Place then scrambled behind the bar to grab the key to her boat before tossing Dane a quick look.

"Go. I've got Rosey's. I'll call the Sheriff." Dane turned to Trent. "Go with her."

"What?" Jillian's hand tightened on the floaty attached to her key, her fingers digging into the spongy material. Dane had to be kidding.

"Let's go." Trent bumped into her, wrapped both hands around her upper arms. "No time to stand here."

Heat from his fingers blazed through the thin cotton of her T-shirt to spiral into a tight coil in the center of her belly. *Dammit.* She didn't need this kind of reaction. Not now. Certainly not with one of Ben Garrett's rescue cases.

With one harsh shrug, she shook off Trent's hands. She leveled a quick, dark look at Dane.

He'd pay for this. Later.

Her small power boat, tied to the railing at the back side of the pier, sat rocking in the disturbed Gulf waters. With her steps sure and agile, she made her way onto her boat. She had it powered up and purring before Trent had the ropes undone. He pushed the boat away from the pier and leapt on board with an agility that spoke of much time spent on the water.

But then, Ben had loaned him his boat, hadn't he?

Behind the wheel she remained standing, her hands sure on the controls. Without a word, she slowly accelerated until she was away from Rosey's. After that she opened the throttle. The boat bounced on the waves as she wove to avoid the bits of debris from whatever had exploded. Sea spray hit full in her face, stinging her cheeks, but she didn't slow down.

Someone could be hurt. Hers was one of the closest boats.

Next to her, Trent gripped the metal tubing along the top of the console. He kept his mouth shut, for that she was glad. Maybe he did know his way around boats, but that was about all any of Ben's friends were worth. *Damaged goods* her grandmother had called them. Men wounded inside, down-and-outers. Freeloaders who never had a pot to pee in or anything else to call their own.

Like her own *freeloading* father. Not that she'd call her dad wounded. Manipulative, charismatic and cagey. But not wounded.

She slid a sideways look at the man next to her. Maybe they weren't all like her father, but her grandmother's warnings still rang clear in her head. Stay away from Ben's friends.

Especially the handsome ones with a touch capable of turning her insides to liquefied jelly.

With hard won resolve, Jillian shoved those thoughts aside and steered her boat around the spit. She sucked in a startled breath.

Large chunks of charred debris floated on the water while the hull of what once might have been a sailboat still burned. The Oasis. No one on board could have survived when she blew.

Trent swore low and under his breath. He stood beside her, his mouth tight. A nerve along the edge of his abraded jaw throbbed.

She held her boat at an idle. Under her lashes she

glanced at the furious man next to her.

Was he thinking about having to tell Ben they'd found his boat, only there was nothing left? Or was he thinking about finding the thief and beating him to a pulp?

She bet the latter. A shiver trembled along her spine.

All that fury, justified or not, she'd hate to have it turned on her.

Chapter Four

FROM TRENT'S SEAT, with his back against the only real wall in Rosey's Place, he watched Jillian Rose wipe the same spot on her bar for what had to be the tenth time. In between filling drink orders for the full crowd of customers.

People curious about the earlier explosion, those looking for information and gossip. They just kept coming. Good for business, obviously hard on Jillian's nerves. Even around the full smile she aimed at everyone she talked with throughout the evening, she looked tired. Shadows full of worry darkened the honeyed brown of her eyes.

About more than Ben Garrett's blown up boat?

Why the hell does that answer matter? He wasn't here to get involved with the locals. Not beyond finding that asshole prick. *Then I'm gone.* Out of here like yesterday's bad bourbon.

Night had barely settled. The musician – Dane Patrick – strummed his guitar and sang some kind of slow, sad country song. Couples swayed together in the small clearing at the center of a sea of full tables.

Jillian glanced his way, her look pointed at the cell

phone on the table in front of him. He gave a short shake of his head. Ben hadn't returned their call. Trent settled further back in his seat, his legs stretched out as far as he could, given the crowd.

Dammit, Ben.

Everything Trent had brought down from DC had been on that boat. His Federal ID, credit cards. His cash. The clothes he now wore he'd borrowed earlier from one of the local deputies. The deck shoes belonged to one of the Marine Patrol officers who'd fished him out of the Atlantic and been near his size.

Not that he was ungrateful. He'd used the twenty the deputy had spotted him to pay for his earlier beer along with the one he now nursed. That left a few dollars in his pocket. Not enough for a motel room or even a taxi to get him to that room.

Man, he wanted this past him. Wanted to be back in DC. Hell, he'd even take Minnesota, as cold as it was at the headquarters for the covert psychic agency Ben headed. Right now, Trent wanted to be working whatever case had his Task Force boss unable to call him back. He cursed Ben all over again.

On the table, Jillian's cell phone vibrated. Trent slammed his mug down and snatched the phone. With the cell to his ear he could barely hear Ben. "Hold on. Let me find a quiet corner."

He caught Jillian's eye. She jerked her head toward the area of the pier where she'd tied her boat. He nodded before heading that way. Once away from the crowd he breathed a quick sigh of relief.

Maybe all this crap was about over.

"Ben –"

"You're going to have to stay put, for a couple of days at least."

"Son of a bit—"

"Cussing isn't going to fix it, buddy boy." Papers shuffled. "That digging you did earlier this month panned out, but we can't talk about it on this phone."

"Then I should be there, not stuck here—"

"Trying to avoid suspension. That hasn't changed."

Trent blew out a pent up breath. He leaned his elbows on the wooden railing. Ben was right, much as it stuck in his craw to admit it. "When—"

"A couple of days at most. I'll get some money wired to Jillian tomorrow. Enough to hold you over."

"My ID?" A tickle of a breeze brought the smell of something being grilled. His stomach grumbled. He hadn't eaten since he'd left DC the day before. "How about a gun?"

"Soon as I can."

"Meanwhile?"

"Ask Jillian to take you in. I'm sure she could use the help. They're always understaffed."

"You want me to tend bar?"

"Yeah." More papers shuffled in the background. "And Trent? While you're there relaxing, find out who stole my *friggin'* boat. And why they felt the need to blow her to pieces."

The call disconnected. Silence echoed in Trent's ear.

"Son of a fucking bitch."

"You swear a lot, don't you?" Jillian's soft voice came from behind him.

His eyes closed for a brief moment. With his thumb and forefinger, he rubbed at his aching temples. He hadn't *felt* her behind him. Not an inkling. Nothing. That fact coated the lead ball at the center of his stomach. He consciously loosened the tightness in his jaw before facing her. "Stress reliever."

"Does it work for you?"

"Are you a goody two shoes who never swears?" He held her cell out to her.

"No." She laughed, the sound gentle on the softness of the breeze. "Just wondering if you have any better luck with that than I do."

Her fingers brushed his as she claimed her phone. An electric current shot through to his feet. He straightened and stepped away until his back braced the railing and the wood bit through his shirt. Her eyes narrowed. She touched her upper lip with the tip of her tongue. With effort, he pulled his gaze away from her mouth. *Damn pretty woman.* Feisty, not afraid to defend what was hers. Those guarded eyes were wary and shadowed with their own secrets.

Bad combination for his peace of mind.

"So." She glanced away from him and then back. "What did Ben have to say?"

Ben? Oh yeah. His boss, who'd left him stranded. "To stay put. Find who stole his boat and why."

She frowned as she shook her head. "That's a job for the Sheriff's Department or for the Coast Guard. Not us."

"He didn't say us. He told *me*."

"On my cell phone."

"What does that have to do with anything?"

"Nothing at all." Her frown deeper, she tilted her head to the side. "I suppose he also expects me to take you in tonight. Feed you. Give you a bed."

Ouch. Trent worked his jaw. Shrugged. "He mentioned you might have room for me. Just until I can get this straightened out. Figure out what I need to do next."

"Hmmm. Right." The slightest level of derision coated her voice. "Come on then. Of all nights, my bartender called in sick. I could use the help." She lifted her chin, squared her shoulders and moved away from him. "You may as well earn your keep."

JILLIAN, FROM UNDER HER LASHES, watched Trent mix the psychedelic pink martini for the dainty blonde sitting dead center at the bar with her bare, shapely legs dangling and toe rings on both sandaled feet. The woman's nails – fingers and toes – were painted a bright, vibrant red.

Clear coat was all Jillian had time to deal with, and that was probably chipped. Irritated with herself, and refusing to examine her own nails, she swiped the damp cloth over the section of bar nearest her.

Trent sure knew his way around mixed drinks and beautiful women.

Why did that bother her so much? It wasn't like she

should care one way or another.

So why did she?

The stack of glasses behind her rattled, clinking against each other.

Her mouth tight, she lifted her chin and threw a narrowed glance behind her. "Okay Rosey. I get it."

"Excuse me?" From his corner of the bar Trent's warm voice melted over her.

Forget the warmth and humidity of a Keys' winter evening. That gravel in his voice was all she needed to heat her insides. With a shake of her head, she internally cursed the man. Cursed herself. Her grandmother. "Never mind."

He shrugged one shoulder and gave the blonde her change along with a huge smile before throwing Jillian a quizzical look.

She tossed her rag onto the shelf under the counter.

Let him wonder.

Not that she was normally this pissy, but why did she care what he thought? Mr. Trent – only here for a few days – Sawyer, what made him so different?

She shot a glare over her shoulder at the now silent stack of glassware.

"Jillian? Trent?" Deputy Ted Mathews, with the Marine Enforcement Division of the Sheriff's Department, picked his way through the crowd. The starched white of his uniform shirt still looked pressed and neat. Impressive feat, especially given the humidity level of the Keys and the amount of time he spent on the water.

She plucked at her wilted Rosey's Place T-Shirt then

wiped her hands down the thighs of her worn jeans.

The little blonde's face screwed up in a pout when Trent moved away. A small lilt of satisfaction shivered its way up Jillian's spine.

Silly woman.

Her or the blonde, she wasn't sure.

"Ted." Trent, moving to stand next to Jillian, leaned across the bar to shake the officer's hand. "Any word on how the Oasis managed to blow herself up?"

"Why don't we move this out to the back of the pier where it'll be more difficult to overhear?" She aimed a bright smile at the scowling blonde before catching the eye of one of her waitresses. The woman would cover the bar while they talked with Ted.

A tiny bounce in her step, Jillian led the way to where her boat arced and dipped in the swell of water bumping against the wooden pylons. The balmy night breeze tickled her hair across her cheeks, bringing with it the briny scent of the Sound.

"How do you two know each other?" She leaned back to brace her elbows on the wooden railing. Trent and Ted stood facing each other, bracketing her.

"This morning I took the stolen report about the Oasis." Ted grinned, a quick flash of white teeth in the dim light. "Found some clothes he could borrow. Since it was Ben's boat, I dropped Trent off here once we were through."

"And loaned me twenty bucks." Trent pulled a few bills from his pocket.

Ted frowned, but took the money.

"She's a slave driver. Making me work for my board. But the tips are good."

Even in the low light, humor glinted in Trent's eyes, stabbing her right at the center of her chest, stealing her breath. She lowered her lashes to stare at the railing on the opposite side. The man was handsome when he smiled. Dangerously handsome. The swollen eye and abrasions only added to the ruggedness, that aura of danger.

Nothing she needed in her life. Not even temporarily. Once Ben wired Trent his money and sent the other things he needed, Trent Sawyer would be gone.

The sooner the better.

Jillian straightened and shoved her hands into the front pockets of her jeans. "So why did the Oasis blow?"

Ted tucked the money in his pants pocket. He shifted his weight, spread his feet a little further apart. "Found a couple of witnesses who saw someone racing away from the Oasis in a dinghy just before she blew. Matches your description of the man from earlier."

"The same one who stole her in the first place." Trent's face tightened.

"Looks to be." Ted pulled a small notebook from his shirt pocket. "These witnesses say the man aimed and fired what appears to have been a flare gun towards the galley of the boat. Moments later she went up."

"Propane? From the galley stove?" Jillian glanced between the two men.

"That's a strong possibility." Ted met Trent's stony gaze. "The dive team will be on this at first light."

"What about the man?" Trent ran a hand over his head, then his knuckles over his jaw. "Where did he go?"

"That's the kicker. The blast pulled the witnesses' attention away from him and, as they put it, he up and disappeared. Dinghy and all."

"Son of a bit—" Trent snapped off the last word. He twisted away and smacked the railing with his open palm.

Jillian flinched.

Dammit, when would she stop doing that?

No man would make her his punching bag, not ever again. Those days were long over. She lifted her chin and deliberately ignored the angry buzz in Trent's gaze. Shutters slammed down over his eyes. Total blankness stared back at her.

God. Where did he go? Just like that?

The urge to rub her hands over her bare arms, even in the balmy February air, rose inside. She fisted her hands in her pockets and deliberately angled away from Trent's empty stare.

Screw him.

She faced Ted, instead. "Now what? Do you get hold of the Coast Guard?"

"We've been in contact." Ted glanced between the two of them then flipped several pages over in his notebook. He shook his head. "Any ideas about who this guy is and what he and his buddies wanted with the Oasis?"

"Buddies?" Jillian flicked a quick glance at Trent.

His expression had melted into one of wary watchfulness. "There were at least three."

"Smugglers? Pirates possibly?" Ted stuffed the notebook into his shirt pocket before he speared Trent with a direct look. "I'd say you being alive messed with their plans. Might want to watch your back. Hate to see you end up on the sea floor along with the Oasis."

Chapter Five

"PIRATES?" TRENT SCRUBBED a hand over his face, rubbed at his right temple. Light spilled from the open door of Rosey's, illuminating a small section of the wooden planking, and threw odd shadows along the darkened areas of the pier. Noise emanated from Rosey's in a vibrant murmur behind Ted, Jillian and him.

He slid a quick look at Jillian's pale face.

A short time earlier, when he'd slammed his hand on the wood railing, she'd gone instantly white. That reaction was something he planned on revisiting later. In his world, there was only one reason a woman reacted that way.

"Not pirates." Trent shifted his focus to Ted and pushed away from the pier railing. "They didn't know I was there. I wasn't a prize."

"Smugglers might be a better guess."

"This thief then shows up here, at Rosey's." Jillian pulled her hands from her jeans pockets and rubbed her bare arms. "And there you are."

"Very much alive." Trent's jaw twitched. "And pissed."

"The questions are—" Ted tugged on his ear lobe.

"What are they smuggling and why did they feel the need to sink the Oasis?"

"What are they afraid of me discovering?"

"Like I said earlier, the dive team will be down there first thing in the morning. If it's there to find, we will."

As if there would be much of anything left after that explosion.

HOURS LATER, Jillian pressed her hands to the small of her back and stretched before taking a quick glance at the intricate wrought iron wall clock her grandmother had long ago attached at the back of Rosey's bar, above the opening to the kitchen and open grill. The last gift a grandfather Jillian didn't remember had given to the love of his life.

Where had that morose thought come from?

She glanced at the stack of glasses, finally quiet and motionless, then again at the clock. Last call, nearly thirty minutes ago, emptied the place out. Only she, Dane, and Trent remained.

But this long, exhausting night wasn't over. Not yet.

She snuck a sideways look at Trent. He stood with dishwater up to his elbows. A down on his luck stranger. One she'd let Ben invite into her home.

Lord, I'm not turning into Rosey, am I? Taking in all the strays, feeling responsible for them? Maybe that's why her grandmother had been so restless and *noisy* all night.

Jillian had enough to tackle just with taking care of this place and Hayden. Not that her sister actually appreciated the effort. But as Rosey always said, usually in regards to her son and his ex-wife, *family is family. We don't choose them, but since they keep coming back, we might as well love 'em.*

Trent Sawyer certainly wasn't family. Nope, not even close. One shot deal here.

When he was gone, he was gone. End of story.

Nodding once, she brushed her palms together. Grateful Trent had stepped in to help, grateful he didn't need training, she'd be more grateful when he was gone and not her headache any longer.

The cook and her two waitresses had departed after the last of the customers. Dane would leave as soon as he finished packing his guitar and other equipment away.

With the rest of close down to get through, Jillian couldn't afford any wayward thoughts.

Like how the hell she'd let herself be talked into taking the man into her home.

Her mouth dry at the sudden image in her head, she yanked the wide windows down at the west side of the building. She flipped the locks attaching them to the solid wooden railing before moving to the other windows along the southern side of the restaurant. At the opening to the end of the pier, she rolled the door down from the ceiling, kicked the bolts through their latches along the solid floor and slipped the locks through, latching the movable door to the floorboards. Afterward she collected the last of the dirty glassware from the unoccupied tables.

Trent had received quite a bit of tip money during

the night. And not just from the petite blonde who'd parked her skinny, little butt on top of that bar stool, front and center. There was the leggy brunette, and the redhead with the … well, the stacked redhead. Trent probably had enough to pay for a room. Not a nice room, but a room.

Not that she'd renege, even if she'd much rather leave him someplace where he couldn't bother her equilibrium. Leave him to the redhead, the brunette or even the blonde.

With those darks thoughts, she swung towards the bar. The stack of clean glasses rattled, the sound loud in the nearly empty space.

"What causes that?" Suddenly Trent stood right beside her, his hand warm on her forearm. He took the dirty glasses from her. "Water hitting the pylons?"

How had she lost track of him? She wiped a hand over her brow. "Probably."

"It's Rosey." Dane glanced up from his equipment, a twinkle in his dark eyes. "Trying to get your attention for some reason."

Jillian glared at him.

"Rosey of Rosey's Place?" Trent's curious gaze bounced between them. "Your grandmother, right? Still hanging around? This place, and you, must still be important to her."

"Jillian kept the doors open while Rosey was sick." Dane aimed a gentle smile at Jillian. "It would have broken Rosey's heart for someone else to have this place."

Jillian pressed her fingers to her eyes for a brief moment. "I still miss her."

"How long has it been?" With a frown lining Trent's forehead, he set the dirty glasses in the sink of sudsy water.

"Several months." The corner of Dane's mouth lifted. "Now this paradise is all Jilly and Hayden's."

Hayden. Jillian's lips tightened. *I sure hope you're having a damn good time, sister. Abandoning me like this.*

"Who is Hayden?"

"My sister." Jillian snapped the words between clenched teeth and snatched up two empty plates from the table in front of her. She took a moment, forced herself to count to ten then moved towards the bar.

"Try a cuss word or two." Trent, a bland look plastered to his face, again took the dishes from her. "Usually helps me."

Her eyes narrowed, she shook her head. Then relented. "Hellfire and damnation."

"There you go. Next time try something a little stronger. Something with more kick behind the words."

"I'll try to remember that."

Dane, a twinkle in his eyes, glanced between the two of them. "I meant to ask you earlier, what are Jazz and Hayden doing?"

"Jazz snagged a charter. I guess Hayden's crewing for her."

Dane's dark eyes deepened, the humor gone, his face closed off. "Eric go with them?"

"She didn't say one way or the other."

Another reason to kick her sister's butt. And Dane's.

He looked so *pissed.*

This was a change. "Dane —"

"Hayden is a grown woman, Jilly." He touched her cheek then nodded at Trent. "Not a thing anyone can do about it."

Or is willing to do.

Dane, his guitar case slung over his shoulder, made his way through the maze of tables to the back wall. With a backhanded wave he slipped out the far door.

"How long has he been in love with this sister of yours?" Trent rinsed the last plate and pulled the plug on the drain.

"Forever."

"And?"

"He thinks he's too old for her. She doesn't recognize his feelings." Jillian rubbed a hand over the back of her neck. She massaged the knot that always seemed to be there these days. "Nor does she want to. I guess it's easier for her that way."

"Aren't we all a bit like that?"

She glanced at the clock over the bar.

Maybe he was right.

MOONLIGHT LIT TRENT AND JILLIAN'S WAY across the open water of Blackwater Sound, so bright he hadn't used the flashlight she'd handed him when they'd left a locked down Rosey's Place less than fifteen minutes before.

Waves slapped the boat's hull. Sea spray dampened his cooled skin. So different than a mere twenty-four hours ago. Tossed in the sea on the Atlantic side of the Keys. Left to drown.

Not dead, yet. Not ready to die, either.

Ben would probably appreciate that news flash.

Trent rolled the barrel of the flashlight between his palms. Exhaustion wavered along the fringes of his mind. The steady rhythm of the boat tempted him to simply lean back, enjoy the damp, cool breeze coming off the water.

Let the beautiful and feisty Jillian Rose lead him wherever the hell she wanted.

Why now? Why with this woman at the helm of her little boat? Attraction or not, he didn't know her well enough to let down his guard. Especially with his hunter skills, along with his ability to shield and protect himself psychically, so completely non-existent.

He blinked several times, squeezed his eyes shut for a short few seconds.

How many times in the past had he been stretched this far? Working a case, spending what small amount of free time he had hunting – on the sly – the piece of shit who'd killed his baby sister. *This was nothing compared to those days.*

But in those days he had *abilities* to lean on, innate talents to depend on, to save his ass.

Then he had vengeance to get him through. What did he have now?

Stripped down. Vulnerable. No gun.

He rotated his head, worked at the kinks in his neck with his free hand.

Like the dull throb in his head, this was nothing more than an annoyance.

Right.

An annoyance and a blown up boat.

Leaning forward in his seat, he lifted his face to the breeze.

Along the stretch of horizon clouds hovered with light from that bright moon casting a silver glow to their edges.

Silver lining. As if there were such a thing.

Blackwater Sound.

Beautiful, yet somehow eerie. An alien world, different from the rivers in Oregon where he'd been raised. Or even the waterways near DC. More dank, darker. The smells of the Sound stirred something primeval inside his chest. Ominous, this place was more dangerous in a completely different way.

A slight shiver twisted around his spine.

Squeezed.

He *needed* his damn weapon. His gun.

"Get ready to shine that light in front of us." Jillian's words broke his thoughts, yanked him forward. Into the *now.*

His feet braced, he stood to hold onto the metal tubing above the console as he flicked his gaze over her. She handled the boat like someone who'd been raised on the water. Like him, she probably had. If not all her life, then the important parts.

Where the hell had that thought come from?

But it *felt* right. This was her environment, where she was comfortable. *In control.* Something important to this particular lady.

The boat slowed then made a graceful arc through the black water.

Trent flipped the switch on the flashlight then played the powerful light in front of the bow. Thick, tangled roots made what appeared to be an impenetrable stand of trees rising directly out of the water. Jillian steered through a slight opening in those mangrove trees, one he hadn't seen until they were almost upon it. He ran the light over the twisted branches.

Great place to hide and wait. To launch an ambush from the water.

Not that he was paranoid.

Much.

After several feet, their watery path opened into a wide expanse of moonlit ripples. Behind them the wall of mangroves seemed to close again, trapping them in what could be a lake surrounded on at least three sides by mangroves. Several boats bobbed along the inside stretch of trees, moored for the night or permanently anchored. He couldn't tell which.

If not for the senseless destruction of the Oasis that could have been him. Here. Now. Lulled to sleep by gentle waves rocking his boat.

Asshole mongrels. He'd find them. That blond giant and the others.

For now, in this saltwater world with the steady hum

of this boat's engine, he was going to stand here and see where Jillian Rose took him. The briny scent of the sea and the moistness of the air washed over his skin. Squinting, his tired eyes strained to see beyond the black shapes outside his circle of light.

After a few more minutes of slow motoring, they slipped down a wide side canal then into another narrower canal. A few yards in, Jillian frowned. Standing next to her, he sensed more than saw her body stiffen.

Wait. The first spark in weeks, of any kind of *extra sense*, and he'd sensed *her.*

His gaze flicked across the water as he leaned forward to stretch his senses outward, away from Jillian, while she eased the boat to a bare idle.

Sharp, painful, needles pierced his skull from the inside.

Dammit. Not an effing thing beyond the tension radiating from Jillian.

If his abilities hadn't deserted him, he'd have been able to narrow in on whatever constituted a threat in a fraction of a second. Instead, ignoring the ache in his head, he visually scanned the few houses lining one side of the canal with his borrowed light. The other side was empty, open space.

Nothing stirred. At least not that he could see. "What's wrong?"

"Someone's in my house."

Trent switched off the flashlight. He tightened his focus to the only house with a lit window. Upper floor, appeared to be a middle room. He again stretched his senses out, this time towards that house. Met a solid blank wall. *Fuck.* "Your sister? Does she live with you?"

"Yes. But that's not her." Jillian killed the motor and used the swell of water to ease the boat against the dock. "She lost her keys and would have had to come by Rosey's to get mine."

"No one else has keys?"

"Only the ones Hayden lost." Her expression close to unreadable in the moonlight, she stared at the house. "Or possibly the ones she lost last month."

"Meaning that could be anyone."

She nodded.

"You could call the police."

"We could."

Or I could find out who is inside. "Stay here. Call the police."

Flashlight stuck in his back pocket and tie down rope in hand, Trent leapt onto the dock. He secured the boat. Jillian jumped out, bat in hand.

"Where the hell did that come from?" Trent twisted it out of her grip.

"What are you doing?" Her voice low and seriously upset, she tried to snatch it back. "That's my bat. My house."

"I'm the guy trying to keep you from getting yourself killed." The words hissed out of his mouth. She needed to stay out of his way. Keep her mutinous expression and curvy body on the fucking boat. *Do what he damn well told her to do.*

Like that would happen. In the few hours he'd

known her, he already knew better.

"Shit." He hefted her bat. Not his gun, but he'd make do with what he had. "Stay behind me."

The moonlight that had lit their way here was now a problem. He spared a quick glance at the middle window. A shadow passed across the curtains then was gone.

Whoever was up there hadn't shifted the curtain, hadn't looked outside. But all it would take was one glance out the window. One look and whoever that was would see Jillian's boat tied to the dock. And then chaos would break loose.

Again.

Chapter Six

TRENT HEFTED JILLIAN'S BAT and glanced around the moonlit expanse of her yard. Cement stretched from where they stood next to her docked boat all the way to her house. They both wore deck shoes so at least their footfalls wouldn't echo across and announce their arrival.

Now's as good a time as any.

Shoulders hunched forward, he crouched low and dashed across the cement yard. Jillian stayed right behind him. At the left corner of the house, he pressed his back against the wall, eased to a position a few inches from the edge. Next to him, Jillian mimicked his stance. The touch of her bare arm sent electric shocks through his left arm.

He took a deep breath, tapped a finger to his mouth as he pulled his arm in closer to his body. They had an intruder to catch. He twisted his head to the side, peered around the corner.

Nothing stirred. Even the air, heavy with humidity, seemed to choose that moment to still.

No one in sight. That could be good. Could be bad.

Two kayaks, their bright blue color almost florescent

in the moonlight, leaned against the far wall of the otherwise empty carport.

"Your car?" He pulled back to glance at Jillian.

She pointed to a side building several yards away.

He nodded, leaned forward again. Several other cars and one pickup truck lined the street beyond the chain link fence. All those vehicles appeared to be empty.

Now to check the other side of the house.

Before he could move, a sound, like a cross between an out of tune piano and a seriously pissed off alley cat, rat-a-tatted across the yard.

What the hell is that?

A man, staggering along what passed for a sidewalk, whistled and ran some kind of metal cup over the chain link fence. The intruder's lookout? Or a drunk stumbling home?

Trent flattened his back against the wall. With one eyebrow raised, he glanced at Jillian.

"Next door rents to the vacation crowd. I think that guy's been there four or five days already." Her voice barely above a whisper, she shrugged. "He's a little early tonight."

The man stopped then rattled the gate in front of Jillian's carport. A curse split the air before he made his way to his own door and disappeared inside. Trent waited a few more heartbeats. He nodded once to Jillian. She fell in behind him. They slunk to the other side of the back wall of her house then peered around that corner.

Nothing moved.

Hopeful the intruder was ignoring the neighbor, he leaned forward, checked the lit window. Satisfied no one stood there watching the back area, he dashed toward the front corner of the house. Jillian stayed with him.

More cars lined the street, from the front of Jillian's place down to where the road ended at the wide canal. All the vehicles appeared empty, but without shining a light into each one, he wasn't going to bet on vacant.

Over his shoulder, he caught and held her gaze. "How many of those cars belong on this street?"

"All of them." She pressed the flat of her palm to his back.

Heat from her touch seeped through the thin material of his borrowed shirt. *Focus, Sawyer.* On the intruder. Not on the way the moonlight streamed over her hair, darkening the deep tones of it, and glinted off the sheen in her eyes. Or the tension he could *feel* emanating from her body. Prickles of that tension echoed down his spine.

"Or none. Hard to say." She shrugged one shoulder. "Vacation homes, vacation rentals. I gave up trying to figure what belonged when I was a kid."

What had they been talking about?

Cars. The street.

He did a mental head shake. *Focus.* Whoever was in the house could be operating alone. Without a lookout. But this was close enough to the time he imagined Jillian routinely arrived home after work.

Did the person in her home lay in wait for her? If so, why leave Hayden's light on?

Unless the person wanted her to believe her sister

Chapter Seven

TRENT LAY STRETCHED OUT on the king-sized mattress, his hands pillowing his head. Sunlight had just begun to break the hold of night, barely peering through the wood slats of the shutters covering the wall of windows across the room.

A large paddle fan hummed overhead, moving the air in the room, keeping it comfortable. Pleasant even. He should be sound asleep. Not laying here in a pair of light sweat-pants belonging to the father of the woman just down the hall. The woman who blushed with every wayward thought.

Such a sexy shade of pink on her sun-kissed cheeks.

The woman who's scent wrapped around him and squeezed. Whose touch lit fires better off banked. Who stirred the remnants of whatever psychic ability remained in his tired soul. The woman who wouldn't stay put and let him protect her.

Right.

Gotta get the hell out of here. Out of here and back to DC.

Back to work.

Before the thoughts making her blush collided with

left that light shining.

As if reading his thoughts, Jillian's fingers curled against his back. Her breathing hitched once.

Maybe the light was on for the simplest of reasons. The mysterious Hayden herself. Maybe she'd found her keys and waited for her sister to walk through the door.

Hefting the bat, he hoped it was the sister, miraculous finder of keys. *Not going to chance it, not going to chance being wrong.* "Why don't you wait outside –"

"You're wasting time flapping your jaws."

"Right." They were going to have a talk about her sense of survival. After they finished with the possible intruder. "Your keys?"

She dropped a small ring of keys into his open palm. "The one with the plastic top."

With his back to the house, his gaze scanning the area, Trent pushed away. In a low crouching run, he skirted the bushes lining the walkway before he took the three steps to the front door.

He tucked the bat under his arm and gripped the door knob to slip in the key but the knob turned easily in his hand. The door opened a fraction. A small sliver of light etched itself over the front steps. He glanced back at Jillian. The thin set of her lips told the story.

Hayden wouldn't leave the door unlocked.

So much for key-finding miracles. He slipped Jillian's in his front pocket then hefted the bat. His fingers tight on the hilt, he used the tip to slowly push the door open the rest of the way. Light from an upper story room spilled over the wood and metal banister, illuminating the foyer.

Slight noises, stealthy and almost non-existent, drifted from upstairs. *Someone going through drawers. Shifting things around, searching for something specific.*

Trent's grip tightened on the bat. He slipped inside the house with Jillian right behind him. The tips of her fingers rested at the small of his back.

Near the base of the circular stairs leading to the next floor, he paused when she stepped away. With effort, he tamped down his disappointment at the loss of her touch. One foot on the bottom step and she touched him again. He spared a glance over his shoulder.

How many freaking bats did the woman own?

And where had she gotten that one?

Her fingers wrapped firm around the hilt of an aluminum bat, a fierce light blazed in her gaze. He read the dare in her eyes and shook his head.

Whatever floats her boat. Considering these two bats were the only weapons they had, he refused to complain. Not out loud anyway.

With considerable patience he didn't feel, he eased a foot onto the next step. Seconds passed like hours. He repeated the process until he stood only a few steps from the top landing. Jillian followed behind him, one slow step at a time.

At the press of his weight on the next stair, a squeak vibrated through the house.

Shit. Now what?

Trent raised his free hand. Jillian stopped below him. The metal of her bat glinted in the light from the open bedroom door. That light switched off, casting the landing and stairs in near complete darkness. Silence, like that breathe not yet taken, stretched.

Trent lifted his bat, braced his feet.

This moron might not be the one who'd blown the Oasis to bits. *But this guy isn't getting past me. Not happening again.*

Steps, heavy on the wood flooring, pounded with a sudden rush of air. Trent swung the bat, blind and hard. He connected with something large and solid. The thud vibrated up his arms. He pulled back to swing again.

"What the hell?" The unmistakable, deep male voice of the blond giant echoed.

A fist snapped Trent's head back, rattled his teeth. Shoved him to his knees on the stairs. His grip on his bat loosened.

The sound of Jillian's metal bat hitting the banister reverberated overhead.

"What the fu –" The blond's voice jumbled into the racket of his big body crashing down the stairs.

With his bat as a crutch, Trent shoved himself into a standing position. He ignored the ache as he shook his head to clear the sudden dizziness.

He yanked the flashlight from his back pocket, threw the switch to the on position. His movements fumbling, he swung the light towards the noise at the front door, just in time to see the back of the intruder limping his way through the open doorway to disappear from view.

With only a slight pause to shake his head clear again, Trent took the stairs two at a time. He blasted through the front door and hit the chain link gate. Slamming it out of the way, he aimed the flashlight in a circular pattern, but the bastard had disappeared.

Vanished as if he had never been there.

How did someone so big do that?

Trent stopped, sucked in deep breaths. With the bat gripped in one hand and the flashlight in the other, he bent over to rest both fists on his knees while listening for any unusual noises. Nothing. Not a car motor speeding away, not a boat, not even the thud of anyone's shoes hitting the asphalt.

The piece of shit had gotten away.

Once again.

"YOU'RE SURE IT WAS the same man?" Ted Mathews, sitting at Jillian's table, glanced up from his notebook. A frown marred his forehead.

Outside the curtained kitchen window, darkness still held sway and would for several more hours. Inside, she wanted to scream. Stomp her foot. Something.

Instead, her hands on Trent's shirtless shoulder, she smoothed the bandage she'd layered over his latest abrasions. The ones he'd gotten when that intruder had shoved him against her banister. "His cologne."

"Excuse me?" Ted lowered his pen.

"His stinky cologne." She rubbed her thumb over the taped edges. Trent really should put a shirt on, but the one he'd borrowed was now torn, in a heap on the floor, and belonged to Ted. *How nice of Ted not to say anything.* She wiped a hand over her brow. Tired and punchy, she needed to get to bed soon. Before she said or did something really, really stupid.

Like invite the shirtless hunk up to her bed. Not to sleep, even though that was what they both needed. Sleep. Not sex.

"The man who had Ben's dinghy wore the same stinky cologne as the guy who broke in here and tried to shove Trent down the stairs." Her fingers tingling, she rubbed the tips. Really, she had to corral her thoughts before they got her in trouble. *Really.* She stepped away from Trent and leaned her hip against the counter.

"Just a couple of stairs." Trent grimaced when he rotated his shoulder. He aimed a thankful smile at her.

Her insides fluttered.

Dammit all. She pressed a hand to her stomach. *Fluttering.* Over a stupid smile.

She spun around. *Coffee.* The aroma from the freshly brewed pot called to her. Rescued her wayward thoughts. They all needed coffee. Now. Anything to keep her shaking hands busy.

"He was the same body size and mass." Trent's words flowed over her. He was addressing Ted. That was a good thing. "There can't be that many big, bulky body-builders here."

"You'd be surprised." Ted rubbed the back of his neck and gave her an absent smile when she set his cup in front of him.

With a cup for Trent and one for herself, she set both on the table. She reached for the scissors and tape, but Trent's hand covered hers.

"Sit down before you fall down."

She frowned, ignored the traitorous desire to turn her hand over, link her fingers with his.

Stupid.

"Please. Sit down. Drink your coffee."

For just a single moment, her eyes flitted close of their own accord. She opened them to meet his warm gaze. Her stomach quivered. "All right."

She sat, wrapped her hands around her cup, and leaned her elbows on the table.

"As far as you can tell, nothing is missing?" Ted laid his pen and notebook on the table before he picked up his cup. "And the entry wasn't forced. So the place was either unlocked when he arrived or he had keys."

"He was looking for something specific. He wore latex gloves. I felt them when he punched me. So no prints." Trent also picked up his cup before he gingerly leaned back in the chair. Grimaced. "Did they send you to take this report because we think it's the same guy?"

"Partly." Ted shrugged. "I was off shift, but with the body they found, in the mangroves over near Crocodile Lake, taking most of our resources this afternoon and evening – along with the Oasis being blown up – I stayed on to help."

"Body?" Jillian straightened. "They'd said Shamus was out sick and his trainee was working a case, but I thought – I guess I didn't realize someone had actually died. Who …?"

"No one any of us know. Male, late thirties. No

identification at this point."

She nodded, wet her lips.

"Anything to do with the Oasis?" Trent lifted his cup to his mouth.

"Too soon to tell."

They drank in silence for a few moments.

Ted slid his notebook and pen into his shirt pocket. He stood, nodded at the shirt on the floor. "I might have another spare in my duffel in the trunk. Want me to check?"

"Thanks, Ted. But my dad has a whole closet full of clothes he's not using." She answered before Trent could open his mouth. Much as she hated to admit it, her dad's things would probably fit him well. "I'm sure I can find something Trent can wear."

Ted grinned. "Don't let your father see him in his duds. As hard as Trent is on clothes, your daddy will have a fit."

Trent stood, his mouth now set in grim smile. He shook Ted's hand. "That's done with."

"Hope you're right." Ted touched two fingers to his forehead. "I'll see myself out, Jilly."

After Ted left Jillian busied herself with collecting the cups from the table. She shut off the coffee pot, wiped the table and counter. Anything to avoid facing Trent and the flutters making a return visit to her stomach.

Dammit all over again.

When she'd wrung out the cloth in the sink and had nothing left to wipe down, she braced herself and spun to face Trent. He stood in the archway, leaning against the wall, watching her. His deep blue eyes were almost black in the shadowed light, the swelling under his right eye giving him an air of danger.

To her peace of mind.

His bare chest rose and fell with each breath he took. With the cuts and scrapes over his face and body, he could be a modern day pirate standing there, waiting for the opportunity to pillage and plunder.

Oh Lord. I'm too sleep deprived for this.

"Let's get you settled for the night." With a hand to her stomach – as if that would help – she faked a wide smile. Careful to not touch him, she hurried past, checked the latch at the front door, and kept moving until she was half way up the stairs.

Realizing he wasn't behind her, she turned to find him still framed in the kitchen archway. Still watching her with his own smile just barely lifting the corners of his mouth.

She spun around and all but ran the rest of the way up the stairs.

Damn man.

his not so good intentions.

✧ ✧ ✧

CUP OF COFFEE IN HAND, Jillian ran her other hand through her hair and swept it back from her face. She'd been up for over an hour, pacing, calling herself stupid more times than she cared to count.

Stupid for letting Trent Sawyer get to her. Stupid for not living through the moment.

The way her sister would have done.

Trent was as attracted to her as she was to him. She might not have Hayden's way with men, but she recognized the look in his eyes. That heat hadn't been a trick of the light.

Instead of standing here staring out the kitchen window at the mid-morning light sparking off the water in the canal, she could be snuggled in bed, just waking up, wrapped in his arms. Sated from a night – or what had been left of the night – of lovemaking. Aching for more.

And then what?

Her lips pressed together, she stared at the ceiling. If only the answers were tattooed up there. She wasn't Hayden. No matter how much she sometimes wished to just throw away all her concerns, she didn't do that. Not anymore.

The one time she'd tried she'd ended up with an obsessive, violent boyfriend who'd put her in the hospital and left her not trusting her own instincts.

No, she didn't live that way. Not for any reason.

The doorbell's sudden, shrill ring echoed, disturbing

the quiet of the house, the direction of her thoughts. Her back stiffened. They didn't get unexpected visitors, for the most part anyway. With a hard swallow, she scooped up her metal bat on her way to the door.

No sense taking chances. Not after yesterday.

Her doorbell shrilled again. She glanced at the landing at the top of the stairs, not surprised to see Trent striding from her father's room, sweat-pants slung low on his hips and his chest bare. A sleep line creased his right cheek, disappearing into the two day stubble along his jaw. The slice on his cheek didn't seem as swollen or as angry. Wide awake awareness, similar to a sharp, blue laser, glinted in his eyes.

On his way down the stairs that gaze connected with hers, sending fissions of pure heat spiraling through her body, tightening her stomach and pooling between her legs.

Lust. Primal in its desire, in its need. There, no longer just below the surface, but right there to be touched. Stroked.

Caught in the dark blue depths of his gaze, she couldn't look away. Her lips parted, her breathing quickened, and her head tilted back of its own accord. She couldn't look away.

Oh, trouble. So much trouble.

Loud pounding on her front door pierced her mind. A slight tremor shook her body. Trent blinked several times. Frowned. He sent a quick glance at her bat. She tightened her grip.

Find your own damn bat.

Strike that, he could return the one he swiped from her the night before. The one that belonged on her boat.

On a deep inhale of breath, she shook her head to clear it before spinning on her heel and taking the few steps to the front door. She peered through the peep-hole. A dark-haired man stood there, his body angled away to face the street. Impatience radiated from the set of his broad shoulders under the crispness of his pale yellow, button-down shirt. Not island casual, not professional business, either.

She threw a glance over her shoulder at Trent. Shrugged. At the base of the stairs, he nodded then positioned himself to the left side of the door. Her eyes narrow and her one-handed grip tight on her bat, she opened the door a fraction.

The man outside swung to face her, that impatience evident along the tautness of his clean shaven jaw, the censure in his dark eyes. At the sight of her, his chin lifted a fraction.

"Devon?"

Shamus' trainee. Brand, shiny new Homicide cop. He held a thin stack of file folders in his hand.

Oh, no. Jillian swung the door open. "Hayden?"

"Is she here?" Devon tilted his head, his body, to get a look behind her. Jillian recognized the moment he spotted Trent standing to the side of the door.

An inane giggle tickled her throat. Because of the detective's now stiff posture or relief over Hayden, she wasn't sure. She covered her mouth and shook her head.

Disappointment clouded Devon's eyes. He glanced

between her and Trent. "Can I come in? I have a few questions for you."

"About my call to Shamus yesterday?" She pressed the bat she still gripped to her chest. "You didn't have to come by here for that."

Devon frowned, eyed the bat. "Shamus is still out with the flu. Can I come in, please?"

She shrugged but stepped back. He entered, casting a suspicious glance at Trent who stood with that glower stamped on his face and his arms crossed over that naked chest.

"Devon, this is Trent Sawyer."

Devon's eyes widened for a fraction of a second. "You're the agent from Ben Garrett's boat."

Trent nodded.

Agent? Jillian slid a sideways glance at Trent. What kind of agent?

"Detective Devon Jackson." He offered his hand.

"You're from Homicide." Trent's tone matter of fact, he shook the man's hand. "Is this about the body they found yesterday?"

"Partly."

In the mangroves, Ted had said. A shudder skidded down Jillian's spine. "Let's take this in the kitchen. I have a fresh pot of coffee made."

She stashed her bat. Trent headed upstairs for a shirt, *thank goodness*, then joined her and Devon in the kitchen where she soon had them settled at the table with steaming cups of coffee in front of them. A slight breeze through the open window over the sink stirred the curtains, brought the aroma of someone in the neighborhood frying bacon.

Her stomach grumbled. She ignored the reminder she'd skipped dinner last night. Instead she leaned her elbows on the table and wrapped her hands around her cup. Breakfast would have to wait a bit.

Third time in two days, talking with a local cop on official business. Twice over coffee in her own kitchen. She glanced at Trent. All since he'd shown up at Rosey's Place. *So much violence.*

Ben needed to keep his freeloaders away from her.

Freeloading agents. As in FBI? CIA? Insurance?

Let it be insurance. They could take their policies and shove them somewhere else.

Although with the Oasis gone, freeloaders probably wouldn't be an issue any longer. She just needed to get through the chaos surrounding one Trent Sawyer.

Why does that sound so much easier than it feels?

Devon pulled a photo from one of his files, laid it on the table in front of Trent. Jillian glanced down. The scent of the neighbor's bacon clogged her throat, tipped her stomach sideways. She didn't recognize the dead man, or what was left of his face. Her lips pressed together, she averted her gaze to stare into her coffee.

"He's one of the men from the Oasis." Trent's voice flat, he pushed the picture towards Devon. "He went overboard. Last I heard, they were going to fish him from the water and throw me over."

"So you didn't put that bullet in the back of his head?"

Although Trent's stomach churned, he kept his gaze level with Detective Jackson's. *It'd be a pisser if the bullet in the dead man's head had come from his gun.* "He was alive when I'd been relieved of my weapon."

Jackson nodded. "Did they call him by name? Any kind of identifying reference?"

"If they did, I didn't catch it.

Frown lines furrowed deep on the detective's young forehead. He stared at the photo for a long moment.

"No ID?" Trent settled back in his chair, coffee cup cradled between his hands. "Fingerprints?"

"Working on it. Issues of some kind, but they're working on it."

Obviously, Jackson was stalled, no place to move forward from. Trent would like to help him. Not for the squat redhead – *he could continue to rot* – but the dead man was a direct link to the other men who'd been on that boat.

Jillian, her eyes still averted from the photo, stared into her cup as if it held all the answers.

He knew it didn't. *Been there, done that.* He caught Jackson's glance, arched an eyebrow at the photo, and tilted his head slightly towards Jillian.

Jackson swallowed once, fumbled the photo but got it stashed back into the folder. He mumbled a low apology.

She aimed a tight smile at him. "Thank you, Devon. I—"

"You're not used to seeing photos like that. I understand."

Neither are you, kid. Trent lifted his cup to his mouth and took a short sip. Green didn't quite cover the kid's complexion. "Is that all you needed? To see if I could ID the man?"

Jackson blinked a couple of times before he glanced around the kitchen. "No. You being here was actually a bonus."

Cup cradled back over his lap, Trent waited.

"Hayden—"

"Isn't here." Jillian's own smile seemed stretched, insincere.

"Do you know where I can find her?"

"Somewhere on the water between Biscayne Bay and Ft. Myers. Jazz snagged a charter for the Symphony. Hayden is crewing for her. I think they left before dawn yesterday morning." She angled her head slightly to the side. Frowned. "Why? I'm sure she doesn't know that man any more than I do."

"This isn't about the John Doe." Jackson tapped the folders. He puffed air out of his nostrils. Swallowed once again.

The man was green in more ways than just his skin tone. Another detective's trainee, if Trent remembered correctly.

"Felicity Chambers was found dead yesterday evening. At the foot of Rhys Blackthorne's stairs." Jackson grimaced before he met Jillian's shocked stare.

Wait a minute. Trent stiffened then frowned. "*Another* homicide, not simply an accident? What does this one have to do with Jillian's sister?"

Jillian's quick glance radiated gratitude. He gave her a short, lopsided smile. Kept his fingers tight around his cup and resisted the sudden urge to pat her hand. That constant ache in his head had to be turning his mind to mush. He was nobody to depend on. Raging instincts be damned. *Damn wrong.*

"We don't know yet if it was a homicide. Felicity is – was – the ex-wife of Eric Chambers." Devon swallowed once. "Eric is Hayden's current boyfriend."

"So?" Belligerence soaked Jillian's voice, darkened the honey of her eyes.

"The last notation in Felicity's cell phone calendar was an appointment late the night before. With Hayden."

"She didn't say anything about that." Jillian's gaze shifted between the detective and Trent. "She would have told me if she went out to see Felicity."

"You're probably right." Jackson looked even greener around the gills. His eyes filled with deep set remorse and he wouldn't meet Jillian's gaze.

Was this guy another fool part way in love with the sister?

"Did she work at Rosey's that night?" Jackson's half pleading gaze bounced off Trent's to land square on Jillian's. "Before she took off to meet Jazz?"

Jillian jerked, the movement so slight Trent wouldn't have seen it if he hadn't been watching her. She rubbed the tip of her nose and bit her bottom lip before swallowing once. "No. She didn't."

"Do you know where she was before she left on the Symphony?"

Jillian shook her head. "But you know Hayden. You know she wouldn't – Hayden couldn't hurt anyone. Not intentionally."

Trent lifted his cup and took another sip of coffee. People were capable of a lot more than their loved ones realized.

The detective nodded then sent a sideways glance at Trent. "Felicity probably slipped and fell down the stairs. I just need Hayden to tell me if she was there that night. If anyone else was there."

"When I hear from her, I'll make sure she calls you." A tight smile barely lifted the corners of Jillian's mouth. She rose to accompany Jackson to the front door.

Trent followed.

Once the detective was gone, she leaned against the door. Ran a hand over her closed eyes.

"You're positive she didn't have anything to do with this woman's death?" Trent, his gaze locked on her, leaned an elbow on the banister.

Jillian's eyes snapped open then narrowed. "I'm sure. My sister's a lot of things, murderer isn't one of them."

Maybe not. But the possibility was still there. "Jackson shouldn't have told you as much as he did."

"Why not?"

"He's in the middle of an active investigation. A possible murder investigation. You're the sister of their chief person of interest."

"You heard him, he just needs to talk with Hayden."

He arched a brow. Was she really that naive?

"How would you know what he should tell me or

not." Her chin dropped to her chest. "Unless you're law enforcement."

"Yes."

"That's it? Just yes?"

"What do you want me to say? Name, rank, serial number?" Trent shook his head. Ben headed his own agency, one with ties deep inside Homeland Security. Not exactly government. But as close as they could get and not quite be sanctioned. "FBI."

"Ben is FBI, also?"

"No. He's the head of the federal task force I'm assigned to. For the most part, I answer to him. What difference does it make?"

"I thought – Never mind."

"What did you think?" Trent settled on the stairs. He stretched his legs, crossed them at the ankle. "That I was down and out? Freeloading off Ben?"

"The thought crossed my mind."

"You don't think much of the people who stay on Ben's boat, do you?"

"No."

"That's it? Just no?"

She lifted one eyebrow. "No, I don't think much of the people who've stayed on Ben's boat."

That stung. Bothered him that it did. Trent studied his bare toes. "Why is that?"

"Are you the company shrink, too?"

A bark of laughter choked him. "Hardly. Just wondering which one of them burned you so badly you want nothing to do with any of us."

"None."

"That's hard to believe."

"That none of them burned me? Or that I haven't let one of them get close enough to do any burning?" She lifted her chin and pushed away from the door. "Don't think you're going to be the first, either. I have no use for any of Ben's friends. FBI or freeloader."

Chapter Eight

THE GOSSIP GAVE JILLIAN a major headache.

Rosey's was packed. A gentle breeze coming in off the water kept the evening temperature perfect. Not too cool, not too warm. Humid still, that didn't change no matter what time of year.

But the gossip—

Jillian ran a hand across her forehead. She resisted the urge to cross her arms and rest her head on the counter. All anyone wanted to talk about were the two deaths.

Who did what to who ... or was it to whom?

Felicity Chambers fell down the stairs. No, she was pushed. Was her death connected to that unidentified man found in the mangroves? Had the mystery man thrown Felicity down the stairs? Had he killed Felicity and then himself so he wouldn't have to face Rhys Blackthorne?

Rhys was headed back from Europe, but had he actually even gone? Or had he faked his trip and been here all along? Had he been the one to throw Felicity down the stairs?

At least the gossips were leaving Hayden out of it all. For now.

In spite of what Jillian had said to Trent, she worried

about her sister's involvement. Hayden wasn't a murderer, but just what did her sister know? Why had she run? How could Jillian protect her if she didn't know what to protect her from?

"Who is Rhys Blackthorne?" Trent's steps quiet, he set a stack of dirty plates in the plastic bin behind the counter.

That stupid frisson of awareness sizzled across her skin. With a frown she arched her neck to stretch out the kinks in her back. "Felicity Chambers' rich boyfriend. He has a fancy place to the east of here, on the other side of Crocodile Lake. She fell down his stairs."

"Ahhh. The plot thickens." He leaned his elbows on the counter and linked his fingers. He threw her a sideways look, his eyes hooded and enigmatic. "She was a princess, you know."

"I'd heard that." Among a host of other things.

"No, really." He smiled, a mere stretch of his lips. His gaze scanned Rosey's. "According to the couple in the corner and the older ladies over by the railing. Some small European county. Her father's the king – which would make her the princess – and she has either two or three older brothers. The princes. At one time, there was a sister, her twin, but they'd both been kidnapped when they were babies. Felicity was the only one they found."

"You're serious?"

"Yes ma'am." Dimples flashing in his cheeks, he winked at her. "They're all serious as they can be. Me, on the other hand, I'm going to have to verify all this intel."

"Sure." She blinked. Jeez, he was potent when he

actually smiled. "Mr. FBI agent in action."

"Mr. Special Agent to you, missy."

"You're in a good mood, all of a sudden." Maybe he should go back to scowling. Safer for her heart.

"I do better with something to focus on." He smiled again, this one lop-sided, before he snagged a towel. "A case. A cause. A table needing a good wiping down. All I need is a focus."

She watched him saunter away. Tension lining the set of his shoulders belied his loose manner. That and the shadows haunting his eyes. Shadows that never quite disappeared. He nodded at the two older ladies as he passed their table along the outside railing before he stopped to wipe down an empty table next to them.

Jillian, with her head tipped back and her throat dry, studied the roof line. *Why can't he simply be a grouchy freeloader with no redeeming qualities?*

The man helping her this evening tempted her in ways she didn't want to contemplate.

A soft clink, of glass against glass, echoed behind her.

Don't start, Rosey. Ben needed to get Trent *gone.* Away from her before she did something stupid. *Like kiss the jerk.*

"Jillian?" Eric Chambers' demanding voice startled her.

Her mouth tightened. Well, that certainly detoured her thoughts.

"Could I talk with you? In private?"

Really? As if there were such a thing in this place.

Especially today, with the gossip on overload and not many empty tables. And now Eric wanted to talk with her in private. Wasn't that just peachy? She scrubbed a hand over her face. "This isn't a good time, Eric."

From the corner of her eye she spotted Trent's sharp, sideways glance.

"Please, Jillian." Behind Eric's wire framed glasses a tiny measure of pleading sparked in his hazel eyes. He held her gaze and lowered his voice. "Hayden's not answering my calls. I'm concerned."

"She's out of town. I'm sure she'll get in touch with you when she gets back."

Momentary panic rimmed his gaze, darkened his eyes. His wide shoulders hunched forward. "But, where—" He swallowed once.

"Did you two have a fight?" That might explain some of Hayden's hyper behavior the other night. Of course, a dead woman and knowing how she got that way might also make for hyper behavior. Jillian shoved the thought aside.

Eric glanced around while shaking his head. "Could we at least talk on the other side of the pier?"

"Now isn't a –" She pinched the bridge of her nose, caught Trent's eye. His were narrowed and his gaze went from hers to Eric's. "Trent, can you cover for a couple of minutes?"

"Sure." He straightened before crossing his arms over his chest and lowering his chin. "I'll be right here if you need anything, boss."

Great. Now she had male, territorial hormones staining the air.

But was that a bad thing, considering she really didn't want to be alone with Eric? Not that she feared him. If that had been the case, she would have moved the ocean itself to keep her sister away from him. No, right now she was just tired of all the drama.

She led the way through the maze of tables, well aware of Eric at her back. Then there was the other male watching until he couldn't see them any longer.

Men.

Once through the door of the back wall and near the pier railing, she swung around to face her sister's boyfriend. A brief hint of some spicy cologne he wore tickled her nose. Mimicking Trent, she crossed her arms over her chest. "What is it?"

Eric blew out a breath before he pressed his lips together and rested his open palms on the wooden railing. He stared at the water, looking like a man with more weight than he could handle, even with his broad shoulders and deep chest.

An ever so slight sense of remorse crawled around Jillian's stomach. Felicity had been his ex-wife. In spite of the divorce, he probably had feelings for her.

Look at her own parents. Two children and four divorces later – three from each other – they still couldn't leave each other alone. Relationships metered out nothing but heartache and trouble.

"Eric." Jillian shoved both hands through her hair. "I am sorry about Felicity."

His eyes closed for a moment. When he opened

them he pulled off his glasses and stuck them in his shirt pocket. He looked at her, the hazel in his eyes more green than brown. With a nod, he gave her a soft, half smile. "I—It's hard to take it in. Hard to believe she's actually gone. She seemed to be doing so well. Never looked better. Seemed to –"

Jillian touched the back of his hand. He pressed his own hand over hers. Squeezed then stroked his thumb across her skin.

She jerked back, away from him. "Eric."

With his hands balled in fists and his jaw tight, he didn't say anything. He stared out over the water with tension emanating from him, the tautness, reeking of barely contained violence swelling with the breeze. She took two steps backwards, ready to bolt.

He had never hurt her in the past, never hurt Hayden that she knew of, but he'd never come so close to coming on to her before, either. Maybe she misread him, misread his intent, but she wasn't going to give him a chance to use those fists on her. Violence because of a perceived slight was something she'd dealt with in the past.

She'd deal with him if she had to. She was no man's victim.

Not ever again.

"I'm sorry, Jillian." With an obviously conscious effort, Eric opened his fists then gripped the railing in front of him. In the low light moisture glistened across his eyes. He shrugged. "I hope they find Felicity simply slipped. That she wasn't drinking again. That no one else was involved."

Without moving forward, Jillian tucked a strand of hair behind her ear, crossed her arms over her stomach this time. "Me, too."

"Hayden—" Again he pressed his lips together then shook his head.

"Hayden what?"

He tilted his head to stare at the clear evening sky. After a few drawn out moments, he heaved a deep sigh. "Listen, I know Felicity asked Hayden to drop by that night. I just don't know if she did."

"Why? That doesn't make sense. It's not as if they suddenly became best friends over night. Nothing against Felicity, but we just don't run in her circle."

Besides, what would they talk about? *Eric?*

He angled his head and caught her gaze. The bleakness in his rattled her.

Her uncharitable thoughts clogged her throat. The man *hurt*.

Eric smiled, bitterness rode the curve of his lips. "You're right on that. They didn't exactly admire each other or want to exchange recipes."

"About Hayden – what does it matter if she stopped to see Felicity?"

"The detective was by, asking me about the two of them getting together."

"He asked me, too." Jillian shrugged, although nonchalant didn't come close to what tightened her chest. "But right now Hayden's either out of phone range or she has the damn thing turned off. If the police want to find her that badly, they'll track down the Symphony and ask her themselves."

"What if Hayden —"

"My sister didn't kill anyone. Why am I the only one who believes that?"

WITH THE LATE EVENING air heavy and thick through the open framework of Rosey's Place, Trent let the ebb of customers' voices flow over him. He swiped his rag across one of the small, glass topped tables that used angles and mirrors to show the water directly below the pier. Soft light from underneath cast that water in an eerie green glow. Fish swimming beneath appeared almost ghostly.

Perfect, considering the ghosts haunting him, taunting him.

And that was without the one rattling the glasses behind the counter.

He had enough stacked on his plate without getting involved in Jillian Rose's business. With all the damn bats she had lying around, she didn't need, or even want, his protection.

Nor would having him in her corner do her any damn good. He was no one to count on, so wasn't it a *fucking* good thing Jillian didn't need him to protect her?

His mouth in a semi-snarl, he glared in the direction she'd taken Eric Chambers. The sister's boyfriend.

Jillian's sister.

Sisters.

No one to count on.

He'd more than let his sister down. Then his partner's. Now, here in Key Largo, a third sister. Hayden Rose. *Trouble comes in threes.*

Dammit. He hadn't met Hayden, why did he care one way or another?

From his position at the edge of the bar, he couldn't see Jillian or even hear what was said between her and Chambers, but through the wide open doorway he could see their faint shadows stretched across the wooden planks of the pier.

He couldn't pick up the slightest sense of *anything* off the man. Nothing to show for his effort but a deeper throb to the constant ache at his temples. Nothing beyond a faint aura of unease emanating from Jillian.

But that could be due to her dislike of Eric Chambers. Trent didn't need any kind of *extra* ability to read her animosity towards the man.

And if Jillian didn't care for Chambers, he saw no reason to give him any benefit of any kind of doubt.

As Trent had done with every man who'd walked into Rosey's, he compared Chambers to the vague mental image he had of the man who'd called the shots on board the Oasis. His gaze on the shadows outside, he pursed his mouth and narrowed his eyes.

Maybe. Something was off, though. What?

Size? Chamber's build could be right.

Attitude? Yeah. Chambers didn't ooze the right mix of authority and power.

Still, he raised Trent's hackles. And it went deeper

than Chambers' obvious appreciation of the thin, grey T-shirt Jillian wore. The man had a girlfriend. Jillian's sister. He also had a dead ex-wife, one who died under possible suspicious circumstances.

Then there was the bullet through the squat red-head's brain.

Trent scanned the bar, zeroed back on the shadows outside. Chambers *probably* had nothing to do with the man's death, but murder was always an excellent reason for Trent to keep his senses as sharp and focused as he could manage.

He rolled his shoulders.

Which, considering his *extra special* skills were MIA, weren't all that sharp. He'd find a way to compensate.

Somehow.

Jillian and Eric came through the doorway, her back stiff and a fire snapping in her honeyed eyes. Chambers' mouth was tight, his posture just as rigid.

They'd pissed each other off.

Good.

With a grin Trent tried to contain, he flung the towel over his shoulder, let it rest there while he gathered more dirty dishes, and trailed behind them. He set the dishes in the plastic bin and raised a brow at the heated glare she threw him.

He liked the way ire brought out the burnt gold in her eyes, when he, himself, was the cause. Someone else being responsible, that bothered something deep inside he didn't want to examine too closely. Nor did he want to examine his sudden need to charge to her rescue.

Nobody's hero.

A few feet from where Chambers now leaned against the bar, Jillian stood behind the counter. She faced the wall of liquor bottles. Her deep breathing and tense jaw told their own story.

Trent fixed a glass of ice water to help cool her down. Of course, fireproof gloves might also be in order. He touched her arm anyway. A slight tremor belied the stiffness of her stance.

Not meaning to, his touch turned into a light and lingering caress over her arm, down her back. The muscles under his stroking hand loosened. Warmth sparked between her and his fingertips. Her shoulders slumped. He handed her the water, wrapped her hands around the glass with his own.

"Drink this. Then go, take care of that new crop of customers sitting over there." He jerked his head to the side. "I'll deal with Mr. Prickly here."

Gratitude flashed through her eyes. There, then gone. "You're awfully pushy for hired help."

"Yes, ma'am."

She lifted the glass. His hands dropped from hers as she downed the water then rubbed the glass over her forehead. With a nod she set the glass on the counter and strode away, not once glancing at Chambers.

Trent, his gaze on the subtle sway of her hips, wiped his still tingling palm down his pant leg and ran his thumb over his fingertips. She got to him. Physically, at least.

She squared her shoulders then stepped to the full table with a wide smile on her lips. *Shit*. He scrubbed a hand over his eyes, his mouth. Her appeal might be more than physical. *Man, I need to get out of here. Leave town. Get back to my real work. My real world.*

Before he could make a fool of himself, he scooped another glass of ice, added water and set it in front of Chambers. Trent let his elbows rest on the counter when he crossed his arms. "What can I get you?"

"A beer." Chambers gave him a dark look, sent another sideways one in Jillian's direction. His nostrils flared. "That specialty one they keep on tap."

Trent pressed his mouth closed. He shoved away from the counter to pull the draft. After setting the full pilsner glass next to the untouched ice water, he again leaned forward on his crossed arms. "So you know Jillian's sister?"

Behind his glasses, Chambers narrowed his eyes and studied the multi-colored bruises along Trent's jaw. Trent lifted the corner of his mouth in a half smile that wasn't a smile. With the additional bruising and swelling beneath his right eye, he knew he looked dangerous. Looked like he wasn't afraid of a fight.

Right now, he'd love for Chambers to take a swing at him. Any excuse to punch the man in the mouth.

Chambers glanced down. "You're new here?"

Trent nodded again. "Filling in. Strictly short term."

"Between jobs?"

"In a manner of speaking."

Eric made a quick face. "Hayden is my girlfriend. At least, I think she's still my girlfriend."

"Problems?"

"I'm not sure." His arms crossed in front of his beer, he traced a pattern through the condensation on the glass. "I hope not."

"Women."

Chambers slid another glance towards Jillian. "Yeah."

Trent also glanced her way. She stood with one hip against the railing and one foot crossed over the other ankle, chatting with customers as if they were old friends. At least her shoulders had loosened and relaxed.

He forced his attention back to Chambers. "So, was your ex-wife really a princess?"

Eric's mouth tightened into a thin, bitter line. He pulled his arms back a fraction, protecting his beer within the circle of his arms. "Yes."

"Wow. That must have been interesting. Sorry I never had the chance to meet her."

"Not all tiaras and roses." Over his glasses, Eric rubbed the bridge of his nose. "Her father has already called."

"Expressing shared loss or threatening you?"

"Why would he threaten me?"

"You're the ex. His daughter has … passed away."

"We're amicable. I'm still friends with her brothers." Definitely defensive. "The brothers and I even own property together."

"That's right. You're the real estate guy."

"What are you, the local gossip monger?"

"Nah. Not local at all."

"Oh, that's right. You're just filling in." Chambers tapped the top of the pilsner glass with both index fingers. "You're Jillian's new guy. I heard you're staying at her place."

"You heard right." He didn't bother to hide the edge in his voice. Or to correct the assumption of relationship. None of this guy's fucking business.

Chambers' eyes widened a small fraction. His hands flat on the counter, he eased back. "The guy from the blown up boat."

A nerve jerked in Trent's cheek, but he nodded. "That would be me."

"Tough luck." Chambers glanced around the room again. He nodded at several people before settling against the back of his seat, a study in casualness missing the mark. "For both of us."

"I only lost a boat." Trent pressed a hand to his chest. "You lost an ex-wife.'

Chambers pushed his glasses up on his nose then wiped his hand over his mouth. He tossed money on the bar and pushed his chair back. With a dark look, he took his untouched beer and circled the room, nodding and chatting with several people before he ambled over to where three older ladies patted his arms then made room for him at their table.

Man could be a damn politician.

Trent rang up the beer, pocketed the measly quarter change and wiped the condensation from the counter.

Had Chambers lost his girlfriend, too? Had Hayden had anything to do with the ex's death?

Why did he care? *Sawyer, bide your time. Don't get involved.*

Right. Was it already too late?

Chapter Nine

"**W**HAT IS HE STILL doing here?" Dane Patrick's deep, raw voice cut across Jillian's dark thoughts.

She, too, wondered why the hell Eric still blessed Rosey's with his presence. Not like she'd made him feel welcome. Quite the opposite. "He came in looking for Hayden."

"That was hours ago. Since she's not here, shouldn't he be gone?"

"Tell me how you really feel." She set an unopened bottle of water on the table next to his guitar case, noted the mic was in the off position.

In the middle of a well-deserved break, Dane stood and stretched. His fingers linked behind his head, elbows out, he twisted from one side to the other.

She needed a break herself. "I've thought about throwing him out. Except he's a paying customer tonight."

"He hasn't drank more than a quarter of anything he's bought since I came in."

"But he keeps buying. His waste is on him."

"Tough being a shop owner."

The pace had slowed, people had filtered out, and only a handful of diehards remained. Along with Eric. This was so unlike him, it set her on edge.

With her forearm, she wiped her brow. She was tired. Tired of the gossip, tired of keeping a smile plastered on her face, tired of dodging Eric's cryptic glances.

Dane's shadowed gaze followed the man in question. "Did Hayden take off because of him?"

"I'm not sure." Jillian touched his elbow. "Dane."

His chin lifted, nostrils flared. Stiff, he lowered his arms to his sides. Obviously she wasn't the only one Eric set on edge.

"My sister —" Oh, jeez. How was she going to get through to this stubborn, proud man? "You should —"

"She's a grown woman, Jilly. I can't make choices for her."

"No?" Both hands on her hips, she sucked in several quick breaths. Otherwise she might strangle him. "How about letting her know that prick over there isn't her only choice?"

"That's on her."

Their eyes narrowed, they stood facing each other for a long, heavy moment.

"Jilly." Dane closed his eyes for a brief moment then ran a hand over his face. "The crowd has thinned. You're as strung out as I am. Why don't you go? I can hang around to help close down."

"So you can thump Eric?"

"I don't thump."

"Hayden wouldn't appreciate it, you know."

"She'd never have to know."

"Dane —"

"Go home, Jilly. Have your newest employee take you out of here."

"I don't need anyone to take me anywhere."

"What a pair we are." Dane gave her a lop-sided smile. Touched her cheek. "Both full of good, solid advice the other won't listen to."

"When you have some, I might actually listen."

"Trent." Dane motioned as the other man ambled by picking up dirty dishes and wiping empty tables. "Talk some sense into this woman. Get her out of here."

"If you signed my check, I'd be happy to oblige, Patrick." He tossed the towel over his shoulder. "Since you don't, I can't until she's ready."

"Like anyone will be taking me anywhere." On a pivot she stalked away from the two men. Trent's soft chuckle followed her across the room, sending small, electrified tingles down her stiff back. *Chauvinistic males.*

Behind the bar she grabbed a clean rag and another towel. Too much pent up energy. Too much … wanting what she shouldn't want. She needed to displace some of that energy, somewhere. Somehow.

The sight of Trent, dimples winking in and out of his cheeks from something Dane said, swirled the embers of that banked fire at the pit of her stomach. No matter how stupid an idea, she wanted Trent Sawyer.

And when he leaves?

She hadn't known him two full days and she already had him breaking her heart as he jumped on the nearest plane he could find.

A faint clink of glass against glass stiffened her spine.

Dammit, Rosey. Even if Trent managed to stick around, *he's a freaking FBI agent.* Not afraid to use his fists.

Obviously.

The bruises and abrasions along his jaw, the cut on his cheek and the nicks marking his knuckles told their own tale. He didn't walk away from a fight. He met it face on. *Literally.* So much violence. Too much violence.

Jillian pressed her fingertips to her forehead and rubbed her thumbs over her temples. He hadn't raised a hand to her.

Not every man was like the one who'd put her in the hospital.

But she didn't trust her own judgment when it came to men.

Didn't trust her heart not to lie.

Rosey's glasses rattled again, louder this time.

Keep it up, Rosey, and I'm going to invest in plastic glasses. The kind that don't rattle when you stick your nose into my business.

As if that would stop her grandmother.

Lowering her hand to her neck, she caught Trent's amused gaze. A smile widened his mouth and he winked. The blue of his eyes, caught by the dim light of the softly lit lanterns hung over each table, deepened to almost black.

Those embers in her belly flared, leaving her skin flushed. An image of Trent, his mouth ravaging hers, imposed itself in her mind. Unable to look away from him now, her breath caught and her fingers curled over her heart.

"Jillian?" Eric's voice scraped along her raw nerves.

She blinked. Her shoulders slumped, the momentary spell Trent held over her broken. That damn FBI agent was dangerous to her well-being. To gain a few moments to ease her quickened breathing, she kept her gaze on the floor's wooden planks.

"Jillian?" Eric had a great voice. Not like Dane's, not all full of gravel like Trent's, but easy on the ears. Rich. Tonight, with its barely restrained edge of irritation, Eric's voice grated.

She lifted her head and met his hooded gaze. A few feet away, lines furrowed Trent's forehead as he frowned. Dane again set down his guitar. Chins raised, both Trent and Dane took two steps toward her. She shook her head. In other circumstances she might appreciate their overbearing concern, their white knight action, but tonight it annoyed.

"What do you need, Eric?" She swiped her towel over an imaginary spot on the counter. "Another beer you're not going to drink?"

All right, then. She hadn't meant to say that out loud.

Eric's brows drew down but then he blinked behind his glasses and smiled. "You got my number, don't you? You always have."

She tipped her head to the side, let her brows rise in question. What kind of game was he playing now?

"I didn't want to be alone tonight. With what's happened to Felicity, and Hayden … not around, I just—"

He shrugged and pushed his glasses to the bridge of his nose. "But drinking too much didn't seem like a good idea, either."

Jillian swallowed then set her rag and dry towel on the counter. He might be a jerk with a huge ego, might have made her so mad she wanted to choke him, but he hurt. In spite of his whacked out ideas about Hayden, he'd lost someone he once cared for enough to marry.

And divorce – that small voice inside whispered.

She plastered her fake smile on her face. "How about some coffee, then? On the house."

Gratefulness flashed bright in his eyes. He nodded and settled more easily in the high-backed stool. After giving the order to her bartender, she patted Eric's hand and collected her rag and towel. He might have played on her sympathy – for a short bit—but she wasn't going to listen to anymore bullshit.

She could still taste the bitter ire of his earlier words.

How could he profess to love her sister, yet think her capable of murder? Dane didn't spout that nonsense, but then Dane knew Hayden better than Eric ever would. Her good points and her flaws.

Dane.

Maybe he was right. Maybe she should call it a night, get away from here for a while. Take her newest, temporary employee and hit the road.

Why the hell did that conjure up images she didn't want to face?

✧ ✧ ✧

TRENT KICKED A ROCK OFF the edge of the road, listened to it bounce into the dark water along the canal beside them. Clouds rimmed the horizon, but for now bright moonlight lit their way. Although they'd taken the boat to Rosey's Place earlier, Jillian wanted to walk home.

Considering she walked by his side, the two of them alone on this deserted side road, he didn't complain. The late night air pleasant. Jillian lifted her face to the soft breeze while it played with the ends of her long hair.

He stuffed his hands into his pockets, curled his fingers into his palms, to keep from touching those loose strands of her hair, to keep from stroking her arm, taking her hand.

He forced his focus to the road and their surroundings.

They'd strolled along in quiet companionship for the last mile. Not much traffic. Even the few sailboats moored in the Sound near Rosey's Place had, for the most part, been quiet. Not much activity.

Not completely sure, this being his first time to Jillian's by land, but they should be near her home. Close to the end of this peaceful interlude. A peacefulness he'd underrated in the last few years. He lifted his own face to the breeze, let it wash over him.

"What did Chambers do to piss you off so badly?" Damn. He couldn't leave well enough alone after all.

The line of her shoulders tensed. She lowered her head to stare at the road. "He told me Felicity had made a play to get him back, that my sister was jealous. That she was furious with him."

"And?"

"That he blames himself for whatever Hayden may have done."

"Wow. That's quite a leap." He kicked another rock to the side of the road. A soft splash echoed. Why the hell couldn't he leave well enough alone? "You don't buy it?"

"No."

"Why not? People do stupid things all the time in the name of love."

"Hayden doesn't love Eric." She sent a quick, sideways glance at him.

"So they're in a relationship because of serious, mutual lust?" He took her forearm, steered her around a lurking pot hole. "I can respect that."

He settled his arm around her shoulders, pulled her closer. Their steps meshed, slow and measured in the moonlight. When she didn't pull away a small thrill tightened his groin.

You didn't come here for sex, mutual attraction or not. He slid his palm down her bare arm. Her skin was soft. Like sun-warmed silk. Her hair smelled of some exotic mixture of spices concocted to drive a man to things he'd be better off avoiding.

Like relationships based on mutual lust.

He lightly squeezed her elbow then let go. Stepped away. She gave him a long, considering look from under her lashes. But she didn't say anything, simply lifted her face again to the light breeze, let it play with the ends of her sultry scented, tempting hair.

He couldn't fool himself, much as he wanted to hold on to the delusion. He wanted Jillian Rose with an intensity that meant he wouldn't be able to walk away from her unscathed.

Safer to walk away without giving in to that temptation.

"I thought Felicity had her own boyfriend." He kicked another rock. "That rich guy you told me about. Rhys something or another."

"Blackthorne. As if you didn't remember. I have a feeling there isn't much you miss." A small smile played over Jillian's lips.

God, he'd love to kiss that mouth. Devour it and—

Focus, Sawyer. Focus. "Why would you say that?"

"I watched you tonight. You watched everyone and everything happening around you. You didn't miss much."

"You're too generous. I'm sure there were all kinds of things that escaped my notice."

"Sure." She slipped a strand of hair behind her perfectly shaped ear.

He'd like to nibble on that ear. Start at the lobe … *slow down, Sawyer.* He had it bad, this mutual lust thing. With a shake of his head, he stared out over the black water of the canal, out over across the empty stretch of land on the other side. "We're close to your place, aren't we?"

She nodded. Her lips curved, that secret little smile that didn't bode well for his resistance. So tempting, those lips.

"That's my house, two doors down from here. I told you, you don't miss much."

Now, why did that statement please him?

They walked in silence. Once at her place, she unlatched the gate and pushed it open. Her hand on the metal hook, she tilted her head and looked up at him. With the moonlight streaming down, her honeyed eyes took on a burnished silver glow. He could get lost in those eyes. A drowning man happy to be sinking into whatever the night brought.

And what about tomorrow?

She laid a hand on his arm, stroked his skin with her thumb. The knot at the center of his gut clenched in on itself.

On an oath, he pulled her into his arms. Crushed her mouth with his.

Heat blazed through him, scorching his already damaged soul. Her lips parted and he plunged his tongue deep into the heat of her mouth. God, she tasted of ambrosia. A nectar of honey and spice meant for him alone.

Their mouths locked and her hands bracketing his face, she pressed the length of her body to his. He cradled her bottom, rocked his erection against her.

This was asinine. On so many counts.

She sucked on his tongue and stole his breath.

How fast could they get inside the damn house?

He backed her against the gate before he lifted her. She wrapped those long, sexy legs around his middle.

Squeezed. Dammit, he was going to come unglued out here.

He moved a few steps forward, stopped to gasp for air. She nipped at his bottom lip. He pulled hers into his mouth, sucked. Her gasp of tortured pleasure sent tremors through his loins.

An off-key whistle broke through his lust-induced haze.

What the—

The fucking neighbor.

Jillian rubbed her forehead over his overheated one. She unlinked her ankles and slid her legs down his. He traced his hands up her back, along her spine. Her eyes half closed, she shivered and leaned into him.

Maybe if they ignored him, the neighbor would disappear.

The whistling stopped a mere foot away. Trent rested his cheek on Jillian's head then angled to look down at the shorter man.

"Is this here guy bothering you, Jillian?" The drunk swayed, but managed to stay on his feet. He stretched his fingers, touched a strand of her hair. "So beautiful."

"No touching." Trent settled Jillian to the side and behind him. He didn't know if she minded or not, but he did. *Big time*. He gripped the man's shoulder and turned him away from them. "You need to go home. Now."

"Righto." The man nodded several times then dug into his jeans' pocket. He pulled out his keys but dropped them. Bending over to retrieve them, he fell. And stayed there, face down on the ground.

Trent shoved a hand over his head then rubbed at his neck.

"We can't leave him there." Jillian's hands pressed warm on his arm.

"I can."

"No." Jillian glanced up at the moon, now partially covered with silver lined, threatening clouds. A rumble of thunder echoed in the distance. "He'll get drenched and we'll feel guilty."

"You'll feel guilty. I won't."

"Trent."

Shit and shit again. This was why he didn't do relationships. "Let's get his sorry ass home."

Chapter Ten

THUNDER BOOMED, close at hand, as the late night storm dumped its rain in earnest. Jillian and Trent made a frantic dash across her yard and through her gate to her front door.

Dammit. With a tremble in her fingers she couldn't quite hide, she scrambled for her keys and got the door open, but not before they were both soaked.

The neighbor slept sound in his own bed, in spite of Trent wanting to leave the guy flat on his living-room floor to sleep it off. Now, here in her own house, she just had the matter of what to do about Trent.

She wanted to continue what they'd started. Wanted Trent inside her, rocking her world.

But what about tomorrow?

The neighbor would probably have one huge hangover with a major headache to deal with.

What would she have?

Heartache?

Guaranteed.

Trent flipped the light switch inside the door, chasing the darkness to the edge of the illuminated circle of light. He wiped rainwater from his face and gave her a rueful grin. "You've changed your mind."

Was she that transparent? "I—"

"It's okay, Jillian." He stroked the back of his hand down her cheek, caressed her ear lobe. Gave her a gentle smile. "It was a bad idea, anyway. Neither of us need the complications of an *entanglement* right now. Even one built on mutual lust."

Speak for yourself. She bit the words back. No matter how much she wanted him to be wrong, he was right.

He dropped his hand then stepped back from her. "Go get dry. Get some sleep."

As if that would be possible.

She gave him a small smile. Nodded once then locked the front door and fled upstairs.

Once in her bedroom, she shut her door and leaned against it in the dark. Tremors she'd managed to contain finally broke free, shaking her to her core.

God, who was she to give Dane advice when she wouldn't let herself try? When she was so bent on protecting her own heart she was afraid to reach out?

An entanglement. Not a relationship.

They'd known each other little more than, what? Thirty-six hours, give or take.

Sex with him would be crazy.

Crazy wild and passionate.

Heat, like tiny prickles of pain, spread through her body, pooled between her legs. She bent at the waist to rest her palms on her soaked knees. She needed to get out of these clothes. Put on something dry. Climb into bed and forget Trent would be sleeping two bedrooms away.

Dane was the smart one. She needed to follow his example. Protect herself the way he did. Hayden would only take his heart and shred it into pieces so tiny he would never be able to put it back together.

Or would he be the one to finally show Hayden not all love was like their parent's relationship?

She shook her head once, sharp. This between her and Trent wasn't a relationship. That word held too much weight, too many complications. Entanglement was probably right. A flash in the dark, a bolt of lightning. No substance to speak of, nothing that could be touched or harnessed.

But, oh, the damage it could do.

TRENT'S THIRD AFTERNOON at Rosey's and he'd already fallen into a vague routine of sorts. Set up the tables for dinner, call Ben for a status report, catch the sway of Jillian's hips across the room.

Chastise himself. Repeat internal warning about getting tangled up with the locals.

No matter how much he wanted to tangle with one particular local. Tangle, kiss, and bury himself in her warm, supple body.

Last night had been a close call. He pulled his gaze from Jillian's ass. A close call he half regretted not taking regardless of the consequences.

Focus, Sawyer.

Ben had yet to return Trent's call today. Yesterday's

phone chat hadn't progressed Trent's agenda one iota. Ben hadn't wired any money, hadn't gotten his credentials replaced. Hadn't sent him a damn gun.

Trent wanted to be involved in *anything* his team was doing. Right now, he'd even take desk time. Anything to be away from the temptation wrapped up in Jillian Rose.

Not that he was sure he even had a team any longer. Besides the possible suspension on the FBI side, there was the matter of his *Hunter* skills being non-existent. Skills that were his entire reason for being on the task force in the first place.

Give it time, Ben had said. *Might only be temporary. Might be. Maybe.* Might also be permanent.

If that was the price, he wasn't sorry to pay it. Wouldn't let himself be sorry.

He damn well wasn't sorry the bastard who'd killed his sister was dead. Or that he'd been the one responsible for that death.

Then there was Jillian.

His gaze drifted back to her ass as she bent to retrieve something she'd dropped.

Yeah. Jillian.

With no customers or other employees on the premises, they had the place to themselves. The memory of last night's kisses burned, so her skittishness was probably good. Good she kept herself busy across the room.

Even though he hated that distance.

He placed another setting of pink napkin, rolled silverware on one of the glass topped tables. The water glowed green in the mirrored reflections from underneath. A shadow wavered across the top of the table. He shifted his position to face the oncoming person as Ted Mathews approached from the open door of the building. Ted stopped, pulled his glasses off and slipped them into his front pocket.

The officer, as crisply dressed today as ever, appeared far more somber than he had the last two times they'd talked. He nodded at Trent as he scanned the area. Once his gaze lit on Jillian, he swallowed several times then looked at the ground.

Not good.

Trent moved forward and offered his hand.

Gratefulness flicked through Ted's eyes. He swallowed again.

Jillian, her steps almost as silent as a cat's, moved to stand beside Trent.

He lifted his arm to wrap it around her waist, to pull her close, but caught himself at the last moment. Instead, he rubbed the top of his head. "Is this about my boat?"

"Ben's boat." Jillian's words snapped in the air between them.

Trent allowed his lips to move a slight fraction.

Ted, looking miserable, shook his head. "I'm not here about the Oasis."

Jillian, wiping her hands on the towel she held, tilted her head. "Then what can we do for you?"

"Jilly, we got a call from Biscayne Bay a little while ago."

She arched her left brow.

Ted swallowed again. "The Symphony exploded early this morning."

Trent blinked. *Crap.*

"What?" Jillian frowned. She pressed a hand to her chest. Shook her head.

"Jazz had the Symphony docked at Sunrise Marina for the last two nights, picking up a charter. Right now, we don't know how many people were aboard."

"Hayden —"

"We don't know, Jilly." He sent a desperate glance towards Trent. "A dive team is down now. Officials on the ground are attempting to find the status of everyone who was supposed to be on board."

"Hayden." Jillian cupped her hands over her mouth.

Trent pulled a chair out from the table beside her. He slipped a hand under her elbow and settled her in the seat. She didn't protest, didn't take her gaze from Ted's.

"You haven't heard from her, have you?" A slight pleading edged Ted's voice.

Jillian, her eyes wide and unfocused even as she stared at the deputy, slowly shook her head. "Not since she left the other morning."

Trent, with one hand on Jillian's shoulder and his other balled into a fist, stood next to her. He angled his head, stared across the too bright water for a drawn out moment. He knew what this felt like. Every single emotion welling inside, threatening to close off the throat. Then forgetting to breathe.

God, Jillian. He knew this one. Intimately.

Ted faced them, his fingers linked in front of him,

his own eyes coated with a sheen of moisture.

"Maybe she wasn't on board." From behind her hands, Jillian's voice wobbled.

Man, he'd been there, too.

Denial.

Jillian brushed her fingers over her cheeks. "What about Jazz? Her grandmother? Has anyone …."

"Devon went down to Marathon to talk with her."

"How is she?"

Ted grimaced, squinting out at the water before he met Jillian's gaze. "She – collapsed. Heart attack. Transported to Miami. She didn't make it, Jilly."

Tears shimmered in her eyes. She blinked, fast and hard. "Give me a few minutes."

Trent squeezed her shoulder lightly. She pushed herself from her chair and fled.

After the bathroom door swung closed behind her, Trent brushed his knuckles along his jaw. "Any idea how this happened?"

Ted shook his head. "Hopefully the dive team will find some answers."

"Any ideas why?"

"Why?" Ted rubbed the back of his neck. "As in foul play why?"

Trent nodded once, slow. The guy was sharp. Although Trent knew it was too soon to know much, he wanted the man's take on the situation.

Ted sucked in a deep breath, let it out. "Not my jurisdiction."

"You've been to the scene?"

He wet his lips, glanced away before meeting Trent's steady gaze. "Yes."

"What does your gut tell you?"

Again Ted glanced away, this time to stare at the ceiling. Trent waited. When he wanted something bad enough, he'd perfected patience down to an art.

"I don't see how this could be anything except deliberate." Ted's bleak gaze swung to his. "They're looking at the charter and the guy's business associates. There's talk of an untenable takeover. Lots of animosity. Not sure how much of that is rumor. They're attempting to sort the facts now."

"And Jillian's sister?"

"Anyone who was on board is dead."

"It's assumed she was on board?"

"They're not assuming anything yet."

"Your gut?"

"She was supposed to be." Misery all over his face, Ted shrugged. "If she wasn't, then where is she?"

Good point. Good question. "Are you buying the business associate angle?"

"No."

"Why not?"

"The Oasis blown up down here. Dead body in the mangroves. Felicity Chambers falling down that flight of stairs the way she did. The Symphony exploding with Hayden on board. Too many random things for my peace of mind."

"Random being the operative word."

"I think—" Ted flicked a quick glance at the still

closed bathroom door. "Hayden is at the center of whatever is going on."

"And that would be?"

"I have no idea." Ted scrubbed a hand over his face, through his hair. The ends stood at attention, messier than he'd ever seen the officer. "You asked about my gut. I have no facts. No proof. I was out the night before Hayden and Jazz took off. I saw them both. Neither one mentioned Hayden crewing for Jazz, although Jazz told me about her charter. Something made Hayden bolt. Something last minute."

All of that, mixed together the way it was, made Trent's own gut take notice. "And the charter, the business angle on all of this?"

"He's a transplant from Illinois to Miami. No discernible ties to the Keys. This trip was supposedly his family's first outing through the Keys. Jazz is one of the best guides."

"Family?" Trent's jaw tight, he leaned his head back.

"A wife and two teenaged sons."

Crap. "So six possible victims?"

Ted nodded. "Jazz had said they were all excited. That the wife was thrilled the husband was actually taking the time to go with them. That business had been stressful but had lightened to the point he could take a short vacation."

"Doesn't mean there weren't issues she knew nothing about."

"Yeah. No assumptions." One side of Ted's mouth lifted in a sardonic smile. "But we were talking about my gut here."

Touché.

The bathroom door creaked open. Jillian brushed her hair back from her face and gave them a small, wan smile that didn't touch her red-rimmed eyes. She glanced around before making her way hesitantly back to them.

"What do you need from me?" She brushed her hands down her jean-clad legs then wiped the tip of her nose with the back of her hand.

"Right now, nothing. Once the dive team surfaces, we'll know more." Ted's expression still miserable, he shrugged a shoulder. "I didn't want you hearing this from anyone else."

Trent ran a hand over the top of his head.

Been there, done that, too. Didn't want the memories.

But still the image of his own sister swam through his mind, mixed with that of his partner's sister. A few years apart. Both his fault.

With the thumb and forefinger of one hand he rubbed at his eyes, trying to dislodge the visions stuck there. *Asinine, really.* He ran his hand over his mouth, his jaw. He hadn't been able to erase those images before. Why would now be any different?

Jillian's hand on Ted's arm, she raised on her toes and kissed his cheek. "Thank you for being the one to come here. I know this wasn't easy."

Ted squeezed her fingers. "Rather it be me than one of the others. Although if Shamus had been on duty and not sick in bed, he'd be the one here."

Jillian's lips trembled. She pressed them together then nodded. "Would you like some coffee?"

Ted hesitated. "No. I should get going."

"Will you—" She stopped, took a deep breath. "Will you keep us informed? Please?"

"Yes. I will." With a quick glance at Trent, Ted pulled her into his arms and rested his chin on her head. After a moment, he gave her a tighter hug then stepped back. He shook Trent's hand and hurried away.

Jillian's arms wrapped around her middle, she stared at the empty doorway.

"Do you want me to call someone to come in?" Trent, unable to keep from touching her – fool that he was – ran his palm down her arm. "To take care of this place for the evening? For tonight?"

Tears shimmering on the edge of her lashes, she blinked several times before looking at him. "No. I need to stay busy. I can't – I can't go home. Not yet."

He knew that one, too. Just as intimately. Work to keep your mind off what you didn't want to think about.

"All right." He handed her the towel she had left on the table earlier. "If this gets out, if anyone has heard about this explosion, they're going to be showing up and asking questions. Are you able to deal with that?"

"Better than dealing with my thoughts going round in circles."

Exactly. Man, that one was real. "Then let's get this place ready for your customers."

Chapter Eleven

NEARLY SIX HOURS SINCE JILLIAN had been sideswiped with the news about the Symphony and business boomed at Rosey's Place.

She set a full tray of dirty dishes on the bar and wiped at her cheek with the back of her hand. Trent had been right. The news had spread fast.

Now her smile was strained, her shoulders tight and her manner short. Either her customers understood or they didn't. She'd fielded too many questions, too much concern about Hayden that had Jillian's eyes stinging with tears. All on top of the concerned glances from Trent. Those came close to cracking the thin shell she'd erected around herself.

"You doing all right?" From behind, Trent's lowered voice washed over her skin.

Why couldn't she just burrow into that graveled voice, wrap it around herself like a cocoon? Ignore everything and everyone else?

"You're sure you don't want to head home, now?" He slipped his hands across her shoulders, his fingers doing that massage thing that had her wanting to lean back and simply melt into him.

She shook her head. What would she do at home? Mope? Dwell? Sit in Hayden's room? She was better off here. When her grandmother had died, she'd done the same thing. Thrown herself into running Rosey's Place. Spent any spare time worrying about her sister.

Hayden.

Jillian blinked several times.

Trent squeezed her shoulders. She steeled herself from turning into him, from leaning against him. Instead she pushed her tray towards the bartender and stepped from under Trent's hands.

His sympathy only made her eyes fill faster with tears she couldn't release. She had to keep busy. Keep moving.

At least Rosey was quiet. Jillian wasn't sure she'd have been able to cope with rattling glasses tonight.

She grabbed an empty tray and hurried to the other side of the room.

Her sister couldn't be gone. If she were, wouldn't Jillian, herself, feel something? Know something?

Hayden. She just couldn't be dead. Or was that what people told themselves when they couldn't accept?

Jillian set glasses from an empty table onto her tray. She added plates customers were finished with from the table next to the vacated one.

Jazz and her grandmother. Dead.

That entire family who'd chartered Jazz' boat. Gone, forever.

The steady drone of voices flowed over Jillian. Louder. More people, more questions.

"Where's Dane tonight?" Trent stood behind her.

Too close.

That urge to lean against him, to let him wrap those strong arms around her and take the weight from her shoulders, simmered below the façade she'd erected around her heart.

Stupid idea.

"I guess he decided not to come." She angled away from Trent. Away from temptation. The dirty dishes on her tray rattled.

Trent gripped her tray, raised an eyebrow when she frowned.

Fine. She let go, lifted her hands, palms forward, in surrender.

A speculative gleam flickered in Trent's eyes. "Dane's not on the schedule this evening?"

"No." She waved him towards the bar and fell in step beside him. "I have acts scheduled on the weekends, but during the week it's first come, first spot on stage. We keep it informal. But when Dane's here, no one else tries. The crowd loves him."

"So where is he tonight?"

She shrugged. "He could be anyplace down the Keys or he could have taken the night off. With Dane, there's no telling."

If she were honest with herself, she'd been relieved he stayed away tonight. She probably should have called him, but what would she say? If he'd heard the rumors … she couldn't worry about that. Unless or until she had something concrete, she would continue to be as vague as she'd been with everyone else tonight. And that included Dane and her parents.

Her parents. No way would she call either of them without having hard facts.

Trent headed behind the bar and stacked the dirty dishes from his tray in the sudsy water. On the customer side of the counter, Jillian splayed her hands on the bar. *A few minutes, that's all I need.*

"Look who the devil dragged in here." The burly bartender leaned forward and braced his elbows on the counter.

Jillian glanced over her shoulder.

Eric Chambers.

Her stomach sank to her knees. Two nights in a row. What was his game this time?

She pressed both hands to her over warm cheeks. Took a controlled breath. Whatever he wanted, she'd deal with it. Send him on his way.

"I take it he's not a regular." Trent angled his head towards the bartender and mirrored his stance, leaning his elbows on the counter. "You don't like him?"

"Not even a little." The bartender's movements efficient, he pushed up from the bar and mixed a rum and coke. He moved off to deliver the drink to a customer sitting at the other end of the bar.

"Jillian." Eric's voice deep, commanding and full of accusation, he stood behind her, not quite close enough to be in her space, but close enough it irritated her.

Not an auspicious way to start a conversation. With the entire bar watching as if this were the main event of the evening.

Maybe it is.

Chin in the air, she turned and leaned back against the bar, her elbows resting on the counter with her hands dangling. She even crossed her ankles. Arched an eyebrow.

Trent came from behind the bar and settled two stools down, his arms loosely crossed over his chest.

Eric flicked a quick glance in his direction before focusing on her. "Why didn't you call me?"

"About?"

"Hayden."

"We don't know anything." She held his gaze. "There's nothing to tell."

"The police—"

"Don't know anything yet. You're jumping to conclusions based on innuendo and rumor."

"You think she's still—" Eric swallowed once, worked his jaw back and forth. "That she wasn't on board the Symphony after all?"

"I don't know." Slightly ashamed of her rigid stance with him, she lowered her chin and let her shoulders slump. Regardless of her feelings about him, he'd suffered one loss and now, possibly, a second.

Hayden.

"Unless they find she wasn't on board, we've lost her." Eric lifted a hand as if to touch Jillian's arm. He slid a quick glance at Trent and seemed to change his mind. Instead he rubbed that hand over the muscle twitching along his jaw.

"Don't say that."

"We need to be realistic."

"Until they say she was on board, I'm not going there." Her chin lifted of its own accord.

"You should have called me. You know what Hayden means to me. You know—"

"Last night you were in here practically accusing her of pushing your ex-wife down those stairs." Jillian fought to keep her voice low, to keep the hiss out of her words. "Now you think I should call you with information on my sister? Not going to happen."

"I was only telling you about the altercation between Felicity and Hayden. I didn't mean to imply—"

"Yes you did. That was exactly what you meant to imply."

"Jillian." Eric extended both hands, palms up. Behind his glasses a spark of anticipation lit his hazel eyes. There, then gone.

Dammit all to hell. "You need to leave, Eric."

Those hazel eyes widened, the color darkening. "You can't be serious."

Trent's movements quick and efficient, he stood at her side.

Eric glanced at him then took a step back. "Jillian."

"You heard the lady." Trent's voice, although low and even, vibrated with a hard unrelenting edge. "You need to leave."

"But—"

Jillian crossed her arms over her chest.

Eric's gaze swung between the two of them. With his mouth tight, and that nerve still twitching in his jaw, he nodded. "Call me when you hear anything."

She arched her brow.

"Please." The word ground out of his mouth.

Trent's hands fisted at his waist. He angled his head then leaned a slight bit forward. "Leave."

Eric's eyes narrowed. He glanced around. With his shoulders and back stiff, he stalked out of the restaurant.

Jillian released the breath she hadn't realized she held. She swung around to face the bar. Her hands trembled. To keep the shake from showing, she pressed her hands to the counter and gripped the edge.

Eric Chambers was nothing but an ego inflated ass-hole. *Remember that.*

After a few drawn out moments, the buzz in the restaurant picked up as people went back to minding their own business. Which probably had everything to do with what they just saw.

I don't care.

Trent laid a hand over hers. Staring at the strength in his fingers covering her own she turned hers up and linked her hand with his. Warmth seeped through her from that simple contact.

"This is where I'm supposed to say thank you." She kept her gaze on their laced fingers.

"Only if you want to."

"I don't want to. I don't want to need anyone to do anything for me."

"I can respect that."

"Can you?"

"Yes. Isn't going to stop me from stepping in. But I

respect what's inside you that makes you feel that way."

Maybe Trent Sawyer is an asshole, too.

"Come on." He squeezed her fingers. "Let's get some air."

"All the windows are open." She waved her free hand in front of them. "We can't get much more air than this."

He tugged on her. "Then let's take a short walk to blow out the cobwebs."

Why not? She signaled her bartender and, with her fingers laced with Trent's, they headed out the door and down the pier away from Rosey's. Brought on the coolness of the breeze, a sweet scent of recent rain flowed around them. Pockets of water pooled in the low spots of the wooden planks.

Diffused light from three separate street lamps lit a portion of the nearly full parking area. Trent stopped. Went still.

What had he seen?

Without moving her head, she scanned the area.

In the far corner Eric leaned against his silver Mercedes Roadster with his legs crossed at the ankle. He held a cell phone to his ear, his mouth twisted in a sardonic smile. Spotting them watching him, Eric straightened and ended his call. With a slight grimace, he yanked the car door open. Once inside, the slam reverberated across the area.

The engine revved, hard and fast, before he tore out of the parking lot.

"I don't know what Chambers' game is." Trent

pulled her forward, squeezed her fingers again, and continued their lazy pace forward around several haphazardly parked vehicles. "But I have a feeling you played right into it tonight."

"At least we both agree he has some kind of game going."

In spite of being irritated with Trent, she continued to hold his hand. Just for this space in time, it felt right. Felt good.

"What type of game? And why?" Trent's thumb rubbed hers. "Unless he's the one responsible for his ex-wife's death."

"Why does anyone have to be responsible? Why couldn't she have simply fallen down the stairs like Devon believes?"

"Because Devon is – green. And sometimes the most obvious answer isn't the right answer."

"If Felicity didn't fall down the steps, what do you think happened?"

Trent shrugged one shoulder, aimed them towards the darker side of the lot, closer to where Eric had parked. "No idea. I haven't been to the scene, no idea what kind of evidence is there. Still, isn't it odd Chambers chose last night and then tonight to be seen at Rosey's? When, according to everyone I've talked with, he doesn't frequent the place."

"Be seen?"

The corners of Trent's eyes crinkled in the low light. "Didn't he strike you as a politician making his rounds? Shaking hands, asking for the vote?"

On point characterization. Fit Eric completely. "In a manner of speaking. Where are you going with this?"

"He had an agenda when he walked in last night." Trent stopped in the empty space where the little silver roadster had been parked. His eyes dark and intent, he scanned the area. "He also had an agenda this evening. From the way he gloated when he was on his phone out here, he was quite pleased with the way things turned out. Although I don't think he expected you to actually throw him out."

"I didn't throw him out. I asked him to leave."

"Same difference." Trent stared out at the water. Frowned. With the hand not holding hers, he pressed two fingers to his temple, almost as if it hurt. He shook his head once before smoothing his palm over his ear to the back of his neck then shaking out his hand. "Whose boat is that?"

She followed his gaze. Dark, except for the orange glow of someone's cigarette, a long, sleek sailboat sat moored a short distance from the mangroves. "Some rich foreigner, I think one of the customers said. People filter in and out on a regular basis. Here today. Tomorrow, who knows?"

"That one was there last night."

"And?"

"Great view of Rosey's Place without really being noticed from your side."

"Okay. Why is that suspicious?"

"Guy sitting there, smoking. Watching." Trent raised their hands, pressed his lips to her knuckles. "Why? Who is he and what does want?"

Chapter Twelve

"**M**IGHT NOT BE ANYTHING." In the nighttime shadows of the parking area outside Rosey's Place, Trent gazed at the moored sailboat and tugged Jillian a step closer. "Might be something. You need to stay aware of your surroundings. There are too many weird, random things going on. I don't hold with randomness."

Especially when I can't get a handle on any damn thing.

The next time he talked with Ben, he'd ask him to find out who owned that particular boat. Maybe Ted's comments about smuggling weren't so far off the mark.

Right now, though, the night breeze, carrying the fresh scent of recent rain and mixing with the brininess of Blackwater Sound, teased his senses and lifted loose strands of Jillian's hair. He resisted the urge to tuck those strands behind her ears. Barely resisted the urge to pull her more fully into his arms.

She gazed out at the vessel, her bottom lip between her teeth.

"I don't know what your sister was involved in, Jillian, but—"

"That's just it." She yanked her hand from his and

ducked from under his semi-embrace. She whirled to stare at the water, then back to face him. "What could she be involved in? Rosey died six months ago. We've only just gotten the place scraped back together. Yes, Hayden would rather play than work hard, but that's not a crime."

No it isn't. But the wrong person could manipulate that. Trent took Jillian's hands. She made a token attempt to pull them back, but he held firm. Her shoulders sagged and she stared at their hands.

Bands across his chest tightened. He rubbed his thumb over her knuckles. "So it's only been six months since you lost your grandmother? And now you've lost your sister, too."

"Hayden isn't gone until – if – they find her body."

God, Jillian. "Sweetheart, I've been where you are right now."

Her eyes locked on his, she shook her head.

"Yes."

This time her movements were slower, but still she shook her head. Tears shimmered on her lashes but she blinked them back. She wouldn't cry in front of him, he knew that as well as he knew anything about her.

Had she cried for the loss of her grandmother? Or had she remained stoic then, too? Shoving the emotions down, refusing to allow them any control in her life?

Something else he knew a lot about. "A few years ago I lost my sister. It was senseless. Unfair. She shouldn't have died."

Jillian stared at him, those honeyed eyes of hers dark

in the dim light. A nerve pulsed along his jaw, taunting him. How was he supposed to help her, when he could hardly help himself?

He tipped his head to gaze at the sailboat. The smoker must have finished his cigarette. Was the person still sitting there, or had he gone inside?

There'd been a time Trent would have known the answer before the thought fully formed. A time when he could pluck that type of knowledge from the air. When he'd *know*. When he could trust what he knew to be completely accurate. When his head wouldn't ache from the slightest mental push on what had once been second nature.

Trent pulled his gaze back to Jillian's.

He'd brought Cassie up, but he didn't want to talk about his sister.

Jillian turned her hands palm up, linked her fingers with his. Warmth seeped into hands he just realized were chilled. Cold all the way down to the bone.

"What happened to your sister?" Jillian's voice, soft on the breeze that played with her hair, echoed through him.

"Cassie was—" His breath burned his throat. At the same time, he couldn't get quite enough air into his lungs. "A beautiful soul. Young. Trusting. My parents' late in life child. Having to tell them she was gone, that it was my fault, was the hardest thing I've ever done."

"Oh." Jillian's hands tightened on his.

Not able to bear the sympathy – or pity – in her eyes, he focused over her head, on the trees at the edge of the property. There, just inside the line of shrubs, movement so subtle he wasn't sure what he'd seen, caught his gaze.

He pulled on Jillian's hands, pulled her into his embrace and behind him in one smooth, quick move.

"What?" Her voice low, she pressed her hands to his back.

"I'm not sure." His senses hit another *damn*, solid wall. He needed his weapon. Any weapon. "Where's your nearest bat?"

"In my car. Back seat floorboard."

"Keys?" He angled his body to keep himself between her and whoever hid along the tree line.

She fished keys from her pocket and pushed them into his hand. He linked his arm around her waist. They strolled, with an easy stride he didn't feel, towards her car.

From the corner of his eye he spotted more movement in the bushes closer to the parking lot, movement that trailed them, following them from a constant distance. Another drunk, like Jillian's neighbor? Eric, back for more of whatever game he played? The blond giant?

At Jillian's car, he unlocked the doors, opened the back and found the bat. As he closed the car door he leaned forward, pressed his mouth just below her ear. "Lock yourself in."

"Not happening." Her breath feathered across his jaw.

"Jillian." *Shit.* He didn't have time for her stubborn streak.

"There is no way I'm sitting here safe and snug in the car while you go fight dragons."

"We don't know what kind of damn dragon that is."

"Exactly."

"I don't need your protection, woman. I have your bat. I'm an FBI agent. This is what I do."

A hesitant light flashed in her eyes then was gone. She straightened away from him, chin raised, hands on her hips. "Then you'd better get on with it."

Heaven help him, he wanted to kiss that mutinous mouth into submission.

"I'm not getting in the car." Her voice low, she pulled her cell phone from her pocket. "But I will stay right here as long as it looks like you don't need me."

As good as I'm going to get from her. Shit. *Will she do as she says?*

Tremors of trepidation scudded down his spine.

Dammit to hell.

Without another word, he hefted the bat and took off in a low crouched run for the bushes. The rustling transformed into full-fledged thrashing as whoever had been there tore through the shrubs to the other side. Away from him.

Trent followed. Pebbles under his shoes crunched, flew up behind him. Once through the line of brush, he found himself on the side of the main road. No cars in sight from either direction. Across the road, dark water stretched outward to meet the moon rimmed clouds in the distance.

Nothing stirred.

In a full circle, one hand gripped around the bat handle and the other fisted, he scanned the entire area.

He stood alone on the highway.

How had the person disappeared so quickly? So completely?

As if they'd never existed.

JILLIAN STOOD JUST INSIDE her bedroom door, in the dark, and shoved both hands through her hair then rested them at her nape. The air was cool from the overhead paddle fan she must have forgotten to shut off before leaving for work. She contemplated simply dropping onto her bed, face first, and sinking into oblivion.

The night had been long. Customers who were usually gone before last call had lingered, wanting to talk. About Hayden. About Felicity. Even about Rosey.

Now, in the wee hours of the morning, exhaustion nipped at the fringes of Jillian's mind. Drained emotionally as well as physically. And neither she nor Trent knew who'd hid in the bushes surrounding the parking area at Rosey's.

One more in a long line of unanswered questions.

On a sigh, Jillian flipped her bedroom light switch and squinted in the sudden brightness. On her bed, in middle of her pillow, sat a square, yellow piece of paper with her sister's handwriting scribbled across it.

Oh, Lord. "Hayden."

Jillian's hands trembled. She stumbled to the bed and

picked up the note. Moisture blurred her vision to the point she couldn't read what was on the page.

"Are you all right?" A frown in Trent's voice, he moved into her room.

She held out the paper. He took it from her shaking fingers, glanced at it then took a second, longer look.

"Sis, please don't worry. I'm fine. Don't let anyone know. I can't explain right now, but I will. Love you," he read out loud. He looked at her over the note. "This is your sister's handwriting?"

Unable to form a coherent word, she gave him a short, jerky nod.

Hayden is still alive.

"So she found her keys." Trent wet his lips then handed the note back to her. "What do you intend to do about this?"

She frowned. *What does he mean, do about this?*

"Jillian. People are dead. She's supposed to be one of them. Obviously she isn't."

"So?"

"So, I'm sure she has information the authorities could use to track down whoever is responsible."

"What am I supposed to do? Turn my own sister in to the police?"

"What if she's done something criminal? Like kill someone?"

"Hayden wouldn't—"

"We are all capable if pushed far enough. What if she knows who blew up that boat and is afraid for her life?"

"Oh, no." *What if he's right? What if—*

"Stop." Trent gripped her shoulders. He lowered his chin to look her directly in the eyes. "This isn't getting us anywhere."

"She said not to tell anyone."

"Do you do everything your sister says to do?"

"That's juvenile."

"It's a legitimate question."

"Telling the police could put her in jeopardy."

"Maybe it would. Maybe it's all drama and a bunch of crap. I don't know your sister."

God, she wanted to stamp her foot. Throw a tantrum. "Why should I tell them?"

He smiled, like a predator who had just cornered his quarry.

Flutters quivered in her stomach, tightened to a hard, solid knot.

"I never said you should."

An iciness slithered around her spine and squeezed. *Asshole.* "Then why?"

"You're so contrary, I wanted to make sure we were on the same page."

Bastard asshole. She showed her teeth, not a real snarl but close. "Why don't you want me to go to the police?"

"For all the reasons you mentioned. In addition, your sister seems to be the fulcrum of several converging points. Going to Ted in the future could be a real, *viable*, option. Right now, though, your sister is safer if we keep this between us."

Relief flooded Jillian, half dissolving the knot tangled in her stomach and around her spine. For now, at least from this direction, Hayden was safe.

Trent's touch light, he pulled her into a quick embrace. His hands stroked down her arms, sending those damnable, unwelcome frissons of heat chasing across her skin. He kissed the top of her head. "Go to bed. Get some rest."

UNABLE TO SLEEP, regardless of the fact it was nearly four in the morning, Trent lay in bed staring at the paddles of the overhead fan as they went around in slow circles. Much like his own thoughts.

Cassie.

If she had lived, she'd be nearing her twenty-fifth birthday. If her life hadn't been taken. Her essence. Her innocence.

If she hadn't been killed for simply being Trent Sawyer's little sister.

Trent pressed the heels of his palms to his eyes. If he could erase the image of her laying there on the ground, her body twisted, her throat slashed and her open eyes staring at nothing, he would.

Although it had taken years, the bastard responsible had paid with his own life.

But even that didn't erase the nightmares eating at Trent when he closed his eyes.

TRENT SET HIS EMPTY coffee mug in Jillian's sink. Strong midmorning sun shone through the slanted blinds in her kitchen. He shook his head. This was winter. He was used to a weak, more northerly sun, not one that would burn you as soon as look at you.

In February.

Jillian breezed into the room, her face pale but her smile genuine. His heart gave an extra little thump, probably to get his attention.

He didn't need that kind of help. Not when it came to Jillian. He ignored the erratic beat and gave her a slow smile.

A flicker of something warm and almost welcoming sparked in her eyes. She blinked twice then pressed her lips together. On an outward huff of breath, she grabbed her keys and jerked her head to the side, indicating the door.

Guess that meant they were leaving.

Probably a good idea, considering the direction his thoughts wanted to take him.

He meandered after her and bumped into her when she stopped just outside the back door. Hands spanning her waist, he griped the top of her hips to keep her from falling over.

"Great." Annoyance coated her voice, almost covered the underlying dread.

"Hmm?" He stopped himself short of nuzzling her hair. The scent, something between citrus and patchouli, gave him thoughts he also didn't need help with. "Did you forget something?"

"No."

Immediately Trent pulled his gaze from her hair and

scanned the area.

A man stood, his back to them, at the edge of the dock. The guy's stance was wide, his hands tucked into the front pockets of his beige slacks. Thick grey hair touched the collar of his understated royal blue and gold Hawaiian silk shirt.

Trent touched his hip with his elbow, checking for a weapon not there. His gaze locked on the stranger, he pushed at his senses and met *annoyance*.

The wall was still there. His head ached from the effort. But threads of irritation filtered through.

He shook his head once to clear it but the fragile awareness, from either Jillian or the man, *not sure which*, still hung in the air. Not much to go on, but right now, he'd take even the slightest edge.

In front of him, Jillian drew in a breath before she squared her shoulders.

Not boding well.

Trent leaned forward to whisper in her ear. "Who—"

She brushed his hands off her hips, fisted her own at her waist before she surged forward a few feet, and then angled to the side.

Probably to keep them both in view, it's what he would have done.

"What are you doing here?" Pissed off didn't quite cover what pulsed through her words.

The man twisted, angling the top of his body towards Jillian. A spark of anger flicked in the depths of his green eyes. A nerve twitched at the edge of his mouth. "That's how you talk to your father?"

"Hello, Daddy." Sarcasm dripped from each word.

"That's marginally better."

"What are you doing here?"

The man raised an eyebrow.

Trent's hands fisted. Father or not, he wanted to punch the man square in the mouth.

"Hayden—" Her father lifted his chin to stare down at Jillian.

"Who called you?" She matched his lifted chin and added narrowed eyes. "I know Ted didn't."

"She's my daughter. I have a right to know what has happened to her."

Jillian flicked an almost non-existent glance his way.

Truth or dare. Which way would she go about the note she'd found?

"No one knows what happened. Not yet." She waggled a finger at her father. "Anything anyone says is sheer speculation."

Her father's brow rose in sudden understanding. He lowered his chin and pulled his brows together in apparent sympathy. "Jillian, dear. There's no way anyone could survive an explosion like what was described to me."

"How, exactly, was it described to you, Mr. Rose?" Trent stepped forward.

The man's eyes widened. "Who are you? Where did you come from?"

How could he have not been aware of Trent standing there? Was the man so engrossed in his private drama he had such little awareness of his own surroundings?

"Dad, he's a friend."

"You didn't answer my question, Mr. Rose."

"Are you with the local police?"

"No. Answer the question. How was it described to you?"

"That the whole boat imploded in on itself. That it burned to the water line before anyone could contain it. That they still haven't recovered all the bodies."

"Your friend's a busy little gossip, Mr. Rose."

"Dad—"

"Since my own eldest daughter doesn't bother to call me, I had to come down here to find out for myself."

"Give it a break. Mom does the guilt trip so much better than you do." Jillian squeezed her eyes shut. Opening them, she speared her dad with a dark look. "You didn't call Mom, did you?"

"*Of course not.*"

"Did anyone else?"

Rose pursed his lips before he glanced between the two of them. Trent arched his left brow.

"No." Rose shrugged one careless shoulder. "I — gave my contact an incentive not to contact your mother just yet."

"You bribed the local gossip king?" Trent raised his own eyebrow.

A smile hovering over his mouth, Rose nodded. "Works exceptionally well. A man needs to know what's going on in his world. Even if he chooses to only visit it once in a while."

"Come on, Trent. I've heard enough."

"The keys to the house, sweetness?" With his hand outstretched, her father eased forward a few steps.

"In your dreams." Jillian stalked back to the side door where she locked it and pocketed her keys.

"Those haven't been too pleasant lately. I need to clean up, take a shower. Get out of these ...." Rose squinted at Trent. "Those are my clothes you're wearing."

"Are they?" He looked down at himself. "Well then, I thank you."

With a wide smile and wave, Trent spun on his heel to follow Jillian to the car, his deliberately off-key whistle buoying his spirits.

Chapter Thirteen

ANOTHER AFTERNOON AT ROSEY'S. Another day without contact from Ben.

With a frustrated glance around the few occupied tables, Trent punched Ben's number into Jillian's cell phone one more time. Twenty rings before a mechanical voice told him his boss' mailbox was full.

Dammit.

Most of those messages were probably from him.

Not worried about Ben, the man routinely forgot to empty voice mail, Trent hit the off button. He'd like to smash his fist against something else instead.

I'm being punished for the Oasis being blown to pieces.

Why else would Ben so blatantly ignore him? Besides the team being at a critical point in an ongoing investigation. An investigation he should be involved with, should be heading.

Right.

Trent tipped his head to one side, then the other, trying to work out the kinks. *Pity they didn't budge.* With his thumb, he scrolled through the numbers called on the cell.

Hayden Rose. Less than two hours ago, lasting less

than a minute. Jillian must have had the same luck reaching her not-so-dead sister as he'd had trying to get hold of his missing boss.

In Jillian's position, he'd be trying to call that damn cell number, too.

The ache at his temples hadn't intensified. Hadn't lessened any since they'd left the house, either, however that glimmer of *annoyance* was stronger than anything he'd had in weeks. Maybe Ben was right. Maybe his senses would return.

Or maybe this would be all he'd ever get back.

He flicked a glance to where Jillian sat several feet away, wrapping silverware in pink cloth napkins. Her last chore for the afternoon. He took a moment to admire the way her hands moved so smooth and efficiently while she ignored her father's latest tirade.

The man leaned forward, his forearms supporting his weight on the counter. She'd fed him, but he'd spent the time since he'd found a place to clean up, along with a ride to the bar, trying to wheedle more than food out of her.

Piece of work. Prince Charming of the bastard, cajoling variety.

As if Jillian didn't have enough to deal with. Trent's hand closed into a fist around the cell phone. How would she feel if he turned her dad into a punching bag?

Too much restless energy. No outlet.

He shoved Jillian's phone in his pocket, nodded at the tourist who strolled in. A man, about Trent's age. Close cut blond hair. Pale blue, calculating eyes.

Trent stopped. Something buzzed inside his head. Like an irritating, bomb-diving horsefly. *Pay attention.* He took a second look at the stranger. The buzzing eased then disappeared.

Son of a bitch. If that wasn't a Fed then neither was he.

The fact his own badge was currently MIA didn't mean a damn thing.

But if the man *wasn't* a Fed, then *what* was he? The alternative to being some kind of agent was worse. Much worse.

In the time it took for Trent to casually make his way to the bar, Jillian had grabbed the opportunity to get away from her father and was setting a glass of ice water in front of the pseudo customer.

Take his order, Jillian. Get away from him.

The man wore white washed jeans and a loose, touristy T-shirt that almost concealed the bulge at his hip. From behind the bar Trent scanned the rest of the customers. Not many, mostly locals. Mostly nonthreatening. No one else seemed to be carrying a weapon.

No one else made his head buzz.

Although that didn't mean any or all of them didn't have a weapon of some sort tucked away for quick use. The *buzzing* was new to Trent, too damn new to trust. Especially without knowing what the buzz meant. Danger alert? New warning system? Brain tumor?

Shove it aside, Sawyer. Focus. His gaze swung back to Jillian. *Come on, sweetheart. Quit making nice and get that sexy ass back over here.*

She smiled at the *Threat* sitting there so innocently,

laughed at something the man said. Once she meandered back he would put her behind the bar, hand her the bat, and force her to stay put.

"Gin and tonic." Rose smacked his hand on the counter.

Trent ignored him.

"I said—"

"Get it yourself."

"I would, but Jilly doesn't let me behind the bar."

"Now why would that be?"

"Well—"

"It was rhetorical, Mr. Rose. I don't really care."

"You're a rude one. No wonder Jilly likes you. You're just alike."

The *Threat* leaned back in his chair and studied the customers the same way Trent had.

Mr. Rose followed the trail of Trent's gaze and, like a rabbit suddenly catching the sound of a rattler's twitching tail, went completely still.

Examine that later.

A second, lower level, buzz vibrated in his head as another lonely tourist ambled into the bar area. Trent locked on him and the buzz disappeared.

Definitely interesting. Something else to examine later.

The second tourist walked completely around the first one to settle on the other side of the restaurant, closer to the railing at the far end of the pier. This one wore shorts but appeared as if he'd shopped at the same cheap T-shirt place as *Threat #1*.

What the hell was going on? Simple surveillance or a

setup of some sort?

And which Rose did it have to do with? Papa over here? Jillian? Or Hayden?

Trent ruled out the simple part. One agent inside would be enough for that.

No acknowledgment, subtle or otherwise, beyond the initial scan each had done of the room. Not FBI. They had no idea *who* he was, nor did they expect trouble or they'd have at least tagged him as a possible problem.

Neither of the two Feds seemed particularly interested in Papa Rose beyond keeping tabs on his whereabouts. They seemed more intent on Jillian.

Again, why?

Just what had her sister pulled her into?

Jillian took *Threat #2's* order, skirted her father to join Trent behind the bar.

"Two coffees."

"How original." Mr. Rose's voice dripped with derision.

Jillian frowned at him while she dumped the dredges of the pot she'd made earlier and refilled the water then stuck a fresh filter in the machine. In a few moments, the aroma of fresh coffee filled the air.

Trent stuck a small stack of dirty plates into the sink behind the bar. Between her father and the two Feds surreptitiously watching her every move, how the hell was he going to talk to her? Without someone eavesdropping?

Once the pot was full, Trent filled two mugs. "You stay here, I'll deliver these."

"Excuse me?"

"Your dad wants a gin and tonic." He lifted the mugs in a mock salute.

"My dad can kiss his—"

"Jillian Marie. Really."

Behind him, Trent heard Jillian fill another mug and slide it across the counter top.

"You're serious? Coffee?" Mr. Rose's voice rose in a soft whine. "How about adding some Bailey's or Amaretto? Maybe a splash of Frangelico?"

Ignoring her answer, Trent set one cup in front of *Threat #1* and held his gaze. "Can I get you anything else?"

The man scanned Trent's face, raised an eyebrow. "Been in a fight recently?"

Trent lifted one side of his mouth in a pseudo smile. "Part of the job."

Threat #1's eyes widened a fraction before sweeping his gaze around the place. He paused for a nano-second at *Threat #2*.

Bingo.

The two worked together.

"Coffee is all for now." *Threat #1* leaned back in his seat. He linked his hands over his stomach.

Trent nodded at the man before heading to make contact with *Threat #2*.

Once Trent was back behind the bar, he positioned himself to watch both men. With a slight turn of his head, he could also see anyone heading into the area through the doorway.

Mr. Rose had moved from the bar itself and now sat – his coffee on the table in front of him – with his back to the wall, away from the two Feds. Rose definitely had a strong sense of self-preservation.

Still no way to talk to Jillian without eavesdroppers hanging on every word.

If Trent had her follow him out, the two strangers would suspect he'd made them. He grabbed a sponge, swiped at the few plates in the sink, rinsed and left them to dry. Scanned the area again.

The few locals had paid their bills, moseyed out. That left the two Feds sitting with their half empty coffee cups and Rose staring morosely into his mug. Jillian sat at the end of the bar near her father's table. She'd resumed rolling silverware into those pink cloth napkins, but watched her father from under her lashes. Probably to keep him from sneaking behind the bar and spiking his coffee.

Another man, possibly mid-thirties, strolled into the bar. His long, dark hair pulled back into a tail at his nape, he wore brown shorts and shirt. He carried a clipboard in one hand and a rectangular package tucked under the other arm.

Special Delivery.

Just how special?

No buzz in Trent's head. So no threat from the deliveryman? From the package? Or the buzz didn't mean what he thought it did.

Neither of the active *Threats* reacted to the deliveryman's presence. Mr. Rose, on the other hand, straightened in his seat.

Without glancing at the two Feds, the man with the package flicked his gaze between Papa Rose and himself before landing on Jillian. "Ms. Rose?"

She frowned then pushed away from the bar and took the few steps to meet him, which put them both right in front of Trent. Front row seat. He couldn't have orchestrated that one better if he'd tried. The delivery-man handed Jillian the clipboard with its pen attached at the top. She took the board, glanced at it before setting it on the bar and holding her hand out for the package.

"You need to sign—"

"Not until I see what I'm signing for." She raised an eyebrow and slightly tilted her head.

Good, Jillian. Good.

That need she had to be in control might pay off.

Deliveryman's mouth thinned but he handed over the package. Jillian turned it over in her hands. In a brown box covered with packing tape, no more than ten inches by six by four, it looked heavy.

From his side of the bar, Trent braced his arms on the counter. He recognized her sister's scrawl across the addressed portion of the package.

Shit.

Threat #1 and *#2* watched from the corner of their eyes.

What the hell is in that box?

"It's from Hayden." Jillian's voice weak and her hands trembling, she set the box on the bar then met Trent's gaze.

"What?" Papa Rose shoved to his feet and scurried to the bar. He reached for the package.

Jillian smacked his hand. "It's not addressed to you."

"Ms. Rose—" Deliveryman leaned into her space. "I need a signature."

"Back off." Trent laced his voice with sharp menace. He leaned forward on his elbows. "Her sister was killed yesterday. You back off and wait until she's ready to sign your damn board."

Deliveryman's head jerked, his eyes widened a fraction but he backed up a step. The flicked glance the man threw to *Threat* #2 tightened Trent's gut.

Papa Rose backed up several steps.

Jillian wiped the back of her hand over her cheek before snatching the clipboard. She signed then handed the board to the man. She waved off his thanks. "Just go away."

By the time the deliveryman had disappeared, without another glance at his buddies, Jillian had stashed the package on a shelf under the bar.

"Aren't you going to open it?" Rose stood with his hands on his hips and a frown pulling his brows down.

"No. Not right now."

"Then I will."

"I told you once, it's not addressed to you."

"Aren't you the slightest bit curious about what's in it?"

Jillian flicked a glance at Trent. She rubbed her hands over her eyes. "Of course I am. This just isn't—" She blinked a few times, swallowed once. "This isn't the time or place."

Trent spared a glance at the two Feds. This had all the earmarks of a controlled delivery.

Set up. Make delivery. See what the mark did with the package.

See who came for it.

"You're going to wait until you get home, aren't you?" Rose's whine passed irritating and slid towards full blown annoyance.

"And if I do?"

"I won't get to see what's in it."

"If Hayden wanted you to have whatever it is, if she wanted you to see it, then she would have mailed it to you."

"She didn't have my last address."

"Do we ever?" Jillian leaned her head back. She stared at the ceiling. "Drop it, Dad."

"Fine." Rose's mouth pursed like he'd taken a bite of the largest, sourest lime on the island.

"Maybe you should open it." His touch light, Trent laid the tips of his fingers on Jillian's arm. Calculated risk, but if he was right about the delivery, they needed to know what the package contained.

She pressed her lips tight but kept her gaze on the floor. After a few blinks she reached for the package and studied it before working one end open. With a frown, she tilted her head and the package then slid the contents out part way.

"What's in there?" Rose edged forward. He angled his head to the side.

"I don't know. But I don't think it's anything good." Her voice low, she angled the package towards Trent.

What the hell?

Plastic wrap surrounded what looked to him like a kilo of some kind of white powder.

Jillian was right. That didn't look like any kind of good.

Or legal.

"Maybe you should call Ted or your detective friend." Put some distance between Jillian and whatever her sister was involved in. "Get his take on this."

"But—"

"If Hayden wanted the cops to have that, she would have sent it to them." Rose reached for the package. Jillian again smacked his hand.

Keep it up, Papa Rose, and you'll talk yourself into a pair of handcuffs.

"Hayden's gone." Trent pulled Jillian's cell from his pocket and set the phone on the counter. "She doesn't have a choice at this point."

Jillian, her eyes narrowed, caught his gaze. "You're right. Shamus will know what to do with this."

"Fine. Do what you're going to do." Her father headed back to his table, his shoulders tight and his chin in the air. The noise he made settling in resounded across the bar.

Jillian shook her head. She gave Trent a sideways look and a rueful smile. "I'm going to make that call and then finish those damn napkin rolls."

Liking the way her honey eyes darkened with amber,

he smiled back. "Want some help?

She shook her head again just as *Threat #1* caught Trent's eye. The man lifted his coffee cup. Trent grabbed the pot. He half listened to the murmur of her voice on the cell as he took his time maneuvering from behind the bar. He topped off the man's half empty cup.

"Thanks." The guy leaned forward, cradled the cup between his hands. "I heard you say her sister died yesterday."

"You heard right."

"What happened?"

Trent frowned. He'd known coffee wasn't what the man had wanted. "What's it to you?

"Curiosity." The man leaned back in his chair. "Nothing more."

Right. Trent studied the Fed and kept his voice low. "Boat she was crewing on exploded up in Biscayne Bay. Everyone on board was killed."

For a quick instant, *Threat #1's* eyes flicked towards *Threat #2*. Man needed to watch that tell-tale body language.

"Yesterday?"

"Let me ask you again." Trent set the pot on the man's table and crossed his arms over his chest. "What's it to you?"

The Fed raised his hands, palms forward. "Not a thing."

Trent let his eyes narrow. "You waiting on someone?"

He shook his head. "Why would you ask that?"

"Here by yourself. Having only coffee." Trent shrugged. "So you're either waiting on someone, for *something*, or have nothing but time to kill."

"Nothing but time."

"Yeah. You and your buddy over there."

The man's eyes widened a small fraction. "Who are you?"

"Now, that's a good question, isn't it?" Trent let a sardonic smile lift one side of his mouth. He held the Fed's pale blue gaze for a long moment before the man blinked.

"Hey." The Fed lifted his hands again. "I'm simply killing a few hours. Not looking for any trouble."

"Make sure you keep it that way." Trent uncrossed his arms then wrapped his hand around the coffee pot handle. "Once the cook gets in from her afternoon shopping trip, you might want to try the grouper sandwich. Goes well with a beer."

The man nodded once. Trent returned the acknowledgment.

Might not have been the smartest move, drawing attention to himself that way. But being on the offensive damn well beat the alternative. Made him feel in control.

Even if that control only existed as an illusionary impression.

He topped off the other Fed's coffee mug. "Sure I can't get you anything else? Something stronger?"

"Not yet. Maybe later."

"Suit yourself." Trent ambled his way back to the bar.

Those two Feds waited for Jillian to hand the damn package off to someone else. Unless her detective friend showed up soon, they might be here for a while.

Trent started another pot of coffee.

Chapter Fourteen

C OFFEE DRIPPED SLOWLY into the glass carafe. The sound melded into the background as Trent scanned the room. Just another boring afternoon at Rosey's Place.

The two Feds, probably DEA, sat at their separate tables nursing their cups of exceptionally fascinating coffee. Both those men needed some serious retraining in their attempts to appear casual after being made as agents.

Not that either of them could be sure they'd been made. But Trent knew they suspected, knew they both wondered who the hell he was and what the hell he was doing at Rosey's. Maybe they'd learn to double check the players before setting up a sting.

Controlled delivery.

A scuffling sound pulled his attention to the doorway.

"I hope you're not going to throw me out again." Eric Chambers, hands in his pockets and a put upon cast to his face, strolled across the room.

This day's getting more interesting by the moment.

No buzzing in Trent's head. But he knew Chambers.

In a manner of speaking, anyway. Was Chambers here for Hayden's package? If so, why hadn't she simply mailed it to him? Why involve her sister in the mess?

"That depends." Jillian smacked the last rolled napkin into the tray. She glared at Eric. "Are you going to make me mad again?"

"I'm going to try not to." Chambers stood a few feet away. He rocked back on his heels. Then he rocked forward. "I am sorry for my behavior yesterday."

Sure you are, buddy. Trent leaned his elbows on the counter and rested his chin in his hand. Funny, Chambers manner struck him as controlled and manipulative rather than contrite. But he'd bet money Jillian had the man's behavior nailed.

The two Feds sat a little straighter. Did they already know Chambers? Was the man a player? Or a not-so-innocent bystander?

Wrong place, wrong time?

This was like a chess game, one without all the pieces.

"More coffee, please." Rose stretched and set his cup on the counter with a flourish.

Trent raised one eyebrow. Couldn't the imbecile see it hadn't finished brewing?

"The vultures didn't take much time to circle." Chambers' gaze, behind his glasses, narrowed on Papa Rose. The corners of Chambers' mouth curled downward. "Before landing to scavenge."

"I'm just as happy to see you, Eric." Rose tilted his head to the side. He studied Chambers as he would a bug, one he debated whether to grind into the ground with the heel of his shoe. "Tell me, did my daughter have the good sense to dump you?"

Chambers rolled his eyes, met Trent's impassive stare. With a frown, Eric pushed his glasses up his nose and shifted his gaze to Jillian. "Have you heard anything else? About the Symphony? About Hayden?"

Behind Chambers, the two Feds exchanged a look. *What is that stuff, to garner so much interest?*

Thus far, Jillian had played this well, for someone who had no real knowledge of the intrigue going on around her. He had to give her serious points for keeping it together.

His hands curled into loose fists as he scanned the area and the men's different positions. He still wanted to use her father as a punching bag. Pound out all that frustration, pummel his fist into the man's face.

Push to shove, however, Chambers would make an excellent substitute.

WITH ONE HAND FLAT on the bar at Rosey's, Jillian rubbed at the spot between her brows. Maybe it was the fact she couldn't do a damn thing to help Hayden. Maybe it was dealing with her father. Or maybe it was Eric showing up, once again, but the afternoon seemed to drag on without end.

She hated this damn helplessness. Hated not knowing what to do, what direction to turn.

Hated second guessing herself.

She'd been doing that a lot since Mr. FBI Agent Trent Sawyer had shown up and turned her world and her emotions upside down. She wanted someone safe … boring, even. Someone who didn't make her want to jump in bed with him without knowing a damn thing about who he was or what made him tick.

Forget the part of her that thrilled to Trent's touch. Forget the near miss two nights before or the fact she could've already had two mornings waking up next to him.

Boring was better.

Safer.

Damn this long day.

Only two paying customers in the place, both irritated Trent for some reason, both only drinking coffee. Hard to make a profit there, especially with her dad determined to spike his with whatever alcohol he could wheedle out of her or sneak from behind the bar.

So tired of the nonsense. Of Eric. Of Dad. Of Hayden's drama.

Hayden has to be okay. If only she would answer her damn phone.

Trent laid a hand over Jillian's and the warmth of his touch sent electric sparks along her nerve endings. *So not boring.* With a light squeeze to her fingers, Trent straightened and her traitorous heart ratcheted into overdrive.

Her gaze lingered on the scrapes across Trent's knuckles. They were healing, like the ones along his jaw and the cut on his cheek. Those bruises had blossomed into a few interesting shades.

So much violence.

"Jillian?" Eric's demanding and not at all conciliatory voice yanked her back.

"What?" She caught the sharpness of her tone but refused to care.

"I asked if you'd heard anything about Hayden."

She bared her teeth in a fake smile and grabbed the tray of rolled silverware. "No. I haven't heard anything new today."

From the corner of her eye she caught the small lift of Trent's lips. An answering wave of pleasure swelled in her chest.

How stupid. Trent Sawyer doesn't matter. He can't matter.

With the tray of silverware braced on her hip, she stalked to the other side of the restaurant portion of Rosey's. Eric followed a few steps behind. She stopped near one of the customers who had Trent's back up.

Half listening to Eric's babbling, she set out the cloth wrapped silverware. Trent shadowed them, supposedly checking salt and pepper levels. The customer behind her exploded from his chair, tearing off for the bathroom, right behind their only other customer.

The door smacked the frame behind them.

"What —" Eric spun around. "Is their problem?"

Trent's arm snaked around her waist. His movements fast and smooth, he tucked her behind him.

"Where's my dad?" Frantic, her hands gripping Trent's shoulders, Jillian's gaze skimmed the room. "Is he in the bathroom?"

The two men came out with her father between them, each holding one of his arms, his hands cuffed behind his back.

Jillian tried to rush forward but Trent wrapped both arms around her and pressed her against his side.

"No." She pushed at him.

"Shhh." He leaned down, his breath tangled in her hair. "They're Feds. Stay calm."

"What?" Eric threw a startled glance at Trent. His eyes narrowed to slits and his mouth thinned. "What has Rose got himself into now?"

"Who knows?" Jillian pushed at Trent's arm again and this time he let go.

The man wearing shorts sat her father in a chair close to them. With a hand on her father's shoulder, he nodded at the other man, the one in white-washed jeans. That man carried Jillian's package. The wrapping was torn at the open corner with the plastic protecting the contents also torn and ragged.

"I *knew* not to take my eyes off him." Jillian smacked the nearest table with the flat of her palm. "First time my back is turned."

She stalked toward one of the men. Feds, Trent had said.

Great. Just peachy.

"Miss Rose." The man in white-washed jeans held up a hand. "Stop right there, please."

"Who are you?" She stopped, fisted her hands on her hips. "And why do you have my father in handcuffs?"

Behind her, Trent choked off a short burst of laughter.

This was funny? She had a few words for him, too. Like why hadn't he told her she had two Feds in her place?

The man in front of her pulled a slim, black wallet from the back pocket of his jeans. He flipped it open. She snagged the identification and glanced back at Trent.

The jerk had his hand over his mouth.

Laughing at her or DEA Agent Simmons?

DEA.

Wonderful. Just what the hell was Hayden mixed up in?

She half expected something like this from her dad, but not her sister.

Trent leaned over her shoulder and studied the ID. Eric stood over her other shoulder. Thank goodness they were the only ones in the place. Less damage control on the gossip front.

Her dad in handcuffs. In Rosey's.

She huffed out an exasperated breath.

Peachy didn't even come close to covering this fiasco.

The agent in front of her plucked his ID from her hand. He slipped it into his back pocket. "Miss Rose, we have a few questions for you."

"I have a few for you." *Like what the hell's going on?*

"Jilly?" The whites showed in her father's wide eyes. His tanned face had paled. "Tell them that stuff isn't mine."

"They know that, Mr. Rose." Trent, with his hand at

the small of her back, guided her to a chair across from her father.

She let him, only because she didn't see an alternative at this point. He sat beside her. Eric scrambled towards the other side of her chair. *No. No. No.* "What do you think you're doing, Eric? This has nothing to do –"

"Eric Chambers?" The agent wearing shorts tilted his head.

Eric's face paled. He nodded.

The two agents exchanged glances then Agent Simmons flicked a glance at her before addressing Eric. "Have a seat, Mr. Chambers. We wanted to talk with you, also."

"But –"

"Bear with us, Miss Rose." The other agent pulled a small notebook from his back pocket then he and Agent Simmons sat, bracketing her father.

Simmons set the package on the table along with a slim recorder switched to the on position. "Do you know what this is, Miss Rose?"

"Jillian is easier. And no, I have no idea what that is." She pressed both palms flat on her table. "Why are you here? Why do you have my dad—"

"We're asking the questions, Jillian."

She smiled, sat back, and crossed her arms over her middle. "If you want answers from me, you'll also answer my questions."

The agents exchanged sideways looks.

She wasn't under arrest, and although it looked like her dad might be, she didn't have to answer diddly squat.

"You may as well tell us what's going on. Get it all out in the open so we can see what kind of help we can be." Trent addressed the agents at the same time he stretched his arm behind her, resting it on the back of her chair. His fingers cupped her shoulder. She wasn't about to examine the way that simple touch comforted her.

While she didn't need anyone, right now she'd take the support he offered. She'd lash him to the spit later. Roast him over an open flame. Teach him to laugh at her. *After* they got her father out of this mess with the two agents.

"Just who are you?" Agent Simmons demanded, his gaze locked on Trent's.

"Trent Sawyer. FBI."

"You said you weren't the police." Her father's whine hung in the stunned silence as each man stared at Trent.

"Technically, I said I wasn't the *local* police."

"FBI—"

"Isn't local."

Beside her, Eric shook his head as if to clear it then leaned forward to rest his elbows on the tabletop. He sent another quick look around her – at Trent – before he laced his fingers together.

"Identification?" The agent held out his hand.

"At the bottom of Blackwater Sound." Trent shrugged. "Unless the thugs who stole my boat found it before they blew her up."

Ben's boat.

Trent's fingers rubbed a circle on her upper arm. A heat she welcomed, for now, radiated through her body.

Agent Simmons narrowed his eyes before he curled his fingers and lowered his hand.

"I'm part of a Task Force with Benjamin Garrett –"

"I know Garrett." The agent in shorts nodded. "You're the one who was on board the Oasis?"

"That would be me." Disgust threaded Trent's words.

"Tough luck."

"We didn't see your ID." Jillian aimed a frown at the man in shorts.

He gave her a small, lopsided smile. Flipped out his ID before turning to Eric. "Do you what this substance is, Mr. Chambers?"

"It's Eric. And no, I have no idea." His smile weak, he shrugged one shoulder. "I'm into real estate, not whatever that stuff is."

"Real estate and my daughter." Her father sneered at Eric.

Both agents, their faces duplicate expressionless masks, looked at Jillian. At Trent's arm around her.

"My other daughter. Jilly has too much self-preservation to get herself caught up with the likes of Chambers." Her father sat back hard in his chair, bounced. "Can't you guys take these cuffs off? I'm not going anywhere."

Both agents ignored him. The one in shorts raised an eyebrow at Eric. "That would be Hayden Rose, correct?"

Eric frowned, but he nodded.

"Considering your *girlfriend* mailed this, you're positive you have no idea what this is?" Agent Simmons pointed at the package while the one in shorts – Turner, maybe? She had barely looked at his ID – scribbled in his notebook.

Eric's skin went a shade paler. "No idea."

"How long have you two dated?"

Eric glanced at Jillian, his brows raised in question. "Five or six months, maybe."

Six long months. She pressed her lips together.

"Do any of you know why, before she was killed, Hayden would send this to her sister?" The agent glanced at Trent then back to Eric.

Eric lowered his gaze to the table, to his hands. Swallowed, but shook his head.

Jillian fought the need to close all of this out, to shut her eyes, press her hands over her ears. She, too, shook her head. "We don't even know what this stuff is."

"Precursor. Used to make a highly controlled legal drug. Comes from only one place. A small country in Europe. Illegal for the average citizen to have in their possession." Simmons pushed at the package, moving it an inch or two closer to them. "They call this *stuff* Darkwater on the street. This one package is worth several hundred thousand dollars."

Jillian blinked. That was an awful lot of money.

"What country would that be?" Trent's voice, deceptively calm, held a wealth of curiosity.

Jillian glanced at him through her lowered lashes.

"Cadeau." Simmons tapped the package.

Trent nodded. Obviously the answer he expected. Beside her Eric went still. He'd heard of this country, too?

Cadeau. French for gift, if she remembered correctly.

"Small country in the Pyrenees Mountains. Tucked between France and Spain." Simmons angled his head as he studied Eric. "Felicity Chambers, Eric Chambers' ex-wife, was their only princess."

Chapter Fifteen

A SUDDENLY COOL AFTERNOON BREEZE wafted through the open structure of Rosey's, raising goose-bumps along Jillian's arms.

Not even Trent's hand cupping her shoulder warmed her skin.

She frowned at the two DEA agents on the other side of the table, at the special delivery package front and center, at her tight-lipped father who sat hunched forward between the two agents.

"Oh, no." Eric shoved up from his seat next to her. He leaned forward with his hands planted flat on the table. "I have nothing to do with whatever any of those people are mixed up in."

Jillian's stomach in knots and her throat tight, she stared at him. What the hell had he, and maybe Felicity, gotten Hayden involved with? Drugs. Smuggling. People dead. Her hand curled into a fist, she pressed it to the base of her throat.

Simmons settled deeper into his seat and steepled his fingers over his lap. Satisfaction tugged at the corners of his mouth. "What people would that be, Mr. Chambers?"

"Felicity's family. Hayden." Eric straightened then shoved his glasses up the bridge of his nose. "Choose any one of them. All of them. I have nothing to do with *any* of this."

"Really?" Trent leaned forward, studied Eric the way Simmons had. "How is it your girlfriend got hold of a substance that happens to only be available from the homeland of your ex-wife?"

"No idea." Eric stared at the ceiling then swung his wide eyed gaze to Jillian. "I told you the other night. Those two were arguing over something."

"Yes you did." Her gaze locked on Eric, she lifted her chin. "And you said that something was *you.*"

"Maybe it wasn't. Maybe I was wrong. Maybe it was over that stuff." Eric jerked his chin at the package on the table.

"Lots of maybes floating around here." Trent pursed his lips. Shrugged. "Either you were a bone of contention, or you weren't. Which was it?"

Eric glared at him.

"Sit down, Mr. Chambers." Turner, the agent in shorts, tapped his pen against his notebook. "Unless you'd rather go with us when we take Mr. Rose in."

"What?" Her father twisted in his seat and sent Jillian a panicked, pleading look. "I have less to do with this than anyone at this table."

"They have you red-handed with the package, Mr. Rose." The corner of Trent's mouth twitched. "Hard to deny that."

"But—"

Trent's right. Jillian bit the inside of her lip. *What are these men going to do to my dad?*

Behind Eric's glasses, his eyes widened even more as he glanced from her father to the two agents on either side. Eric swallowed, his Adam's apple working overtime, before he sat in his seat with his shoulders hunched forward and his hands clasped tight in his lap.

"The problem I have with Felicity wanting you back is the fact she was obviously still with this Rhys Blackthorne character." Trent's glance flicked from Eric to Simmons. "You know she died at Blackthorne's house? She fell down his stairs."

"He's right." Eric's eager gaze focused on the agents. "Have you checked out Blackthorne?"

"That's on our list." Simmons settled further into his seat. "However, it's been verified Blackthorne was out of the country when she died."

Although Jillian couldn't see the agent's feet, she bet they were crossed at the ankles. The man visibly enjoyed Eric's discomfort, enjoyed Trent running the show for them.

"Besides—" Trent, his left eyebrow lifted, tilted his head to one side. "Why would Blackthorne be involved in smuggling this substance when he has access to it through legal channels?"

Jillian started. *What's he talking about?*

Trent, his deep blue eyes impassive, squeezed her shoulder. "Blackthorne has controlling share in the pharmaceutical company holding an exclusive agreement with the King of Cadeau. Felicity's father."

"Oh." Jillian laced her fingers together over her stomach. *When, and how, did he figure all this out?*

"You've done your homework." A flash of respect glinted through Simmons' eyes.

"I've learned to keep my ears open." Trent shrugged. "A lot of information filters through this place."

Jillian scanned Rosey's. *Maybe I need to pay more attention to the gossip.*

"Brings us to the same question for Felicity." Trent slanted that impassive gaze towards Eric. "Why would she have any interest in this stuff? Her daddy supplies it and her boyfriend buys it. Legally. Was she an addict?"

"No." Eric pursed his mouth. "Never in a million years."

"Was Hayden?" Simmons directed his question to Jillian.

Jillian shook her head.

"Neither of my daughters mess with anything like that." Her father huffed and rotated his shoulders forward.

"Just their daddy?" Trent's mouth tightened, like he had more he wanted to say.

"No. I—" Her father looked away. "I'm not saying anything else."

"Suit yourself, Mr. Rose." Simmons' gaze zeroed in on Eric. "With Blackthorne being so involved with Felicity's father, why would she have wanted you back? No disrespect, Chambers, but you're not exactly in the same league. Unless there's something you haven't shared with us?"

"Hayden told me Felicity left you because you didn't make enough money to support her like she wanted to be supported." Although Jillian spoke the truth, she hated the wounded look Eric threw at her.

He shook his head, stared at his hands. "Felicity and I – we loved each other. We just couldn't live together. Money was simply her excuse. I understood that. She did, too."

"Then why this nonsense about her wanting you back?" Jillian frowned.

"It wasn't nonsense." His gaze still downcast, he shrugged one shoulder. "But with Rhys out of town, Felicity thought it prudent to wait until he came back, feel him out. She was never one to jump ship without a lifeboat waiting."

"She was a princess." Jillian hadn't really known Felicity, hadn't had much to do with her one way or another. Hayden hadn't been able to stand her, but Eric had colored that sentiment. With gusto. "Why would Felicity need a lifeboat? Why did she need any man?"

"Cadeau isn't exactly a rich country." Eric flicked a sideways glance at her before again staring at his hands.

Jillian waved a hand towards the package. "Even with whatever that stuff is?"

"That's helped the economy, to an extent." Simmons looked as if he'd settled in for the week. "I believe they get more income from tourism these days."

"Felicity's father keeps all of them on a tight allowance." Already in a frown, Eric's brows lowered even more.

"All of them?"

"She has two older brothers."

Simmons straightened a fraction. "We're looking to talk with them, also. Any idea where they are these days?"

Eric met his gaze then shook his head. "Felicity's father called when he'd learned of her death, but I haven't talked with either of her brothers in over a week. I know their sailboat is still moored here. But I'd assumed their father called them both home."

The other agent, Turner, jotted down several notes. "So, Eric. You're saying Felicity wanted to get back with you and that Hayden knew this?"

"My sister dumped you before you could dump her?"

"No. There was no dumping. I hadn't figured out what to do about Felicity." Eric shook his head again. He straightened in his seat. "About what she wanted. I didn't see how being together would work when it hadn't worked before. But Hayden had been acting ... distant."

"You'd said she'd been angry with you. That you were fighting." Jillian glared at Eric. "How does that equate with distant?"

"Like she was keeping secrets." Eric's tone pitiful, he twisted his hands tighter in his lap. "Like she was fighting with me in order to put distance between us. Or maybe I'm just trying to rationalize it. To make sense of it, for there to be a reason. First Felicity. Then Hayden. I don't see how either of them could be involved in anything like this—" Blinking his eyes several times, he shook his head. Fell silent.

Jillian pressed her lips together and stared at the table. *Is Eric really hurting this much, or is he just that good an actor? I don't know what to believe. God, I'm so damn suspicious.*

Trent's fingers tightened on her shoulder. *Why can't I just sink into that warmth?* Take the comfort offered in those small circles he rubbed over the thin material of her T-shirt?

She squared her shoulders and lifted her chin. Dammit, not a princess by any stretch, she didn't need a man to fix things. "Hayden isn't – wasn't – involved beyond however she came across that package."

"Now, Jillian." Simmons mouth twisted in a slight smile. "By your own admission, that's your sister's handwriting. So she'd done more than simply come across that package. Hard to believe she wasn't up to her pretty little neck in this mess."

Heavily trod footsteps sounded across the pier. Both agents twisted in their chairs just as Detective Shamus Conlon strolled through the door. Sudden tears welled in Jillian's eyes. The legs of her chair scraped along the restaurant's wooden floor planks as she shoved her chair back. In ten seconds flat Shamus' strong arms tightened around her.

She might not *need* any man, but right now gratitude swelled inside her for Shamus' mere presence.

"There, there, child." His voice a harsh rasp, he smoothed her hair back from her forehead and set her back so he could look in her eyes. "Hard couple of days for you, I know. We'll find who did this to your sister.

Make them pay."

Afraid she'd burst into tears if she tried to speak, her chin jerked in a quick nod.

Although not a friend to her father, Shamus was the same age, had been through school with him, and had been a staple in her family for as long as she remembered. His thick white hair flowed back from a high forehead, contrasting with a tan that spoke of countless hours out of doors in the Florida sunshine. That healthy tan seemed a bit paler now, those bright green eyes a bit flat. Dull almost.

That bug he'd been fighting?

"Should you be out, Shamus? Maybe you should still be in bed. I don't want Mrs. Conlon after us all."

"I've had enough mother-henning and pecking to last the rest of my life." He peered at her through narrowed eyes. "Doc says I'm not contagious now so you let me worry about the missus."

Jillian laid the palm of her hand over his cheek. *Not feverish and only a slight bit clammy.*

"Satisfied?"

With a nod, she patted his cheek.

"Who are all of these gentlemen?" Stocky and not much taller than her, Shamus tucked her against him, much the same as Trent had done more than once.

She frowned at that thought even as Shamus turned them both to face the tables.

Trent instantly liked Shamus Conlon who, after introductions were made, grabbed a chair and settled himself between Jillian and Eric's seats. Annoyance marked Chambers' face. Trent bit back a sarcastic grin.

Yeah, he liked Detective Conlon's style.

With barely a glance Trent's way, Jillian brought Shamus up to date, leaving out the part about her sister being alive. Jillian held it together, Trent gave her credit. That sheen of tears, bright in her eyes, when the older detective strolled in, told their own story. Shamus played an important part in Jillian's life.

Another reason to like the detective.

Not getting involved, remember? Curious, yes. Determined to catch whoever had stolen and blown the Oasis apart, also yes. There had to be a connection between the stolen boat and the precursor.

Satisfy my curiosity. Let the DEA agents arrest the bastards. Move on.

Back to Washington DC.

Where it's cold this time of year.

He shook off a sudden chill and slid a glance across the tabletop to focus on Jillian's father. Rose sat, his mouth thin and tight, with his cheeks sunken, as if he sucked on something completely unpleasant but couldn't bring himself to spit it out.

No love lost between the father and the detective.

If you didn't want someone else stepping into those shoes, you should've been more of a father, asshole.

The stacked water glasses behind the bar rattled once, the sound sharp and echoing through the open area. Trent tucked his chin. *So, Rosey agrees, even with the father in question being her son?*

"The biggest question, to my mind, is what Hayden

stumbled across?" The detective – Shamus – his fingers linked and hands resting on the table, drummed the pads of his thumbs together. He met each of the agents' gazes in turn before he threw a side glance at Trent and Jillian. He ignored Chambers.

"Stumbled?" Simmons frowned. "Why don't you think she was into this up to her neck?"

"I've known both these girls from the time they were little. Neither would be messed up in something like this."

"People can fool you. Change. Not be who you think they are." Simmons angled his head.

"True. But not on this. Not Hayden. Not Jillian." The solid assurance in Shamus' deep baritone had Trent leaning forward himself.

Jillian closed her eyes and swallowed once. When she opened her eyes, moisture glistened, trembled on the edges of her lashes. She blinked several times.

Trent fisted his hands, fought the strong urge to pull her into his arms, to press her head to his shoulder, and whisper he'd see her through this mess.

Somehow.

Not a hero.

Slippery road, Sawyer. Straight to the lowest levels of stupidity.

He needed to take that step back, gain distance, and let Detective Conlon comfort her.

No matter how it stuck in his craw.

"Hayden Rose's handwriting." Simmons pushed the package towards Colon. "Addressed to her sister."

Shamus' mouth flattened as he studied the label.

"Jilly is Hayden's touchstone. The one who keeps her world safe. Secure. So her sending this to her sister isn't at all surprising. As I said a few moments ago, how Hayden stumbled into this is the real question."

"You aren't convincing me Hayden Rose wasn't involved in this." Simmons flicked a glance at his partner before focusing on the detective.

"When you actually know people, you understand them. What their motives are. Hayden has none that would lend themselves to what you're suggesting."

"You can't know that."

"Actually I can."

"Aren't you a bit biased in your opinion?" Simmons frowned.

"I see where you might think that." The detective gave him a short nod. "I prefer to view it as being insightful. As understanding the people who populate my world."

"And?"

"Rose over there, he's an opportunist. Won't work an honest job unless he absolutely has no other choice."

Trent glanced towards Rose. The man huffed, rolled his shoulders and turned his head to stare out over the water. Calling his character a bit too close for his liking? *I'd bet money on that one.*

The right corner of the detective's mouth lifted. "Neither of his daughters take after him. Jillian has a responsible streak so wide you can steer a yacht through it. Hayden—Flaky? A bit. Flighty? Definitely. Honest? Absolutely. Both girls take after their grandmother in that way. Sometimes too bluntly honest on occasion. They're not mixed up in this beyond whatever and however Hayden *stumbled* across it.

"My best guess is she sent that to her sister to get Jilly to figure it out. That whoever it belongs to blew up the Symphony to kill Hayden in order to stop her from asking questions. Or to stop her from telling what she discovered. Hayden might be flighty, but she's not stupid. She's Rosey's granddaughter and can think on her feet."

"Might be flighty?" Simmons leaned forward, subtly mirroring the detective's body language. "You talk about her as if she's still alive."

Trent's shoulders stiffened.

Shamus tucked his chin to his chest. His mouth tightened for a fraction before he looked upward and speared Simmons with a direct gaze. "Having trouble believing she's gone."

Simmons slid a sideways glance at his partner, then to Jillian. "We don't mean to be insensitive about that. About your loss."

Jillian lifted her chin, stared at the agent.

Keep it together, sweetheart. Don't say anything we'll regret. Trent held his breath until the man lowered his gaze.

"Mr. Chambers?" Simmons stood and picked up the recorder from the center of their table. "I need a few minutes in private."

Eric's eyes widened but he nodded then pushed his chair back. The scrapping sound over the wooden planks echoed loud through the room. With a backwards glance full of trepidation, he followed Simmons to a spot several yards away, near the bathroom doors.

Turner, the other agent, also stood then clicked his pen and slipped it into the collar of his T-shirt. He tucked his small notebook into the back pocket of his shorts. "Come on, Mr. Rose. Time to go."

"Go?" Rose's panicked gaze swung from the agent's to his daughter's. Awkward, with his hands cuffed behind him, he scrambled to his feet. "Jilly? You're going to let them take me?"

"There's no letting in any of this, Mr. Rose." Under the table, Trent stretched his legs, settled further into his seat, and linked his fingers over his stomach. "I'm sure the agents will be in touch. To tell us where you end up."

Beside him, Shamus lowered his chin. Probably trying to hide the grin twitching his mouth.

A frown marred Jillian's forehead. She threw a worried glance at her sputtering father. "You're really taking him?"

"We have to, Ms. Rose. He tried to steal the package."

"I didn't *steal* anything."

"It wasn't addressed to you." Turner moved the chairs, hooked a hand in the crook of Rose's arm, and maneuvered him around the tables. "Minimum, we have you on mail theft."

Rose's face paled several shades. "But—Jilly? Tell them it's okay. Tell them—"

"I don't think there's anything I can do, Dad." Her head tilted slightly and her eyes narrowed, she swung her gaze towards Turner. "Is there?"

"No, ma'am." The agent fished several business cards from his wallet. He handed one to each of them. "We'll be in touch, but don't hesitate to call."

Turner led a still sputtering and stumbling Rose out past where the other two men stood. Simmons nodded at Turner, but Eric, with his arms crossed over his chest and his mouth tight, focused completely on Simmons.

Jillian's eyes troubled, she watched until her father and Turner disappeared behind the outer wall. Then she sighed, deeply, and the sound skittered across Trent's skin to twist his gut into a tight knot.

He ran a hand over the top of his head. She was better off with her dad otherwise occupied. Let the DEA keep him out of their hair for a few days. Trent was sure this had more to do with having something to show for their time and effort than any real belief in Mr. Rose's involvement. They probably wouldn't even file charges. Not even on mail theft.

So why do I feel so damn guilty for letting them haul her father's sorry ass out of here?

When had any of this become his responsibility?

Chapter Sixteen

TRENT GRIPPED THE BACK of his neck. Squeezed then massaged the tense muscles. He slouched lower in his seat at the table Jillian, Detective Shamus Colon, and he shared at Rosey's. The only table currently occupied.

No customers in the late afternoon hour. Probably good, all things considered.

On a disgusted inward sigh, Trent yanked his gaze from where DEA Agent Simmons *chatted* with Eric Chambers. Through the open door, Trent caught a quick glimpse of Agent Turner leading a still sputtering Mr. Rose down the pier towards the parking area.

None of this is my responsibility.

None of it.

Not Jillian. Not her father. Not the sister.

The DEA had the case. Detective Shamus Conlon and Deputy Ted Mathews both seemed competent. They could help sort out the mess with the sister.

Jillian didn't need him.

So why the hell do I feel so damn involved?

Asinine.

Doesn't learn should be tattooed across my forehead.

Temptation with a capital T. That was Jillian Rose. Jillian with her damn bats stashed everywhere, her big honeyed eyes full of tears she refused to let fall. Jillian, the woman whose kiss drove all sane thoughts completely out of his head.

"Is there fresh coffee brewed?" Shamus patted Jillian's arm while Trent studied the edge of his thumbnail.

In his periphery vision he spotted the grateful look she gave the detective. That damn knot torqued itself tighter in Trent's gut. *Why the hell do I want her looking at* me *the way she looks at Shamus?*

"There is coffee. Trent put it on just before—Well. Let me get you some. Trent, would you care for a cup?"

"Sure." He watched her hurry behind the counter, watched her pause and take a deep breath.

Where does this damn desire to fix this mess come from? He sucked in a lungful of air. *Why am I doing this to myself?*

"Fighting the feeling is futile, son." Shamus scrunched down in his seat, his broad shoulders leaned against the back support and lowered, as if he'd lost what little energy he had left. "Learned that when I found my missus."

Trent's mouth tightened of its own accord.

Right. Time to change that *subject.*

"What's your opinion of Chambers?" He kept his voice low, as much to avoid Jillian hearing his question as the two men still locked in discussion across the room.

"Not sure I know him well enough to have one." A faint smile hovered over Shamus' mouth. "Newcomer to the Keys. From Miami, I think. Strikes me as an opportunist, but more cunning, with different motives than Rose."

The detective struck Trent as being astute and a good judge of character. *Too astute.* He shifted in his seat so he could keep an eye on Jillian. "What about his ex, Felicity Chambers?"

"Working on figuring out what happened to her."

"Your boy, Devon, seemed to think she simply fell down the stairs."

"That's what he gets for thinking." Shamus shook his head, smiled at Jillian when she sat an overlarge, full mug of steaming black coffee on the table in front of him. He sniffed appreciatively. "And that's also why Devon's still my boy and not investigating on his own. He'll get there, just take him awhile."

"So Felicity's death wasn't just a sad accident?" Jillian's voice soft, she set a multi-hued blue mug in front of Trent.

Not the normal cups for Rosey's. He lifted his to his mouth, blew across the surface. She must have had these stashed somewhere behind the counter.

Shamus, his shrewd eyes focused on Trent, shrugged. "Maybe it was. Maybe it wasn't. I haven't gone over all of the evidence yet. Not sure I even have an opinion at this point. At least not one I'm willing to share."

"What's going on around here, Shamus?" Jillian sat, sinking low in her seat and cradling her own softly shaded pink mug between her hands. "Boats blowing up, people dying."

"Working on figuring that out, too." Shamus picked up his cup, this one glazed green and grey. One corner of his mouth lifted. "You still have these mugs. From when my missus talked your grandma into trying her hand at ceramics. Rosey was pretty good. Shame she didn't keep at it." He brought his cup to his mouth, blew across the surface. "Shame I can't talk to your sister, Jilly."

Trent flicked a sideways glance at Simmons and Eric. Neither paid their little trio the slightest attention. Looked like he was right about Shamus Conlon. A hell of a detective.

Good or bad thing? Remains to be seen, since, asinine fool I am, I'm not walking away.

Not yet, anyway.

Beside him, Jillian blinked at Shamus with just a hint of smile. "It is a shame, I know."

"When you're ready to talk about all that, let me know. I'll listen."

With her gaze on the table, Jillian nodded. She traced the tip of her index finger across the rim of her cup.

Interesting. The detective didn't push that point. Must not be part of the game plan.

Not yet, anyway.

Trent took a small sip. "What's your opinion of Dane Patrick?"

Jillian frowned, but Shamus shrugged.

"Another latecomer to the Keys. From Los Angeles, I believe." Shamus took a sip himself, closed his eyes for a moment. "Talented."

"Not much of an opinion."

"Not much to base one on." Shamus set his cup on the table. "Plays guitar, sings at the different restaurants, a few bars. Keeps to himself. Seems genuine enough."

Trent nodded. Same feel he had. At least Patrick didn't set off the type of alarms Eric Chambers did simply with his mere presence. Alarms that had nothing to do with psychic ability.

Across the room Chambers stared out over the water. The line of his shoulders tight, he shook his head, as if to clear it, then headed for the bathroom. As the door swung closed behind Chambers, Simmons came back to their table, asked if Turner had left his card with them.

Jillian nodded. She flicked a worried glance in the direction the other agent had gone with her father.

"He'll be fine, Ms. Rose." Simmons actually smiled, the movement crinkling lines around his eyes. "We need to clear a few things and, unless something else turns up, I'm sure he'll be free to go in a day or so."

Jillian swallowed and bit her bottom lip before lifting her chin. "Thank you for that."

"No problem." Simmons gave Trent and Shamus a small salute. "We'll be in touch."

Trent, Jillian and Shamus sat there, silent, as the agent left the bar. A few moments later Chambers exited the restroom. He scanned the area then pushed his glasses up his nose and rubbed his forehead before approaching them.

What is it about the man that sets my hackles on edge? Besides his arrogance and Jillian's obvious dislike?

Chambers, his hazel eyes dark and agitated behind

his wire rimmed glasses, stood next to the table with his hands shoved in the pockets of his khaki shorts.

"What's wrong?" Impatience edged Jillian's voice.

"They want me to stick around. To stay in the area." His shoulders hunched forward, he addressed Shamus. "Can they do that? Order me not to leave?"

The movement sharp and quick, Shamus shrugged. "That sort of thing is more of a suggestion than an order."

"Didn't sound like a suggestion."

"That was the idea, I'm sure." The detective tilted his head slightly to the side. "You have somewhere you need to be in the next few days?"

Chambers glowered at him. "No."

"Then what, exactly, is the issue?"

"Exactly nothing." Chambers rolled his shoulders. "I just don't like being ordered around like that."

Trent caught Shamus' sardonic gaze.

Sucks to be Eric Chambers.

"They're treating me like I'm guilty by association." Chambers' hands balled in the pockets of his shorts. His jaw tightened. "Because that stuff in their package comes from Felicity's home country, and I stop to see if Jillian heard anything else on the Symphony, I get caught in the middle of it all."

"I don't know about that. I'm sure they would have come looking for you at some point." Shamus stood and stretched.

"Yeah." Chambers rocked on his heels. "Because I'm the princess' ex-husband."

"Exactly." Shamus leaned over to give Jillian a peck on her cheek.

"I can't tell them what I don't know."

"Well then." The detective's eyes gleamed for a bare moment. "How about you tell me what you do know about Felicity's fall down those stairs."

Chambers' face paled. "What's there to tell? Devon Jackson said she slipped."

Shamus held Chambers' skittish gaze for several drawn out seconds before the detective angled his head towards Jillian. "Precious, I'll be back in a bit. Trent, nice to meet you. Eric—" Shamus clamped his hand on the taller man's shoulder. "Why don't I walk you to your car so we can have a chat?"

Chambers, his gaze on the ceiling, shook his head before he pulled his hands from his pockets and rubbed his face. "Why not? That seems like a perfectly normal way to end this bizarre visit."

After they left, Jillian, her mouth in a thin line and her hands palm up in her lap, stared at her fingers. Trent sipped his coffee, letting her have the few moments of quiet, thinking time. He glanced at the clock over the bar. There wasn't much time before the early evening customers would start trickling into the place.

Being busy would be good. Less time to think.

"Tell me about your sister." Jillian tilted her head, nailed him with her topaz filled gaze.

Trent sucked in a scalding breath. *Not what he'd expected.* While his heart thudded heavy in his chest, he rubbed the back of his neck. Memories rushed in, filled the void he struggled to keep empty, filled it and expanded it until his lungs hurt. He scrubbed his hand down his face, covered his mouth.

"You said she'd died."

"I did say that." He stared out at the lustrous blue of the water surrounding Rosey's. The briny scent of seawater drifted on the coolness of the breeze wafting in through the wide windows. A beautiful February, late afternoon in Key Largo.

So many Februarys without Cassie.

Where were all the damn employees when he needed them? The cook? The bartender? The detective? Anyone so he didn't have to think about Cassie. Didn't have to talk about his beautiful baby sister.

"I also said it was my fault." He pulled his gaze to Jillian's. The empathy there, right on the surface of her eyes, punched him in the gut. His hands balled into fists, he consciously straightened each finger. Then he wiped his damp palms over the thin material of his pants.

"You did say that."

"Quite a few years ago, in the Navy, I was part of a special force tasked with taking out a killer who targeted family members of high-ranking naval officers."

"You were a SEAL?"

He ran his tongue over his teeth. "Yeah."

She sat back in her chair with her arms crossed loose in her lap and her body angled towards him. Her eyes radiated sympathy he damn well didn't deserve.

"I've seen a lot, done a lot. What that killer did to those people –" Trent slid further down in his seat. He rubbed his hand over his mouth again. "It crawls in your gut. Stays there. We caught up to him, but something went wrong. He lay in wait for us. One moment I had him, looked him dead in the eye. The next, everything went to shit. We were ambushed. He got away."

The laugh churning in this throat lacked any trace of amusement.

"There was a leak that's since been taken care of, but not before he identified me. He wanted to make me pay for nearly catching him. He kidnapped Cassie –" *Don't go there, Sawyer.* "Killed her. Left her for me to find."

"Trent –"

Jillian's soft voice strummed along his nerves. Hummed, wrapped tight around his chest, made it hard to breathe. He held up his hand. She'd asked. He'd damn well finish.

"After Cassie, he quit killing. Stopped. Disappeared. Rumors flew he was dead. I was pulled off. They said I was too close, couldn't be objective. They were right. She was my sister. *She was killed because of me.*" Trent wet his dry lips. "Eventually the manhunt was dropped. When my time was up, I left the Navy."

"And joined the FBI." Jillian rubbed her arms. "They let you work on your sister's case as an agent?"

"Hardly." He scrubbed a hand over his head. "That's the beautiful thing about Top Secret ops. No one talks. I didn't share about Cassie and neither did anyone else. Her death was listed as accidental. Wrong place, wrong time. End of story."

"But it wasn't."

"I *knew* that bastard wasn't dead. Over the years, I spent every free moment working the case in the background." He was a damn good hunter. Or had been. "I ended up on a special task force with Ben Garrett. With his extended resources, I found her murderer."

"What happened?"

His nostrils flared. He worked his jaw. "I killed the son of a bitch."

Jillian's eyes widened. "Oh."

"He presented me with the perfect opportunity. I took it. He's dead." With his thumbs, Trent kneaded his temples and pressed his palms over his eyes, blocking out the painful brilliance of the water. He'd eradicated the man, but the cost had been anything remotely resembling a psychic gift. "But not before he grabbed my partner's sister."

"You saved her?"

"Barely." He blew out his breath. "She's all right. At least physically."

Mentally, well that's another story. For both of us.

Through half slit eyes, he stared at Jillian. "I intended to kill the bastard. That was always my goal."

"I get that."

"Do you?" A nerve jumped along his jaw. "I'm on administrative leave. Instead of prison. The shooting was deemed justified. Now I wait for Garrett and the higher-ups to decide what to do with me." His hunting ability gone, he had no place on the psychic task force. Where that left him, now, he had no idea. "While I sit here with you, wondering about your sister and what she's involved in. Life is full of ironies."

He met her gaze, expecting censure, surprised by the empathy still shining there. Empathy and a bit of distance. A bit of hesitancy. Both were probably good things.

She lifted her pink mug, saluted him. "To life's ironies."

Right.

Several footsteps pounded along the pier moments before the bartender and cook, carrying the day's fresh fish and assorted fruit and vegetables, ambled through the door. Where had they been when he needed them to stop him from spilling his guts to this woman who had begun to mean way too damn much?

Hostage to Fortune.

While Cassie's killer was dead, that wouldn't stop any of the other sick and twisted individuals he hunted from doing the same damn thing. Anyone he cared for had a huge, fucking target on their back.

No one's hero. No one to depend on.

Life's sick, twisted ironies.

Jillian touched his arm, her fingertips soft against his skin. "Time to get to work."

He nodded. Watched her smile and greet her employees as she pushed herself up and away from the table. Such a beautiful smile.

Wide and genuine.

Warm.

For a few more moments he stared at the gleaming, bright blue of Blackwater Sound. Cassie was gone. He couldn't bring his sister back.

Hayden's still alive.

If they found her, figured out the missing pieces, figured out who wanted her dead so badly they killed all those other people, if they solved this puzzle, he'd find some semblance of peace. He'd tuck this whole Key Largo experience away in a place a certain honey-eyed, bat toting woman wouldn't haunt him.

Right.

Bottom line, they needed to find Hayden, find her hidey hole, before she ended up as dead as Cassie.

WHAT'S TAKING SHAMUS SO LONG WITH ERIC?

Jillian tilted her head to stare over across the Sound before she laid her knife on the counter and pushed aside the cutting board where she had fresh mango, pineapple and cilantro chopped to go into the tropical salsa she made daily.

The fact her salsa was nearly as popular as the grouper sandwich gratified something inside her. Maybe one day they'd be able to serve the fancier foods she loved to cook. Or maybe Rosey's could add a catering sideline.

If she could keep the place from going under.

A few feet over, the rhythmic thump of Trent's knife striking his wooden block as he attacked onions and garlic filled the stretched silence between them. He hadn't said more than two words since the cook and bartender arrived.

A solid half hour ago.

The DEA agents were long gone, with her dad in custody. Hadn't *that* made her feel like a good, dutiful daughter? And Shamus still *chatted* with Eric outside.

In the kitchen area behind her, the aroma of grilled onions mixed with fresh garlic and bell peppers filled the air as her burly bartender helped the cook with her preparations for the expected evening crowd. Neither talked much as they went about their chores.

Even Blackwater Sound seemed quiet.

Waiting.

Jillian wiped her hands on a towel she kept handy, wrapped it around her fingers. She knew Trent expected her to condemn him for killing the man who'd murdered his sister.

But I don't.

She understood standing up for those you loved, defending them. She even understood the vengeance that had run through Trent's blood. If someone *had* managed to kill Hayden, how would she, herself, feel now? About that man, about him being caught and justice being served?

I'd want to take my bat – the heavy one – to the knees of the one responsible, swing it at his head. Beat him senseless.

Tit for tat.

Vengeance. Right there to be stroked. Embraced.

So she understood Trent's not quite easy acceptance of his own role in the death of the man who'd taken his sister's life. She understood, even though she did her damnedest to avoid violence, it was a part of life. That violence twined through Trent's life. Had for quite a while, probably would for a long time more.

A shudder worked its way down her spine.

And I use avoidance of violence to keep others — men — as far away as my bat's reach.

With a soft sigh, she looked at Trent from under her lashes. The hard line of his bruised jaw told its own story. He wasn't anything like the man who'd put her in the hospital. Trent used his fists to protect. To defend. When other options failed.

He wouldn't hurt her, not physically.

She understood all of that.

Inside, though, she still flinched.

"Jilly?" Shamus' voice from near the open door rescued her from her dark thoughts. "Can I go over something with you before I head back to the station?"

"Sure." She glanced at Trent. *Does Shamus know Hayden's alive?* The towel twisted between her hands.

Trent set his knife aside and snagged the towel from her to wipe his hands before following her around the counter. Shamus, standing near the door, raised an eyebrow. Maybe she didn't *need* Trent, but she'd accept whatever support he wanted to give and be grateful for it.

Shamus headed through the door, towards the pier. Towards privacy.

Jillian wet her lips, pulled the bottom one between her teeth.

She didn't want to lie to Shamus. But how did she tell him the truth without jeopardizing her sister? *Of course, there's that damn illegal precursor. Dammit, Hayden.*

Next to her, Trent ran a warm hand down her arm. He cupped her elbow, gave it a light squeeze.

This will be okay. She'd handle whatever Shamus threw at her.

On the pier outside Rosey's, she lifted her face to the moisture laden breeze. They'd have rain before long.

Shamus, with his mouth pursed, stared towards the line of clouds hugging the eastern horizon. "Going to be a wet night."

"Looks like it might be." Trent stood next to her, his solidness tangible in the balmy, rain-scented air.

She tucked her thumbs into the back pockets of her jeans and resisted the urge to just lean against him, to let him support her.

Shamus nodded. From his pocket he fished out a small plastic bag holding a cell phone in a green rhinestone case.

Hayden's phone.

"Where did you find that?" Jillian's breath caught in her chest, made it hard to push the words out. "Not out at Felicity's …."

Trent wrapped his arm around her shoulders, pulled her solid against him.

"No." Shamus' green eyes sharp in the lowering light, he rubbed the tip of his nose. "Hayden may have been the last person to see Felicity Chambers alive. You told Ted she was crewing for Jazz. Even out on the water they should have been close enough to shore for her to get a cell signal, so I called Hayden's phone. Rang several times before going to voicemail. When we received word the Symphony had exploded, I realized my calls to Hayden had been *after* the boat sunk."

"But if the phone was on the boat, it would be at the bottom of Biscayne Bay. It shouldn't ring at all, but should go straight to voicemail." Jillian's cheek against Trent's shoulder, she glanced up at him. "Right?"

"That would be my take."

"Although I'm no technician, that's my take, also." Shamus nodded again. "Which is why I ordered a GPS trace on her cell. Ted found the phone earlier today."

"Where?" Jillian couldn't help the breathless sound of her voice or the way her heart thumped against her chest.

"Under a planter just outside the marina where the Symphony had been docked."

"Hayden lost it?"

"Possibly. We need to know what's on it, Jilly. I can get a court order, let the evidence guys have at it, but chances are that will destroy whatever is on it."

"What do you think is there?" She frowned as the two men exchanged sharp glances.

"A photo." Trent's grip tightened on her shoulder. "They don't need the actual phone to see what numbers she called or to see who called her. They can get that from her phone company."

Shamus nodded. "Might be a long shot, but it's a possibility. One I don't want to see destroyed if there's any way to access it. Hayden's not stupid, Jilly. She sent that stuff to you for a reason. I'm hoping she left us another clue."

"You think I know her security code."

"Don't you?"

God, Hayden. Jillian wet her suddenly dry lips. *Don't let there be anything incriminating on the damn thing.* She nodded and held out her hand.

Time to find out the truth.

Chapter Seventeen

WITH A NONCHALANCE TRENT didn't own, he rubbed a hand down Jillian's arm and shoved his other hand in his front jean's pocket. Otherwise he might do something stupid.

Like grab that phone, throw it across the pier where they stood, and let it sink into the dark water of the Sound.

Which would be another fine piece of asinine behavior.

Sunlight, dipping late into the afternoon and pushing towards dusk, sparked off the green rhinestones covering the phone's case.

He didn't know what was on the damn thing. Didn't know if he'd be *simply* destroying evidence or protecting her from some harsh truth about her sister. Or both.

Protection.

Jillian didn't want his protection.

His fingers curled in his pocket. He'd protect her anyway.

But not by throwing the phone in the Sound.

With the tip of her tongue, she wet her lips before she took the cell. Shamus tucked the plastic bag into his front pants pocket.

"It's okay." Trent, with his arm still around her shoulder, pulled her a little closer.

She pressed the on button at the top of the phone, her eyebrows lifting when the cell actually powered up, then slid her fingertip over the screen in a path to unlock the phone. With her hand trembling, she clicked open the photo file and tapped the last image.

Taken at night, without a flash, shadows darkened the edges of the photo. But there, in the center, stood the blonde giant, his face lit by light from a nearby lamp, staring at them from Hayden's cell phone. The deck of the ill-fated Symphony spread out behind him.

"Son of a bitch." Trent pulled his hand from his pocket and wiped the back of it across his mouth.

"I take it you know this man?" Shamus glanced from the phone to him.

"He helped steal the Oasis. Blew her to hell."

"Looks like he might also be responsible for the Symphony."

THE PROMISED EARLIER RAIN had fallen and clouds still hung low by the time Jillian and Trent called it a night and shut Rosey's down.

Exhausted, mentally as well as physically, Jillian pulled her car out onto the empty main road and headed south towards home. A pair of headlights suddenly appeared in her rearview mirror. "Where did they come from?"

Slouched in the front passenger seat, arms folded over his stomach, and his chin nearly to his chest, Trent's narrowed gaze remained on the side mirror. "The edge of the road. Question is, were they waiting for us?"

Her gaze flicked between Trent, the rearview mirror and the road. Since the photo they'd found on Hayden's phone, those had been the most words he'd said at one time in a long time. Hours had passed with little more from him than a few grunts.

"What do you want me to do?" Jillian wet her bottom lip. "The turn to my house isn't far."

"If that car is actually following us, they probably already know where you live. No sense taking them by there, though." He straightened in his seat. "Turn down another street. One with a way back out. Use your signal. Act like this is normal. What you intended."

Her fingers tight on the steering wheel, she nodded.

As she neared the right turn that would wind its way to her home she eased her foot off the accelerator and flipped on her left signal. This time of night traffic on the Overseas Highway was usually light. At this moment, however, the highway remained empty except for them and the car behind.

She slowed more, made her left turn. The other vehicle continued on its way. The breath hadn't realized she held exhaled in one long sigh.

"Don't get too comfortable." Trent hit the window control and his window slid down, letting in the heavy, sea-tinged breeze with its fragrance of recent fresh rain.

Moonlight played hide and seek in the low lying

clouds, making the night dark. Soft sounds from the life in the mangroves filtered through the open window.

Beside her, he continued to stare at the side mirror. "We're not off the hook yet."

"Oh." Her palms damp against the wheel, she flexed her fingers before taking the sharp curve that took them along the road towards the northeast end of the island. She accelerated, glanced at her mirrors.

"There." Trent straightened more and leaned slightly forward in his seat.

A pair of headlights swept around the corner behind them. They looked the same as before.

"Now what?" Her grip on the wheel tightened in concert with the knot at the very pit of her stomach.

He scanned the area lit by her car lights. She ran the tip of her tongue over her dry lips. Dark silhouettes of mangroves on both sides of the empty road, illuminated by their headlights, narrowed in on them.

Isolated them.

"Where does this road take us?" He glanced at her before he again shifted his focus to the side mirror.

"If we go straight, it ends up at Ocean Reef. Near Rhys Blackthorne's place. But there's a turn coming up that will lead us back around to the Overseas Highway."

"Good. What's on that road once we make our turn?"

"One place along the straightaway. Then, when we turn again, there's another house on the right. That road curves into a more populated area after that."

She let her foot off the gas, didn't break or signal,

and took the sharp right turn. Her shoulder brushed his for a moment before she straightened the car. Tingles scudded down her spine. From his touch or from the adrenaline rush roiling just at the top of her stomach, she wasn't sure. She hit the button to roll her own window down, letting in more of the rain soaked breeze.

The car behind them made the turn and fell in a distance behind them.

"So either they decided to take this route home, or they really are following us."

"Money on following us."

"Yeah." She bit the inside of her bottom lip.

A short distance ahead, on the right side, palm fronds wavered in her high beams, marking the driveway to the only home on this straight stretch. A large, 1920s home with mature palm trees to block the view of the house from the street.

"There's no real side of the road out here, is there? Nowhere to pull off?"

Her head jerked. She threw him a quick glance. *He's kidding, isn't he?* Pull over out here with no one around, no way of protecting themselves? No idea *who* was behind them. *Bad idea.* "No. After we turn again that other house is on the right, then a short distance later is a dive shop, a restaurant and more houses. Maybe that's an area we can pull over."

Where there are people. Even if they're all asleep. Someplace where there's someone else to hear if I start screaming.

"We need to pull over *before* we get there."

"Trent –"

Ahead, a black wall of vegetation loomed. She sucked in a breath, cranked the wheel and pressed the gas pedal. Her car careened around the sharp corner. They flew past as the road curved gently around the home on the right.

Only her grip on the wheel kept her from falling into Trent.

"Let your foot off the gas." He pressed his shoulder against hers. Heat from his skin radiated through the thinness of her T-shirt. His breath fanned her neck. "No brakes."

She let up on the accelerator, kept her fingers wrapped round the wheel.

What she wanted was to rub her hands over her face, scrub this whole incident from her mind. Wake up, go to work, her only worry if she'd have enough grouper for the dinner crowd.

"On the left side, coming up. What is that?"

This is dumb. They were both going to be dead before dawn had a chance to push the night away. She gripped the wheel even tighter. "That's access to a really small patch of beach. Garden Cove. There's a dive shop nearby. Kayaks to rent. That sort of thing."

Trent glanced at the mirror on his side. "Use your emergency brake. Slow the car down, tuck us back in there."

She did what he'd told her. Backed her car under a low lying row of trees, slipped the vehicle into park, and flipped off her lights just before the other vehicle's headlights swept around the curve and over the stretch of road they'd just vacated.

"Down." Trent grabbed her arm, and with one hand on the back of her head, he shoved her to his lap. With his head bent near hers, he wrapped both his arms around her.

Her heart pounded a staccato beat in her chest. Several long seconds passed. His warm breath tickled her ear just before he swept her hair to the side and pressed a quick kiss to her temple.

"They went by." He straightened, helped her sit upright. A soft glimmer of moonlight, there then gone, picked out a gleam in his darkened eyes.

She swallowed around the knot suddenly lodged in her throat. He ran his index finger down her cheek. Heat followed in the wake of his touch.

"We need to – Figure out what we do next." Huskiness thickened the graveled timbre of his voice. "About whoever's in that car."

"Yes." Her hands on his thigh for a moment, she pushed herself back into her seat, brushed her hair away from her face. *What next?* She reached to twist the ignition.

"Wait." Trent, his voice now low and urgent, laid his hand over hers.

Instead of the other car's engine noise fading into nothing, it seemed to be coming closer again, this time just above an idle. Jillian's stomach muscles clenched, shoving bile up into her throat. The trees blocked them from view before, but they'd be visible to anyone coming down the road from the other direction.

Jillian swallowed hard then sucked her bottom lip in between her teeth. She swore the other car's engine changed pitch, even now more ominous, more threatening.

His touch light, Trent gripped her chin, angled her face to him. "We need to get out of the car with the dome light in the off position. It can't go on when we open the doors."

She nodded. Her hands shaky, she twisted the dial to off and bit her lip harder.

Trent squeezed her shoulder. "Ready?"

"As I'll ever be." Her voice cracked, the words hung in the air.

"Stay low. Duck behind the car, then head to the trees with me." He brushed her mouth with his thumb. "Let's go."

Her lips tingled, but she set her jaw and shoved the sensation aside. He pulled her bat from the back floorboard. She yanked the key from the ignition, shoved it into her pocket at the same time she forced her door open just enough to escape. Crouched low and hunched forward, she pushed her door closed. With a gulp of thick air, she darted behind her car.

Trent grabbed her hand. Together, they dashed towards the scraggly barrier of trees. A thin layer of damp sand coated the asphalt parking area. They both slipped, Jillian nearly went down.

Hell no, sweetheart. Trent wrapped an arm around her waist, half carried her across the asphalt. With several thin tree trunks as minimal cover that would have to do, he squatted, pulled her down beside him, and held her close with his cheek pressed to her head.

Headlights swung across the area as the other car eased forward around the far line of trees. The vehicle stopped, its engine idling. From where they hid, the glare of the other car's headlights silhouetted Jillian's vehicle.

A car door slammed.

Jillian's fingers gripped the arm Trent wrapped around her waist. He tamped down the urge to pull her more fully against him and instead squeezed her once, then dropped his arm. He braced one hand on the ground in front of them, his other on the bat.

The beam of a flashlight bounced off Jillian's car door.

In the dark, Trent inched forward. Whoever held that light circled Jillian's vehicle.

Searching.

Shit. How the hell were they going to get out of this?

The flashlight beam swept over the sandy asphalt, paused at the area where they'd nearly gone down. Male laughter, sinister as the dark night, echoed across the open area and followed the beam of light along the row of trees to the right of where they crouched.

Come closer, you moron. Trent's fingers tight on the bat's hilt, he shifted a fraction of an inch. *All I need is one swing.*

"I know you're there." The sudden rustling of the breeze through the branches above them underscored the menace in the man's voice.

The blond giant.

Time to end this.

Trent, with his fingertips light on Jillian's elbow, indicated she stay put. Even in the darkness he could *feel* her frown. *Please stay put, sweetheart.*

The blond giant's beam approached, constantly sweeping the trees and parking area.

Silently Trent counted to three. The beam swept the area above them and he launched himself out of hiding. He swung the bat low, aiming for the man's knees.

With a grunt, the guy went down, his flashlight flying, its beam of light wild across the dark sky. A clatter of metal against asphalt then the light dimmed.

Trent jumped on the man, shoved him onto his stomach, and kicked Blondie's gun out of his hand. His knee on the asshole's back, he pressed the bat across the shoulders, leveraging his weight to keep the blonde giant in place.

A beam of light played over them as Jillian hurried forward with the flashlight. She collected the man's weapon, crouched, and tucked the flashlight under her arm with the beam directed to the ground between them. Both hands gripping the gun's handle, she pointed Blondie's weapon just where the moron could see the barrel aimed at his face.

A small thrill of satisfaction welled inside Trent.

Good job, Jillian Rose.

"Are you going to cooperate?" Trent dug his knee into the guy's back. "Or should she shoot you now and get it over with?"

The man swore, and with his cheek mashed against the gritty sand, he glared at Jillian. He spat, the spittle doing little but further dampening the sand near his mouth. Granules stuck to his lips.

Trent pressed harder on the bat. "If I were you, I wouldn't make her mad."

"She's as much trouble as her sister."

"You know –" Jillian's voice trembled, then hardened. "Knew Hayden?"

"Give me back what the bitch stole."

"You're not in any position to be giving orders." Trent leaned more of his weight on the center of the bat. The man grunted. Spit and swore.

Their momentary control could shift at any moment. Trent needed to find a way to secure this guy. Or knock him out. Either way worked.

"Jillian? Is your cell in your pocket?"

"Yes."

"Call Ted Mathews. Tell him to get out here *now*."

"Okay. Yes." The light beam fumbled while she pulled her cell from her pocket.

"You're not turning me over to the cops." The blonde giant arched his back, tried to twist to the side, to throw Trent off the way a wild bronc would a rider.

Trent's knee slipped on the asphalt. He fisted his hands tight around the center of the bat, swung the handle end forward, and smacked the guy along his jaw. The man went limp.

Glass jaw. Trent sucked in a breath. *Hope I don't have to remember that.*

Jillian slipped her cell back into her pocket and aimed the flashlight at the man laying prone on the ground.

"Dispatch said they'd get hold of Ted, get him out here ASAP."

Trent nodded. With one hand still holding the bat, he patted Blondie's pockets. Empty. "No ID."

Blondie wore dark jeans, dark polo shirt, and dark shoes. Along with black gloves on both hands.

A man bent on serious business.

Still crouched beside the guy, Trent traded weapons with Jillian. The bat for the gun. Glock, semi-automatic. Not his own gun, but that would have been too easy.

He scanned the area around them. "Do you have anything in your car we can use to tie him up?"

"Those bungee cord things."

"Perfect."

Jillian hurried towards her car. The blonde giant groaned. Trent squatted to press the gun's barrel against the man's temple.

Scuffles sounded near Jillian's car. A muttered curse.

"Jillian?" *What the hell was happening?*

"You bast –" More scuffles sounded from her direction.

The blonde giant's weak, guttural laughter lashed over him.

Trent raised the gun to smash the butt against the moron's head as the flashlight played over him and the man sprawled on the ground.

"Jillian?"

She moaned.

He squinted at the beam of light. Someone had hold of her, was forcing her forward while shining the beam his way.

"Jillian?" Trent tried again.

A muffled curse then the sound of scuffles and a grunt from whoever held her. Then the resounding smack of the flashlight against bone.

"Jillian?" Trent's nostrils flared even as his grip tightened on the butt of the gun.

The beam of light wavered to the side, obviously indicating he should let the blonde giant go free.

"Forget it." He shoved to his feet, with that light blinding him, as the rasp of Jillian's breathing quickened, became shallower, like she was trying not to scream.

She's still conscious. For how long?

Chapter Eighteen

*T*HIS ISN'T HAPPENING.

Trent twisted to keep himself at an angle between the blond giant still stretched out on the ground and the idling car to the right. The beam of light pointed in their direction wavered towards the vehicle.

Hell, no. You bastards aren't escaping that easy.

He widened his stance, kept the gun aimed at Blondie on the ground. With the flashlight blinding him, he couldn't risk shooting in that direction and possibly hitting Jillian.

Cassie's image flashed in his mind. There, then gone.

No. These two pieces of shit aren't going to hurt Jillian.

How he'd prevent that, he had no idea.

"Police are on their way." Blondie shoved to his knees, staggered to a standing position, and planted both feet. "Probably be here soon."

The light waved again, three short flickers, between the blonde man and the idling vehicle.

"You're not taking that car." Trent rocked forward onto the balls of feet.

"There are other alternatives to the car." Blondie rubbed the back of his gloved hand along his jaw then shook his head once.

The light beam shifted as whoever held it eased towards the shoreline to the left of where Trent stood. The blonde giant rolled his shoulders then swung his fist. Trent blocked the man's punch. He shoved his left fist into the man's gut and smashed the butt of the gun across the guy's jaw.

From behind a thinning section in the wall of clouds, the moon peered out in a meager glow of light as Blondie staggered, shaking his head. He twisted his big body and, with a lopsided gait, tore off towards the shoreline.

As quickly as the moon-glow had lit the area, the wall of clouds thickened, extinguishing the light. Darkness swallowed Blondie.

Jillian's sudden gasp struck at Trent's heart. He swung towards her as the sound of her being shoved to the ground echoed across the area.

Shit. His grip tightened on the gun. *Can't shoot. Can't risk Jillian.*

He rushed forward, but the man with the flashlight ran faster than Blondie.

Trent found Jillian at the edge where asphalt met beach. On her hands and knees, her breath came in ragged bursts. He pulled her to a standing position then wrapped an arm around her shoulders, pressed her against his chest.

God, she's okay.

"Go. I'm fine." She pushed at him. "Catch them."

He threw a quick glance at the light from the flashlight as it wavered along the shoreline. In that instance the man hit a set of stairs leading to a dock. The light beam bounced with every step he climbed.

Trent brushed his lips over Jillian's forehead. "Stay put."

The gun clutched firm in his hand, he tore after the men. Sand slowed him some, but as he made the dock the beam of light played over the wooden slats a mere few yards ahead.

An unmistakable sound of revving engines ripped through the air. The light beam bounced again then distinguished. Just ahead, running lights glowed in what appeared to be a low slung power boat.

Could be a freaking yacht for all he could tell in the darkness.

The pitch of the engines changed, idling as the boat's lights eased away from the dock.

"Another day, fucker." Blondie's laughter followed the sounds of the big engines and the churning water as the lights framing the boat's gauges moved further away.

Trent braced his feet and aimed the gun at those glowing lights.

Squeezed the trigger.

The bullet exploded outward, the reverberation tensed the muscles in his arm, down his spine to his feet. The sound echoed across the cove.

One set of gauges went out accompanied by a loud string of curses.

"Take that." Trent let his arm drop, pointed the gun at the ground.

The moon again peeked from its veil of thick clouds. Sea foam, looking like wisps of frosting on a black cake, followed the boat as its big engines churned the water in its wake.

Dammit to hell.

TRENT STOOD AT THE CENTER of the sandy parking area of Garden Cove with Ted Mathews. Jillian sat in the driver's seat of her car, the door open and her head back against the head rest. Although her eyes remained closed, Trent knew she didn't sleep. She'd refused medical treatment, had sworn she'd be fine. No broken bones, just a few bruises.

From the sound of the whack she'd taken, those bruises would soon turn ugly.

Asinine move, sending her back to her car. Should've known Blondie wasn't alone. No fucking assumptions.

Not with Jillian's safety.

I know better.

His hands balled into fists. He sucked in a lungful of thick, balmy air.

Rain threatened again. The forensic crew gathered around the lot needed to hurry. Their equipment lit the asphalt and beach area like a damn baseball field. The darkness of the early morning hour clouds pressed heavy against the edge of their lights.

Ominous.

Jillian's bat lay across her lap, her hands resting at its center, her fingers spastically gripping it then loosening.

"Car was reported stolen last week in Georgia." Ted frowned.

Trent nodded. Blondie was too slick to use his own vehicle in a tail.

Arnie.

The name had been written in bold, black ink on a local coffee house's to-go cup, sitting pretty as you please in the driver's cup holder. Once they tracked down whatever barista had been working yesterday evening, Trent knew in his gut she'd ID the owner of the cup as Blondie.

As the same man in the photo on Hayden's cell phone. The same man who'd blown the Oasis apart.

Ted moved a few feet away to talk with another deputy. Shamus had been informed of the night's events. Maybe the techs would be able to get DNA off the lid. *Maybe.* Arnie had worn gloves. Trent doubted the man left any fingerprints. Their luck, Arnie hadn't even had a single sip of whatever was in the cup.

Of course, the drink itself could always belong to the man Arnie had brought along with him.

No. The cup belonged to Blondie.

But who was the other man?

The squat redhead was dead. That left the man from the shadows on board the Oasis. The man who pulled Arnie's strings.

Who the hell are you? Trent studied at the abandoned vehicle. *How do I track you?*

Earlier, as he and Jillian had left Rosey's, that weird warning buzz had vibrated in his inner ear, only to disappear the moment he'd spotted the vehicle on the side of the road.

Like an early warning system.

Buzz. Identify threat. Buzz stops.

How do I leverage that to my advantage?

Trent shoved his hands into his pockets. Ted now had Arnie's weapon.

And Trent's. Another surprise stashed under the driver's seat. Another unanswered question. Had Arnie kept it as souvenir?

Whatever Arnie's reasons, Trent wouldn't be getting the gun back any time soon. Although the weapon had only been missing a few days, ballistics would still need to be done to make sure it hadn't been used in the wide swath of crime shadowing Key Largo these last few days.

Ted's immediate boss wasn't thrilled with Trent right now. Firing the gun at a fleeing boat was probably just the tip of the boss' *displeasure*. Trent didn't blame him, but he wasn't sorry he'd taken that shot. As for the rest of it, there wasn't a lot he could do. At least not at this moment.

"There's a deputy sitting outside Jillian's house." Ted stopped next to Trent, stood shoulder to shoulder, and stared at the empty car. "He's to check the inside of the house before you go in. Why don't you take her home?"

"Is there an officer at the back of the house, also? Those morons stole another boat this time, not a car. Do you have any idea how easy it would be –"

"Trent –" Ted shook his head. "Take her home. Lock the doors. With you inside –"

"With only a bat for a weapon. Been there, done that." His jaw tense, he set his fists on his hips. "We need to find that boat. Haul them in."

"In these waters, that's like hunting for that needle in a haystack. They could be anywhere, tucked into a cove somewhere. Or they could have abandoned the boat the way they did this car. They could be half way back to Georgia by now."

Tell me something I don't know. God, Trent knew he was being unreasonable. Wanting answers, demanding results *now.* "Her house isn't safe."

Ted sucked in a deep breath. Nodded. "Let me know where the two of you end up."

"Thanks." Trent scrubbed a hand over his face, over the top of his head.

Ted nodded again. "Take care of her."

"Damn straight."

WITH RAIN BATTERING THE ROOF of Jillian's car, she sat in the front passenger seat. Her fingers, wrapped tight around the bat in her lap, trembled. Trent sat in the driver's seat. Darkness surrounded them, the light over the front steps of her house the only outside illumination. She stared at the front door, at the officer who slipped her key into the lock.

A nerve twitched under the swelling along her left cheek, where the man who'd held her had hit her. Her right shoulder throbbed from the way he'd twisted her arm behind her back.

Deal with the aching muscles and bruises later, right now they aren't important.

"Hey." Trent, his features shadowed by the dim white glow of her car's gauges, twisted in his seat, laid a hand over hers, and squeezed. "The deputy has already secured the perimeter. We'll be okay for the few minutes we'll be here."

"What if they got inside before he did that?" Hating the way her voice shook, she lifted her chin.

"That's why he has your key and we're waiting for him to give us the all clear."

Which chafed him. She'd seen the tense set of Trent's jaw line when he'd handed the house key through the car window. Letting someone else secure the place didn't set well with him. But gratitude wormed its way through her heart, gratitude Trent sat with her, in her car. She didn't trust anyone except him.

When had that happened?

This all-consuming trust when it came to her safety? She didn't do that. Not with anyone except *maybe* Shamus.

"Thank you." The words hardly more than a whisper, she let go of the bat and turned her hand over to twine her fingers with Trent's.

His eyebrows drawn down, his gaze swept over her face.

"For being the one out here, with me."

One corner of his mouth lifted and with their hands linked, he settled back in his seat.

After a moment, the foyer light blinked on, then the

one in the kitchen.

Trent's fingers still entwined with hers, his gaze locked on the progression of lights through her house. "Where would your sister stash another kilo of that stuff?"

"Why do you think she has another kilo?"

"Either Arnie didn't get word the DEA snatched what Hayden had taken, or your sister managed to get more than one package. From what little I've learned about your sister, she strikes me as smart enough to hedge her bets."

"She can be sly when the need is there."

"So where would she stash it?"

Jillian stared at her house, at the lights glowing room by room upstairs. "Rosey's safe."

"There's a safe at Rosey's?"

"No." She jerked her chin towards the house. "Years ago my grandmother put a small floor safe in the den. My dad –" She swallowed, made a face. *What a mess.* "When my dad was in town, Rosey needed a place to *stash* the day's receipts where my dad couldn't find the money. As far as I know, he still isn't aware of its existence."

"But you and Hayden both have the key or the combination?"

"Combination. Yes, we both do."

"Is it big enough to hold a kilo?"

She nodded. "And Hayden was here the other night, when she left that note for me."

The deputy, now standing on her front steps, waved

at them.

"There's the all clear." Trent squeezed her fingers again. "I guess we're doing more than collecting a change of clothes."

Oh, God, Hayden. What the hell are you involved in?

Jillian and Trent made a dash through the rain to the front door.

"The back sliding doors are locked, the blinds closed." The deputy handed Jillian her key. "I'll wait here on the steps while the two of you collect what you need."

With her bat in hand, water dripping down her face and her smile strained, she thanked the deputy then followed Trent into the house. She waited while he locked the door behind them. "What do we do first?"

"Clothes. Enough for a couple of days, at least." He took the stairs two at a time. At the top of the landing he glanced over his shoulder. "Then we'll check the safe, see what we see."

Jillian hurried to her room, quickly changed then stuffed clothes into her duffle without caring if she wrinkled them or not. Tried not to think about Hayden doing the same thing only a few days ago.

She shoved thoughts of her father away. No one could help him right now. Maybe once they figured out what Hayden had got herself mixed up in, they could find a way to deal with her dad. But no matter how she looked at it, she needed Trent's help to find those answers.

That thought didn't chafe the way it had only yesterday.

Trent stopped at the door to her room with a black duffel in one hand. Her father's, left from a time he'd beat his own hasty departure. Like the clothes Trent now wore. As she had, he'd changed, this time a pair of khaki trousers and a dark blue polo shirt that only served to darken the blue depths of his shadowed eyes.

She pulled her gaze to the bat nestled on her bed next to her bag.

"Ready?" When she nodded, he took a few steps in and grabbed her duffle from the bed. "Grab your weapon and lead the way, lady."

She tucked her bat under her arm and hit the light switch with her palm, throwing the room into partial darkness, before leading the way down the stairs to the bottom floor then to the back of the house. The deputy had left the lamps on the side tables on, the light softly casting a warm glow to the room.

Even here, in her grandmother's sanctuary, the sense of being exposed prickled along her skin. She scanned the room, relieved to see Trent doing the same.

Nothing abnormal. Nothing out of place.

With a last glance at the white shuttered blinds, she hurried behind the overstuffed brown leather couch and flipped back the edge of the throw rug. On her knees, she raised the tile covering the safe. Without hesitation she spun the locking mechanism and in a few moments had the safe unlocked.

Trent knelt beside her.

With a shallow swallow, she wet her lips. Now or

never.

She sat back on her heels and lifted the heavy safe door.

There, at the bottom of the floor safe, sat a matching kilo of the stuff Hayden sent in the mail.

Chapter Nineteen

"T ELL ME AGAIN WHY we're sitting outside Dane's place, instead of being checked into a hotel, getting some sleep?" Jillian drummed her fingers on the passenger door handle of her parked car. Outside their lowered windows, dawn had just broke on a grey, dismal morning with clouds promising another soaking before too much time passed.

And to think, a few short hours ago she'd worried they wouldn't make it through to dawn.

Would they make dusk?

"Sleep is overrated and I'm curious." Trent, settled snug in the driver's seat, stared out the windshield.

They sat backed into a vacant lot up the street from Dane's house. The recent storm cooled the air just enough to cut the stickiness of the humidity. A breeze wafted in through the windows, bringing with it the brininess of the nearby open water. Dane's home sat at the end of the street, two houses down from where the car sat, less than half a mile from her home. Although most of the houses on this street didn't have water access, his did.

From this vantage she and Trent could see the front

of the house and the side abutting the canal. By car or boat, they'd see Dane once he made it home. At least in theory. As long as he actually came home.

"Dane is probably already in bed." She leaned her head back on the headrest. "Asleep. Like we should be."

"Later." Huskiness lined Trent's voice but he continued to stare forward.

Sleep. Waking up with Trent beside her. She shifted in her seat, barely stopped herself from squirming. Their near misses with each other played through her head. *Stop dwelling on what –ifs.*

Not that dwelling on the kilo of precursor made her feel any better. They'd left the package in the safe, secure for the time being.

Now, like Trent, she concentrated on the view outside. Or at least tried to focus. Her mind drifted with the hint of whatever aftershave he'd scrounged earlier in the day. The scent teased her, messed with her senses.

As if she were a teenaged girl *parked* with her first crush.

I'm beyond pathetic.

She lifted her chin, mentally chastised herself one more time. Then straightened in her seat.

Aftershave.

"Whoever was with Arnie, I know him. I mean, I've come in contact with him somewhere before."

"I know."

"What do you mean, you know?"

"He wouldn't speak. Used that flashlight like a talking stick. He didn't want us hearing his voice. Which means one of us knows him. Since you're more local than I am, my money's on you."

"That makes sense."

"How did you figure out you know him?"

"His aftershave."

"Like with Arnie after he broke into your house."

She nodded. "But I can't place this, it's like I should know who it belongs to, but can't quite place it."

"Eric?"

"That would tie everything up in a nice, neat little bow, wouldn't it?"

"So it's not Eric?"

She shrugged both shoulders, huffed out a breath. "Eric's one of those guys who wears whatever cologne appeals to him at the moment."

"So you're not ruling him out."

"No, I guess not."

Trent angled his head towards her. "You sound disappointed."

"I don't like Eric. But I don't want it to be him. I don't want him to be the one wanting to hurt us, hurting Hayden."

"This guy *did* hurt you." Trent's gaze lingered for a moment on her cheek. "What about Dane? Could he be this guy?"

"No."

"Because your first instinct says no? Or because, like Eric, you don't want it to be him?"

She rubbed the tip of her index finger over her bottom lip and stared at Trent. At the way the bare vestiges of dawn shadowed his face, his eyes. How the dark stubble along his jaw almost hid the new swelling from Arnie's latest attack. Later, she and Trent would likely have matching bruises. They were both a mess. "My first instinct. But thinking on it, Dane doesn't have the same body type, the same build. This guy was a bit shorter … bulkier, maybe. More meat across the shoulders. But solid."

"That's good." Trent's hot gaze sparked those smoldering embers low in her body. He broke contact to stare out the windshield. "Rules out Dane, but not Eric."

"So we should be sitting in front of Eric's place, not Dane's?"

"Later."

Something *not* to look forward to.

"Your sister is the key to this situation. Eric doesn't know where she is. Doesn't know she's still alive."

"You think Dane does?"

"He hasn't been around since *before* you got the news about that boat Hayden was on."

"How does that equate to him knowing she's still alive?" Jillian also stared out the windshield. She squinted, but in the feeble light everything seemed flat without much differentiating between shifting shadows.

The breeze drifted over the bushes and palm fronds, making them dance. There was a lot of movement in those shadows. Dane, someone else, or a fat palm determined to fool her?

Hard to tell.

"No one knows where he's been these last couple of

nights." Trent's words low, he stared forward.

She shrugged. "I don't think it's anyone's actual job to keep track of Dane."

"From what I gather, someone almost always knows where he's playing."

"Doesn't mean *they* always know." Jeez, she was playing devil's advocate.

"His house is empty."

"You can't know that. When you did your skulk around the place, you said several of those windows had closed curtains. He could be snug in his bed, snoring, and we won't be the wiser until he stumbles out sometime this morning."

"He snores?" Trent raised an eyebrow and sent her a sideways glance.

"Speculation."

Trent pursed his mouth then nodded once. "Speculating, he could be completely out of town. Miami maybe. For the night. For the week."

"No. Dane rarely leaves the Keys."

"What's he hiding from?"

"Why does he have to be hiding from anything?"

"He doesn't. Just strikes me that he is."

"Like you are?"

"Why would you say that?"

"No particular reason, just strikes me that you are."

"You already know my demons." The side of his mouth she could see lifted in a small, sardonic smile. "And we were talking about Dane, not me."

"Maybe you're more interesting."

"Maybe I am." He tilted his head, looked directly at her. "Maybe that's an area you really don't want to explore."

"Maybe I do." *Did* that *really come out of her mouth?* Where was the duct tape? Her words hung in the air between them, as thick as the humidity.

"Jillian –" He angled his head to stare out his side window for a moment, then twisted back to focus on her. "What about you? What demons are you hiding?"

She lifted her chin but couldn't look away.

"The other day you flinched when I smacked the railing. Why? Chambers sets off every single alarm bell you have. Again, why? And why the proficiency with the baseball bat?"

"Who says I'm proficient?"

"Who was he?"

She swallowed. Closed her eyes. Opened them to stare at the car's ceiling. "Why do you care?"

Silence.

What was this? *You shared your wounds, now I share mine?*

"An ex-boyfriend. Same old tired story. Charming man, too charming to be real." She touched the swelling on her cheek then laced her fingers tight in her lap. "That little fact was brought home when he decided I could be his punching bag. I broke up with him. He decided he didn't want to be without me. Became obsessed. I ended up in the hospital. The police couldn't find him. So Rosey bought me a bat, taught me how to swing. The bastard spent one night at the ER and another couple in jail. Haven't heard from him since."

"Remind me not to piss you off."

"Too late."

From under her lashes she watched that one side of his mouth lift.

"Then remind me to lay off the charm."

"As if you have any."

His smile widened. "So Eric Chambers is too charming for your tastes?"

"Partly." Her grip on her fingers loosened. Talking about Eric was easier than about her previous bad judgment in men. She leaned her head back against the headrest. "Smarmy. And always with an agenda underneath everything he does. What he says."

"Yeah. I got that." Trent's gaze scanned the area outside. He leaned forward, planted the palms of his hands on the dash. "There. Movement near the edge of the water."

"Someone's tying up a boat."

"Looks like two people. A male and a female. Let's go find out who they are."

Hayden?

Jillian sucked in a breath. Slipping out of the car, she followed Trent, both of them keeping to the shadows. By the time they made it to the end of the road, the woman had jumped from the skiff. With jerky movements she grabbed the rope to tie it to the cleat.

Hayden. Jillian moved forward, but Trent grabbed her waist.

"Get back in the boat." Dane's deep voice whispered over the air.

Hayden's head lifted. She dropped the rope, scrambled back onto Dane's skiff. He already had the small engine in reverse.

"Wait." Jillian shoved Trent's arm away. She rushed forward across the scraggly yard. "Hayden."

Her sister, arms wrapped around her middle with her shoulders hunched forward and eyes wide, shook her head several times. "Stay out of this, Jilly."

"I can't." She stopped at the cement ledge, her hand outstretched.

Trent stood next to Jillian, fists on hips, legs braced. "Patrick, let's talk about this."

Dane's hands on the controls, he shook his head while he eased the skiff a little further away. "Keep Jilly safe, Sawyer. I've got Hayden."

"Dane, no —" Jillian pressed her hand to her mouth.

The nose of the skiff lifted as he increased power before they pulled out of the canal and into the Sound.

Away from them.

AN HOUR LATER, with the early morning sun trying to shine through the lingering storm clouds outside, Trent finally had his replacement ID and a credit card, along with a specially equipped laptop computer, his boss had sent by courier to the hotel.

Still no gun. His fingers twitched. So did a nerve along the edge of his jaw.

Settled in a wingback chair, tucked into the corner of the small suite he'd asked Ben to secure, Trent's gaze strayed to the lovely stretch of Jillian's shapely legs in those tight jeans as she prowled across the living area.

She faced the wall farthest from him for a long moment then swung around to pace the length of the room before staring the other wall down.

Restless energy. Trent got that. Better to work it out her way rather than the way crossing his mind while his gaze detoured to that sexy ass of hers as she stalked away from him.

Her way was safer for both of them.

He stretched his legs, linked his fingers over his belly. Didn't mean he couldn't watch her, though.

"She's terrified." Jillian swung to face him. "You saw Hayden's face."

"They tried to kill her." He scrubbed a hand over his mouth. *Gawking time over.* "Did kill her friends. She doesn't want them killing you."

"I don't want *her* killed, either." Jillian stopped pacing and stood several feet away with her arms hugging her middle. "What is Dane thinking?"

"That he can keep her safe." The same thing Trent thought – prayed – about Jillian.

"It's not his job to protect her."

"Why is it yours?"

"Because I'm the oldest. It's always been my job."

"Maybe you should step back. Let Hayden take lead on this one."

"And what? Wait here? Do nothing and see what shakes out?" Jillian's mouth as tight as her arms around her middle, she stared at the ceiling for a long moment while her breathing hitched.

Trent rubbed his hand over his eyes. That or get

caught ogling her chest. Exhaustion muddled his mind, the way he couldn't seem to take his gaze off her body for more than a few seconds.

That lack of control wasn't like him. Not at all.

Although around Jillian Rose it was fast becoming standard operating procedure.

With his hand still over his eyes, he swallowed once. She'd moved closer. Whether it was the change in air vibration, the slightly exotic scent of her washing over him, or that new sixth sense where she was concerned, he *knew* she now stood closer. Right next to him.

"Devil's advocate time again?"

At her words he lowered his hand from his face, got caught in the honey of her light brown eyes. He could lose himself there. Even with the sparks lighting them from the inside.

"Because I'm not going to just wait and see what shakes out." She loomed over him with her legs braced and fists on her hips. "That's not going to happen."

"Just saying."

"Well, don't say." In one smooth movement, she bent forward, bracketed his face with her hands, and pressed her mouth hard against his.

Time stopped. He swore it stopped.

She pulled away, her face a few inches from his. Those honey eyes reflected the same dazed shock he knew must be etched over his own face.

"If you're trying to shut me up –" He cupped her face, skimmed one thumb over her bruised cheek then along her lips. "That's a damn dangerous way to start."

Chapter Twenty

THE HUM OF THE hotel air conditioner the only sound in the quiet hotel suite, Jillian leaned over Trent's chair and stared into the dark depths of his blue eyes. His thumb lightly caressed her bottom lip.

Right now, early this morning, in this place free from prying eyes and overt threats, she wanted *Trent*.

The rest of the world would have to wait.

Between her hands she cradled Trent's chin, her fingers along his jawline. She ran her own thumbs over the stubble roughening his cheeks. New bruises from his last tangle with Arnie darkened patches of his skin.

"So brave." With the tip of her index finger, she lightly traced the edges of one of those bruises.

Trent's eyes half closed, he pressed his own hand over hers, brought her palm to his mouth, and kissed the center. "Are you sure you want to be touching me like this?"

"I'm sure." Who cared what later brought?

Maybe she did, but she'd deal with it when she had to deal with it – when later came.

Right now she wanted him. Inside her, surrounding her. Keeping the worry at bay. For a short time at least.

He wanted her right back. Physically at least.

For now, that was enough.

In one fluid movement, with a gracefulness she was suddenly grateful for, she pushed away from him and stretched out her hand. His gaze never leaving hers, he wrapped his fingers around hers, stood, pulled her to him and, careful of her sore shoulder, wrapped her arm behind his back. He skimmed the knuckles of his other hand over her bruised cheek before he lowered his head and claimed her mouth with his own. With her free hand she clutched the material of his T-shirt over his chest.

His heartbeat matched the staccato beat of her own.

Her senses on overdrive, her nerves sparked everywhere their bodies touched. Even through their clothes. They'd stood like this before, body pressed to body, his tongue dancing with hers, swaying to the music throbbing between them. But she'd let a neighbor and then her own hesitation get in their way.

Not this time.

With her mouth locked with Trent's, she kicked her shoes off then easing backwards, drawing him with her towards one of the two bedrooms.

Under the open doorway, he pulled her into a tight embrace, his cheek pressed against her temple. "Are you sure you want to do this?"

His breath whispered across her hair. She rubbed her forehead over the stubble of his jaw and her own breath caught.

Yes. She wanted this.

Lord, I'm in so much trouble.

She wanted this for more than the momentary escape it promised. She wanted this for herself. She wanted *him*.

"Yes." Her hands now at his waist, clutching the material of his shirt, and his arms tight around her, she stepped backwards into the bedroom.

He pressed his lips to her forehead. Warm tingles followed the path of his hands as he slid his palms down her back to cup her rear. Her head tilted back and suddenly his mouth was there, his tongue caressing her neck, sending wild electric shocks to every nerve ending. She rocked against him and a low moan caught in her chest.

In one move he swept her up into his arms and in three steps had her on the bed. With her head cushioned by the pillow, he held himself over her, his heavy lidded gaze locked with hers. "Jilly –"

"Stop thinking." She traced a finger over the edge of his jaw, along the old and new bruises, then she pressed her finger to his lips. He sucked the tip into his mouth, ran his warm tongue across the pad. Heat spread like fire inside her, a direct line from the warmth of his mouth to the tightness clenched between her legs. Her eyes widened. Her back and neck arched. "Trent."

Some remote part of her brain registered the deep huskiness in her voice. The pleading.

Wicked pleasure lit the depths of his blue eyes. He flicked his tongue over her finger once more then lowered his mouth to trail the tip of his tongue over her neck, to nip at her ear lobe.

Another moan escaped. "Trent."

He yanked his T-shirt over his head, tossing it somewhere behind him. Her hands splayed across his bare chest, over the taut muscles. This time he groaned, the sound guttural and from deep inside.

His gaze locked on hers as he slid his hands underneath her shirt, eased it up several inches to span his palms over her stomach. Electric heat scorched her exposed skin. Her back arched again.

He slipped his hands further under her shirt, up the sides of her rib cage, the heat notching close to explosion range. Gripping the hem of her own shirt, she pulled it over her head and let him toss it in the same direction his had gone.

Cool air skimmed her skin, followed by the barest graze of his knuckles over the top edge of her beige lace bra. She slipped her fingers inside the waist band of his jeans. He covered her hand with his, squeezed.

"Hold on." He toed off his shoes then undid his pants, pushed them and his underwear to the floor, and after he claimed a small packet from his pants pocket, kicked them away.

The shadowy light from the other room played over the toned muscles of his naked torso, making him look like some Greek God standing over her. Her breath caught at the evidence of his desire for her, at the overwhelming need simmering inside her.

"Your turn." He set the packet on the nightstand then leaned over her, unhooked the buttons on her pants and slid them down her legs. His fingers trailed heat the entire way. "You're so beautiful."

Beautiful. That's exactly how she felt right now. With him.

His eyes hooded, his gaze scorched her before he stretched out beside her. With his touch gentle, he traced a fingertip over her stomach and leaned to cover her mouth with his. The kiss deepened. Through the lace of her panties he cupped her, sending tremors of heat spiraling along her nerve endings. She pressed upward, against the heel of his hand.

With his mouth still on hers, he eased her panties down her legs then crushed her body against his, her bra the only barrier between them. He rolled her on top of him.

Her palms flat on his chest, she pushed upwards and slid her legs along his until she straddled him.

"What do you want, lady?"

"You inside me."

"First —"

"*Protection.*" She fished the packet from the nightstand, tore it open, and slid the condom, as slow as possible, over him. Then, with her thumb and forefinger, she traced the length of him. Twice.

"You're killing me, Jilly." The words ended on a groan. His hands spanned her waist, gripped her sides.

"Not yet." Her breasts heavy, needing to be touched, she took his hands, pressed them to her chest.

His fingers slipped inside the lace of her bra, caressed her nipples.

"Ahh." Her hands over his, her neck and back arched, pushing her breasts into his palms.

He bent upwards, one hand still on a breast, the other snaked around her waist. He claimed her mouth. His erection, pressed hot right at the center of her thighs, throbbed between them.

"Trent. Please." She whispered the words against his warm mouth. "Now."

On a low, guttural groan, he thrust inside. Filled her with one upward stroke.

She gasped as her whole body went completely still. He buried his face at her neck, his mouth hot on her skin.

Then he moved. His hands at her hips, he pulled back, shoved forward.

Her calves tight at his side, her palms flat on his chest, she rocked with him, matched him thrust for thrust. Rocked hard against him. Built a cadence that spiraled inside, that had nowhere to go but –

"*Trent –*" Hs name tore from her lips.

Underneath her, inside her, he thrust harder and faster. Frantic, she gripped him tighter. Curled against his chest. He stiffened then suddenly they soared as their bodies lost control.

Together.

IN THE SEMI DARKNESS the heavy hotel curtains afforded in the middle of the morning, Trent traced a finger down Jillian's arm. She sighed, curling against him in her sleep.

Grateful for a past stop at a small convenience store after their near miss with each other – the one the neighbor ruined – and grateful for the cash in his pocket at the time, he'd bought a couple of condoms. Those were gone now, and while he didn't regret the last few hours he still didn't have an answer to how she'd gotten so far under his skin.

So fast.

Trust. All consuming. How could he ever be worthy of that?

Loathing hadn't been in her gaze, either, when he'd told her about his vengeance for Cassie. He'd told Jillian the ugliest part of himself and the look she'd given him had only radiated understanding and acceptance.

This morning, she'd made *love* to him as if he actually mattered.

How the hell did he deserve any of that?

From a woman like Jillian?

He watched a thin sliver of light dance along the break between the curtains as they moved in the breeze created by the low hum of the air conditioner.

In February. Air conditioning.

This place was as foreign as whatever ate at his insides.

Neither of them were one night stand types, but he had a life in D.C. She would have hers back once they found her sister again and took care of this current threat.

Jillian hadn't asked for promises, he hadn't made any.

Where did that leave them?

He scrubbed a hand over his face, over his head.

What's the next step?

ALTHOUGH HE'D ONLY SLEPT a few hours, Trent sat in the hotel suite's living room area with the laptop Ben had provided open on the low table in front of him. Jillian still slept. Room service would soon be here with the burgers and pot of coffee he'd ordered, but he hated waking her. She'd barely stirred when he'd slipped out of bed, her hand curling over the spot where he'd lain.

He shook his head. Not wanting to go where his thoughts led, he focused on the computer.

Ben had come through, at least with information if not a weapon.

Dane Patrick was an interesting fellow.

Once an LAPD cop, Patrick had killed a man – his mother's long term boyfriend – been exonerated then quit the Los Angeles department to disappear off the grid before landing here in Key Largo as a one man band playing the local tiki bars.

One Delilah Patrick now lived as a long-term patient at Tradewinds Behavioral Center, a psychiatric hospital located near the center of Key Largo.

Dane's mother.

What that had to do with the current Hayden situation, Trent had no idea, but it bore delving into further, exploring and seeing where it took him.

Another email hit his inbox.

With a brief glance at the bedroom door, Trent clicked open the email. Read to the end then read it again. Dane owned two pieces of property on the island. The one he and Jillian had visited and another on the eastern side of the island, on a canal opening into Largo Sound.

Is that where you're hiding Hayden, Patrick?

Yet another email hit Trent's inbox. Information on Eric Chambers. The man owed a real estate company specializing in vacation properties, two of which had been off the market for the last two weeks. Not rented, according to what Ben's assistant had sent over, but simply unavailable.

Interesting. Noting the two rentals stood next door to each other, Trent pulled up a map. Those two houses were less than a block from where the Oasis had been docked.

More and more interesting.

Since he had the search engine up, he culled information on the kingdom of Cadeau and their royal family, the Landrys. Trent found current photos of the king and each of the two princes along with information on their personal histories.

Smugglers? The sailboat he'd been so curious about, the one moored neared Rosey's with the smoker on board, belonged to the royal family. So many puzzle pieces. *How do they fit together?*

A firm knock on the suite door pulled him from his computer search.

He stood, touched his side with his elbow for a weapon he didn't have.

Dammit.

Probably their food. Cautious, Trent approached the door from the side, took a quick glance through the peephole.

A waiter with a push cart.

The knocked sounded again. "Room Service."

Trent pulled a few dollars from his pocket before opening the door a slight amount. He handed the man the tip and waved off any help. Once the waiter rounded the far corner of the hallway, Trent pulled the cart into the room.

"What smells so wonderful?" Jillian, wearing his T-shirt and her panties, leaned against the bedroom door. She threaded fingers through her hair, swept it back from her sleepy face, and smiled at him.

His gut tightened and hunger welled inside. Not for the food on the cart between them.

No more condoms, Sawyer.

With regret sharp in his gut, he pushed the cart in front of the couch. "Eat first. Shower. Then we need to take another ride."

She frowned but straightened. To get his mind off the long stretch of her bare legs as she made her way to the couch, he set both burgers on the coffee table, poured them each a cup of coffee. Since sitting next to her would only result in him hauling her onto his lap, he pulled the desk chair to the table so he could sit across from her.

With the table between them.

Self-control only went so far.

With a wan smile he told her he'd called her cook and bartender, asked them to open Rosey's and hold down the fort. She frowned over her coffee cup but didn't complain. Then he filled her in on the emails from Ben's assistant.

"Dane has never said a word about his mother." She picked up her burger, stared at it for a moment before lifting her gaze to his. "This ride you want to take, is it to see her or to check out Dane's other property?"

"Probably both, but the property first."

"Where is it?"

From his shirt pocket, he slid out the hotel notepaper he scribbled the addresses on and read Dane's aloud. With her frown deepening, she leaned over the low table and bit into her burger.

"You know where this place is?" He followed suit, devouring a third of his burger before she answered.

"If it's the place I think it is, all I can say is wow." She held her burger with both hands, her forefingers tapping the bun while she stared into space. "There's this place just off Largo Sound, north of the Pennekamp Visitor's Center, but tucked away. The rumor is some guy is building his own mansion out there, a bit at a time. The property belongs to a trust fund and the gossip mongers haven't been able to figure out who actually owns the place."

"So Dane has nothing to hide?"

She shrugged, took another bite of her food. Her eyes sparkled over the top of the bun. "Wouldn't that be something if it turns out to belong to him?"

"Patrick's other property is in a trust, with him and his mother listed as co-beneficiaries." Trent settled back in his seat with both hands wrapped around his coffee cup. "Finish that and I'll show you on the map I have pulled up on the laptop. See if we're talking about the same place."

"It's kind of funny. Hayden's been fascinated with that place for months now. I wonder if she knows about Dane and his mother."

"If she didn't before, I'm betting she does now."

"You're probably right." She set her half eaten burger on the plate, picked up her cup.

"Then there are those two properties Chambers' company manages. While we're out we can do a drive by, see what's up with them."

She took a sip of coffee and her eyes darkened as she studied him over the rim. "Maybe they're being renovated. Maybe the owners are in town and are staying there."

"And maybe, because they're close to the marina area, Chambers is letting his smuggling buddies have the places rent-free."

"That's a gigantic leap, don't you think? You're supposing he has smuggling buddies."

"Maybe." Trent snagged the rest of her burger, raised an eyebrow.

"I'm done." Her sudden smile sucker punched him, clogging his throat for a long moment.

With his eyes narrowed and *not* watching her, he polished off her burger before again settling back with his coffee. "Chambers. There's something there I can't quite figure out. He fits the build of the third man on board the Oasis. He also fits the build of the man who grabbed you this morning."

For that, for the bruise darkening her cheek, Trent was going to nail the bastard.

"On board the Oasis, did the third man speak to you?"

"Not to me directly. And I don't remember him wearing glasses. But he might have had contacts in. Or I'm just not remembering. The guy was in charge, though. Told Arnie to …." Trent closed his eyes, tried to pull the pieces of that night together. "There's something there, something about the cadence of the man's voice. Makes me wonder if it's Chambers."

"You don't recognize the voice itself as Eric's? His is pretty distinctive."

"No." And that was the kicker. He couldn't get a handle on the man's voice. Stuck in his craw, pissed him off. He forced a reassuring smile. "So first, we go by those two properties. Second, we pick up your boat at Rosey's."

"Doesn't that defeat the purpose of hiding here if we're going to just waltz into Rosey's?"

He let his smile widen. "From the look of Dane's other place on the satellite map, that property has one way in on a long and narrow dirt road. A boat widens our options. Makes it easier to shake anyone following."

"We have to be talking about the same place. And you're right, a boat makes more sense. What aren't you telling me?"

She was sharp, this sex goddess staring at him with so much suspicion lacing her eyes.

"When I checked in with Ted earlier he told me a

deputy doing a drive-by at Rosey's reported some activity near your boat early this morning. Ted and I both believe Arnie may have slipped a tracking device on your vessel."

"Then there's no way we're going out to that property." Jillian set her cup on the table, the thud echoing in the room. She stood, her fists planted on her hips. "No way we're leading him to Hayden and Dane."

The T-shirt she wore – his T-shirt – rode high on her thighs, exposing more of her legs. He set his own cup on the table before scrubbing a hand over his face. Now wasn't the time to get sidetracked, no matter how much he wanted those long legs wrapped tight around his waist.

Again.

No matter how much those angry sparks in her honey eyes turned him on, sent his instincts into overdrive, making him want to throw caution and common sense out the picture perfect window framing that luscious body of hers.

"What we need is to get on board your boat, find the device and dispose of it somewhere in Blackwater Sound where no one can see what we're doing."

Her mouth tight, she stared at him through slitted eyes.

He never knew suspicion could be so arousing.

"Really." He lifted both hands, palms forward. "On the water, as I said earlier, we should be able to tell if anyone is following us."

"What if you're wrong?"

"About the tracking device?"

"Yes. And about spotting anyone trailing us? I'm not risking my sister for you to prove a point."

That struck too close to home. His hands fisted and he lifted his head to study her through his own narrowed eyes. He stood. With his legs braced apart, he set his fists at his waist. "Then I suggest we find every freaking bat you own and stash them all in the boat. While we're at it, pray we don't need them."

Chapter Twenty-One

FOR NOW, AN EARLY AFTERNOON sun shone from a brilliant blue sky and white, fluffy clouds hovered along the horizon, keeping their distance. Humidity, however, kept the balmy air thick.

Jillian let loose the nervous sigh trapped in her throat. From the passenger seat of her car she glanced at Trent, who sat in the driver's seat. They'd already been up and down this short street twice before backing into the empty driveway of a small cottage style house with a For Rent sign in the front window and a jungle of greenery around the yard.

The vacant house sat next door to one of two vacation properties Eric Chambers' company managed. The two properties Trent labelled as suspicious.

Another sigh caught in her throat. This whole stake out thing ate at her nerves.

A five foot rose bush hedge separated them from the driveway next door. Anyone who stood on the other side of the hedge and *happened* to glance their way would see them sitting in her car with their windows rolled down.

She couldn't come up with a single believable explanation for that.

Luckily a white cargo van sat between that hedge and the door of the targeted house. Again, though, anyone coming to the passenger side of the van would see them.

But something else bothered her, more worrisome than the hedge. At least in her view.

Eric's silver Mercedes Roadster sat on the street in front of that house.

So Eric's in that house.

Wasn't that just *peachy*?

And that van sitting there so innocently had Georgia Plates.

Georgia.

Just like Arnie's stolen car.

Uneasiness deepened the trench along the path it scuttled down her spine.

If Eric's involved with Arnie –

If Arnie's in that house –

She shook her head.

A lot of cars displayed Georgia plates here in the Keys. The islands held year round appeal and Georgia was this part of Florida's closest neighbor. Those plates didn't implicate anyone.

"We don't know who owns that van." Conscious of their open car windows, Jillian kept her voice low. She *really* didn't want to be caught here. With hands threaded through her hair, she laced her fingers on top of her head. "The van owners could simply be on vacation. If they just arrived it would be reasonable for Eric to be here. Or maybe that's nothing more than a delivery van of some sort."

"Could be." Trent's half whisper matched hers. He drummed his fingers on the steering wheel. One side of that sexy mouth lifted in a sardonic half smile. "In which case, this will end up being a nice, simple afternoon drive."

"Simple my ass."

Trent's soft laugh shot straight through her. He reached over and patted her thigh. Answering warmth threaded through her body. Her nipples tightened and heat pooled between her legs.

Damn her traitorous body. The sex was supposed to have taken the edge off her response to him. Not increase it. One touch and she ignited as sure as kindling in a parched desert.

Trent's fingers tightened, the side glance he sent her as hot as her thoughts.

At least she wasn't alone in those thoughts.

Trent straightened in his seat. "They're on the move."

Oh boy.

Reality was a pisser. How did he deal with this on a constant basis?

She swallowed against the hard lump in her throat.

From the unobservable side of the van two male voices filtered across the short distance.

"Enough already." Eric's frigid tone hung thick in the humid air. "Time is wasting. Take care of business or I'll find someone who will."

Beside Jillian, Trent went utterly still. She flicked an uneasy, under the lashes glance in his direction then angled her head to look directly at him.

His eyes had gone flat, dark blue obelisks with all traces of light leached away from the inside. A nerve twitched along his locked jaw, pulsing in an angry tempo. "Son of a damn bitch."

ALL ALONG CHAMBERS had been the one.

Trent's grip tightened on the steering wheel of Jillian's car. Beside him, she'd gone quiet. Her eyes narrowed, their color darkening to amber as she stared out the windshield.

With a balmy, early afternoon breeze drifting through their rolled down windows, they sat less than ten feet from the bastards responsible for blowing the Oasis apart.

Enough already. Time is wasting.

The harsh words Chambers had snapped at whoever stood behind the van echoed in Trent's head.

From the time he'd been pulled out of the water from his dunking in the Atlantic, he'd tried without success to pinpoint the voice of the man who'd stayed in the shadows on board the Oasis. The man's words, though, those had come back in a sudden, hot, remembered flash.

Enough already. The night is wasting. Throw him overboard and fish that moron from the water.

Chambers was the one.

The one who'd ordered Trent thrown overboard. The one who called the shots. The one who held Arnie's reins.

A car door slammed then a powerful engine revved, breaking the silence.

Chambers was leaving.

Trent grabbed Jillian's arm, yanked her down onto his lap and sprawled over her to cover her with his upper body.

No internal warning buzz, no overt threat, but they didn't need to be seen sitting here.

Her muffled gasp cut short as Chambers' Mercedes tore down the street.

Away from them.

They could follow Chambers. A part of Trent wanted that bad enough to throw caution aside. But with Chambers gone for the moment that potentially left only one standing in the driveway next to the van.

Arnie?

Trent's lip curled. He wanted Arnie as much as he wanted Chambers.

What do I do with Jillian?

A flash of his sister's empty eyes sucker punched him.

Not going to happen to Jilly.

On an oath, he sat up then brushed a strand of hair away from Jillian's forehead as she straightened in her seat. Careful of her bruise, he trailed the back of his fingers over her cheek and across her full bottom lip. "I don't suppose you'll wait here while I go see what our friend is up to next door."

"You suppose right."

He let his hand drop. "We need to know —"

"Moot point." She pointed towards the rose bush hedge.

Through a thin spot in the greenery, taillights shone and the van's engine coughed then caught. Moments later the vehicle backed out of the driveway.

Trent and Jillian ducked one more time. They waited for the van's engine to fade in the distance before Trent started their vehicle and eased out on to the street. Ahead of them the van made a right where the road intersected with the Overseas Highway.

With his foot pressed to the gas, Trent raced after the other vehicle. At the intersection he braked but didn't stop.

Jillian braced her hands on the dashboard. Winced. *From her sore shoulder?* "You're sure Eric's the missing man from the Oasis, aren't you?"

"Positive." He told her about his flash of memory at Chambers' choice of words. "I still can't place the voice, but the cadence is the same. And the words are too close to *not* be the same person."

She swallowed but kept her gaze locked on the van now only a few car lengths in front of them. The van made an abrupt right into the parking area of a small marina.

Trent continued straight before making a U-Turn a block further down. "All of this is connected, Jillian. Eric's ex-wife's death. The smuggling. The two boats being blown up. It's all connected."

"What about my sister?"

Trent made the left into the marina. He hated the way her voice caught. He hated he didn't have any reassurances to give her. Not Shamus Conlon, Trent didn't have the faith the older detective had in Hayden's innocence. Hayden *knew* something major. "I don't know."

Silence met his statement.

Dammit to hell. Jillian wanted reassurance he couldn't give her.

How involved was Hayden? And how would Jillian handle the truth?

Much as a part of him wanted to, he couldn't protect her from whatever that reality ended up being. Right *now*, though, he needed to focus on *here*.

Five other cars sat in the marina parking lot, all grouped together. The van they'd followed sat idling near a squat building in front of a sidewalk at the edge between the parking area and two gangways each leading to several floating docks. Most of the berths held boats. Sailboats outnumbered any other type of vessel. Two of the closest boats had people onboard. A couple of kids ran back and forth between the building and the two occupied boats.

A beautiful, sun filled afternoon, as long as those clouds hugging the horizon stayed on the horizon. Perfect day for a family outing.

If this went bad, if that was Arnie in the van, any one of those people could wind up being a hostage to fortune. Arnie had no sense of morality.

Trent parked the car at an angle facing the driver's

side of the van, and like the van's driver, he let their car idle.

"What do we do now?" Jillian also scanned the area. "Those kids …."

"We could sit here. Watch and wait." He sent her a sideways look. "Or I could approach the van."

"And I sit here and use my cell to call backup?" Lightly coated sarcasm covered each word.

"Yes." He touched her shoulder. Ignored the strong desire to pull her into his arms. "I don't want anything else to happen to you."

"Like I *want* something to happen to you?"

"I'm the professional. This is *my* job."

"Your job sucks." Her eyes widened. "I mean –"

"Exactly what you said." His turned his gaze towards the van, away from her. He shrugged. "But I'm good at it."

And, *shock the hell out of me*, he liked his job.

He shoved open the car door. "See if you can get hold of Ted. Tell him this may be nothing, but it *feels* like something."

"But –" Her words cut off as her mouth set in a mutinous line.

One foot out of the car, he twisted away from her. Sure those were daggers she aimed at his back with her eyes, he squared his shoulders.

She hated his job, hated the danger. One day she'd probably hate him.

Not a lot he could do about that. No matter how much it stuck in his craw.

Time to find Arnie, get this whole thing solved and settled.

Then what?

He ignored the arbitrary voice in his head and focused on *now*.

Out of the car, his gaze constantly moving, he angled away so he could approach the van from a more direct position but out of view of the driver's side mirror. He slipped behind the van, stole a look through the back window.

Empty.

No cargo. No driver.

Where was Arnie?

Trent quickly scanned the marina. The kids were back on their respective boats while the adults were all busy and oblivious to the drama possibly playing out a few yards away. He threw a quick glance over his shoulder. Out of the car, Jillian leaned against it with her cell phone pressed to her ear.

Small miracles. For right now, she stayed put.

Except for the empty idling van, nothing seemed out of the ordinary.

That left the squat building.

Bathrooms, showers and laundry facilities, according to the overhead sign.

He maneuvered around the side of the van away from the boaters, to the point he could see the front of the building. A shallow alcove held two vending machines. No space for a man as burly as Arnie to hide.

Trent eased away from the van to the parking lot side

of the building.

Men's bathroom on the left. Might as well start there.

His steps cautious, he moved across the threshold and within two feet found Arnie zipping his pants. The blonde giant's face creased in surprise. Trent swung his right fist, aiming to connect with Arnie's glass jaw.

But the big man was quicker on his feet.

Or he'd learned.

Arnie blocked Trent's fist and threw an under-punch towards Trent's stomach. Dancing a step back, Trent managed to protect his gut and landed a blow on Arnie's shoulder, knocking the blonde man back a few inches. Trent kept his fists up but then round-housed Arnie, his foot landing square on Arnie's chin.

With a growl, Arnie charged forward, knocking Trent back through the open doorway. They fell onto the asphalt with Trent taking the brunt of the fall and Arnie on top of him. Pain ricocheted through Trent's spine. On an agonizing intake of breath, he shoved Arnie off and to the side.

Time to end this before I actually get hurt.

Arnie rolled to his knees. Trent's fist glanced off the man's beefy shoulder.

Shit.

Trent scrambled to his feet. Managed not to sway.

Arnie's glass jaw was only an advantage if Trent could connect more than a glancing blow.

Mouth in a snarl, Arnie twisted away to lope towards the idling van.

Oh, hell no. Trent tore after him.

The screech of tires and quickly applied brakes registered in his mind.

Jillian swung her car in front of the van and blocked its getaway just as Arnie yanked the van's driver door open.

Yes. Only a few feet from her car, Trent motioned for her to stay inside.

Arnie's cold gaze flipped between them.

A buzz screeched in Trent's inner ear. Loud, clanging.

Trent met Arnie's cold gaze. The alarm silenced mid scream.

Arnie leapt into the van. With the door still open he shoved the vehicle into gear, spun the steering wheel hard to the right, and gassed the vehicle.

Reverse.

Shit.

Arnie dove from the vehicle, hit the asphalt, and rolled. His laughter filled the air as he pushed himself to his feet.

The van headed backwards, straight for one of the occupied boats.

Adrenaline spurting through Trent's veins, he surged forward. His fingers glanced off the edge of the van's bouncing door. *Not happening.* He twisted his body, grappled with the inside of the door, and threw himself into the driver's seat. His hands around the steering wheel, he hit the brakes, but the gangway loomed too close and braking sent him into a sideways skid.

He was going to hit that boat unless he did something drastic.

On a whoosh of breath, he manhandled the steering wheel to the left and hit the water back end first. Jerked forward, he barely missed hitting his forehead on the steering wheel. His head bounced twice on the headrest behind him.

But he'd missed the boat.

Saltwater filled the van as the force of the water shoved the driver's door further open while the van continued to sink.

Get out.

After prying his fingers from the steering wheel he slipped out and into the cool waters of the marina. With a sidestroke, he swam for the nearest boat. The one he'd managed to avoid. There the adults, no longer oblivious to the drama, pulled him onboard.

He stood dripping on deck, his gaze locked across the gangway on Jillian's frozen, wide-eyed face.

JILLIAN WRAPPED HER ARMS around her waist and pasted a tepid smile on her mouth. The horror of what nearly happened here at the marina, to those people on the boat, to Trent, welled in her mind. Loomed over her as surely as those clouds welling up from the horizon to fulfill the promise of an afternoon squall.

"I'm fine." From several feet away, Trent's voice washed over her. He sat on a bench angled towards her and brushed aside the prying fingers of one of the men from the boat. The man had said he was a doctor and was intent on examining Trent's poor, beat up face.

"You're a hero. That's what you are." The stranger didn't give up, he gripped Trent's chin and turned his head to check out the other side of his face.

"I'm no hero." Trent jerked his head to the side, away from the man's fingers. "This is my job. It's what I do. Thank you, but I really am fine."

From where Jillian stood, several feet away, she scanned Trent's face. New abrasions scuffed his jaw line and that might be a new cut underneath his right ear. She'd have to get closer to tell. Right now she didn't want to be close to Trent. Didn't want to touch him. Didn't want to care about the damn man.

The way her heart clenched, the way it ached, she didn't like this, didn't like what it signified.

She loved the son of a bitch.

And he was going to leave her. If not on a whim then in a coffin.

Just a matter of time.

ONCE AGAIN IN DRY, borrowed clothes and someone else's deck shoes, Trent stood on the marina gangway with his back to the area where the van had sunk. The current hive of police activity barely registered.

He watched Jillian.

To anyone else she seemed to be gauging the incoming clouds.

An afternoon squall approached. That's what she'd told one of the men from the two boats.

But Trent knew better.

There might be a storm coming, hell it had rained every day he'd been here, but Jillian had withdrawn from him as surely as she had when her neighbor had shown up drunk and ruined the moment blossoming between her and Trent.

Back then he'd been grateful. But back then he hadn't had Jillian, hadn't completely tasted her, made love to her. Hadn't realized how far under his skin she'd gotten.

He hadn't known what he'd been missing from his miserable life.

Ted Mathews' patrol car pulled into the parking area, adding to the several Monroe County vehicles already there, and rescued Trent from the direction of his thoughts.

Probably should be grateful.

He flicked a glance at Jillian then spun on the heel of his borrowed shoes and met Ted at his car.

"You need to stop getting yourself dunked into the waters around here." Ted scratched the corner of his eyebrow while scanning the marina.

"Right." Trent slouched then shrugged one shoulder. "Tell me something I don't know."

"Arnold Phelps."

Trent straightened. "That's our guy?"

"Yes." With a nod at Jillian as she joined them, Ted leaned a hip against the front fender of his patrol car. "While you're sure about Chambers' involvement with Phelps, there doesn't seem to be a connection beyond what you two overheard at that house. We're in the process of securing a search warrant for both houses. There's a BOLO for Phelps."

"And Eric?" Jillian's voice low and almost monotone, she frowned at both of them. "Is he just going to be able to run around loose, maybe even skip town?"

"We don't have enough to tie him to anything, Jilly." Ted shook his head.

"But Trent recognized him as the other man on board the Oasis."

Ted shook his head again. "Trent can't actually place him onboard when the boat was stolen. It's all circumstantial. He recognized the words and the cadence, not the voice. A lawyer would argue that Trent's been around Eric how many times and never recognized him.

"In addition, Eric is the property manager for those two properties so it's within his purview to be present there at any given time. While he's a person of interest and we're going to track him down, bring him in for an interview, we need more evidence to hold him."

She rubbed her temples then wiped the back of one hand over her forehead. "Then what do we do next?"

"We go for a boat ride." Trent glanced at Jillian. The mutinous set to her mouth buoyed his spirits. Mutiny was okay. Good, even. Much better than withdrawn and pale. "There's another property to check out."

"Sawyer –" Ted's expression wary, he scanned the horizon. "If I wasn't on duty, I'd go with you."

"I'm not going after Chambers." *Not yet.* "I'll deal with the possible tracker onboard Jillian's boat, Ted.

Don't worry."

"Right." Ted shook his head and swung his gaze back. A half smirk broke loose. "The rain may hold off for a while. You never know who's going to show up on the water out there. Be careful."

"My middle name."

Ted shook his head one more time. "Don't do anything too stupid."

Trent and Jillian watched as Ted headed towards the other officers.

"Taking my boat out *is* stupid."

"Jillian –" Unable to stop himself, Trent ran the palm of his hand down her bare arm. She shivered and glanced up at him with darkened, unreadable eyes.

The edges of her mouth twitched, in a smile or to keep from saying something he didn't want to hear, he wasn't sure.

His money was on what he didn't want to hear.

Chapter Twenty-Two

D AMP, LATE AFTERNOON WIND twisted its fingers through Jillian's hair. With the briny scent of the sea in her nose, she lifted her face to the mist spraying back from the front of her boat while keeping her grip tight on the wheel.

Trent wanted a remote location where he could search the vessel for Arnie's stow-a-way tracker and she could watch for anyone approaching. She knew these waters, had spent part of every summer, every holiday, and the last full year on the Sound. And now, her stomach twisted in knots, she knew just the place.

Only a short distance away.

Once they rounded the long jut of land, and had it between them and the rest of the populated area, she eased back the throttle.

"There." She pointed to a thick outcropping of mangroves. Although there weren't any docks in this uninhabited area of the islands, and it was too shallow near what constituted a shoreline for her boat, she could keep them relatively stationary in this cove of sorts while Trent searched for the tracking device. With the mangroves to her back and open water in front, she had a better chance of spotting any potential problems.

A few days with the man and already she sounded like a cop.

She adjusted the controls then angled her body to give herself the optimum view of the area while still keeping them still. From under her lashes her gaze lingered on the stretch of denim across his ass as he bent over the aft section of her boat searching for the device Arnie had stashed.

What she'd said at the hotel still stood. Hayden's life was worth more than whatever ate at Trent. He hadn't told her everything. Nor had he told Ted. There was some plan there, in the back recesses of Trent's mind, and it involved too much risk. To her sister and Dane. To her. To Trent.

He welcomed danger, thrived on it. She didn't. When he got hold of something, he didn't let it go. The hunt for the man who'd killed his sister. This relentless pursuit of Arnie Phelps. Trent had no qualms about throwing himself in harm's way.

None.

I should aim this boat straight for the closest sheriff's station.

Trent might be FBI, but he was unarmed with only *her* for backup. Not favorable odds.

Why had Ted, knowing about the tracker, just let them go?

But Ted didn't know Hayden was alive.

Maybe it's time to stop playing cops and robbers. Time to tell what I know. Time to own up to my responsibility and stop depending on someone else.

To stop depending on Trent.

She scanned the open expanse of water.

Isn't that the crux of everything? Dependence on Trent, a man who would soon be gone from her life, one way or another.

Her gaze slid over him, over the width of his shoulders, over the ripple of his muscles under the material of his shirt as he moved things out of his way.

Strong, but he wouldn't physically hurt her. Smart and dedicated, he'd find a way to save Hayden. Or die trying.

One way or another, he'll break my heart.

She blinked several times and tried to focus on the water surrounding her boat.

On any bright, sunny afternoon she'd be able to see the shallow bottom, see the fish swimming, the life on the sea floor. Today, with the dark, heavy clouds overhead, the view remained murky and unclear.

Like my emotions. No clarity.

Love. The word whispered through her, wrapped itself into a tight, heavy knot at the center of her chest.

"Why are we out here, Trent?" She angled her head towards him, to where he squatted with one hand braced on the thin railing at the back of the boat. "Why didn't you have Ted's man take that tracker off of the boat?"

Trent stilled for a moment before nailing her with a narrowed gaze from under his outstretched arm. "How would that bring Arnie slithering out from whatever rock he's hiding under?"

"You told Ted you weren't going after him."

"I said I wasn't going after Chambers."

"This is about my sister's life, not about proving whatever it is you've set out to prove."

The corner of his mouth twitched, not in amusement. Not if the pointed stare from those hooded blue eyes was any kind of indicator. "I can drop you anywhere you'd like. You don't have to be here."

"My boat." Uneasiness snaked its way down her spine. She didn't like this, but she wouldn't let him go alone.

He was reckless, but she admitted it was a *controlled* reckless.

Would it be enough to keep him alive? *This time?*

"Suit yourself." He went back to his task.

Her fingers gripped the metal wheel. *This is insane.*

"Found it." He straightened and extended his hand. A small silver square sat in the flat of his palm.

"Now what do we do with it?" The thing looked so innocuous. Just a small piece of metal. At least it looked like metal. For all she knew it was plastic or some weird alloy.

"I'm tempted to throw it overboard, but it's probably waterproof."

"If you did, and it still transmitted, wouldn't they think we're still here? At this spot?"

Trent nodded.

"Why isn't that a good idea?" Let Arnie and Eric think they were out here sunbathing.

Sudden, fat drops splat hard against her head, her temple, dripped down her face.

Of course. Sunbathing in the rain.

Trent shoved the device in his pocket and in a few minutes they had the Bimini top up and secured. Rain pounded the canvas. As long as the wind didn't shift, though, they'd stay relatively dry. While Trent adjusted their position, she fished a towel from the locker underneath and wiped rain water from the seats.

"We need to flush Arnie out. And Chambers, if he's the one pulling Phelps' strings." Trent's hands on the wheel, he looked at her with the darkness of the wet afternoon shadowing his eyes. "That's the only way your sister will be safe."

That tightness constricted again in her stomach. Weighted heavy in her chest. "The police –"

Trent dug the device from his pocket, held it flat in his palm. "You want to go back to the hotel and let Ted and Devon Jackson stumble their way through? Dump this thing here and head back in to where it's safe?"

"Safe sounds like a damn good thing right now." She twisted the towel between her hands. "And both of them are competent."

"I'm sure they are. Personally, I have tremendous faith in Ted. But they're handicapped." His fingers closed around the device then he wiped water off his chin with the back of his hand. "Although Shamus suspects, none of them know for certain Hayden's alive."

Unable to pull her gaze from his, she held out the towel.

He shook his head. "You'll have to tell them."

She slammed the towel on his seat. *Dammit, what the*

hell should I do? "That will risk her life."

"Maybe. But maybe it won't. We don't know. Not for sure."

Underneath the Bimini, with rain beating on the canvas, they stood close, near enough for the scent of whatever aftershave he'd found at the hotel to tease her senses with its spicy earthiness. Close enough for her to be able to reach out a hand, to trace the newest bruises darkening his jaw.

Instead she ran a hand through own her damp hair, gathered it at her nape. "Why do you care?"

He blinked, broke eye contact with her.

"Your sister?" She caught the flicked glance he threw her before he turned to stare at the rain. "Trent —"

"Let it go, Jillian."

"Why? If that is what's driving you —"

His nostrils flared and his lips thinned, but he kept his gaze on the water.

"Trent."

He lowered his head until his chin almost touched his chest then he pursed his lips before angling his head in her direction, although he still didn't meet her eyes. "Cassie is gone. The man who killed her is dead. This isn't about her."

"No, it's not. But is it about you saving the world?" Where had *that* come from? She was nobody's psychiatrist.

His eyes narrowed for a long moment before he sighed and shook his head. He finally met her gaze, the blueness in his direct and maybe a little sheepish. "No.

I'm not interested in saving the world. At least not today. Just *your* sister. Hayden. Not Cassie."

"Okay." *Please let this not be a huge mistake.* But what was one more in the long line she'd made lately. Like falling in love with a man who put everyone else ahead of his own safety.

"Okay?"

"What do we do with that thing?" She jerked her chin at the device in his fisted hand.

One side of his mouth lifted in a dangerous half smile.

Oh Lord. Who's in more danger now? Arnie or me?

"Take the wheel." Trent changed places with her, his body brushing hers and sending spirals of heat across her skin. His eyes widened.

She held his gaze for a moment then he yanked her close. Claimed her mouth. Heat sizzled between them in the few seconds before he lifted his head.

Desire, hot and intense smoldered in his hooded gaze. He lowered his head again, brushed his lips softly over hers then pressed his forehead to hers. "When this is over."

When this is over.

If we survive. She pressed two fingers to her tingling lips. *If I don't run as far away as my bruised heart will take me.*

Trent moved from under the cover of the Bimini to rummage through the locker underneath the back seat. Soaked in seconds by the steady downpour, he found a hammer and sent her a full blown grin.

Her heart stuttered in her chest. "What are you going

to do?"

"Invite Arnie to come out and play." He crouched down and set the device on the floor of the boat.

"Why does that sound like a bad idea?"

"Definitely not for the weak at heart." He grinned again and her weak heart flipped in her chest. With the hammer he tapped the device once before smacking it hard and shattering it into several different pieces. "But I have a suspicion you have the heart of an adventurer, Jilly. You just keep it under wraps."

That grin of his tightened her stomach. She averted her gaze to stare at the fragments of the tracking device. *Better under wraps than scattered like so many broken pieces across the bottom of my boat.* "Beats having a heart attack from all the excitement."

"Live a little, darlin'." He grabbed the towel from the driver's seat, swept all the pieces together and wrapped them in the cloth. Standing, he put the whole mess in the open locker under the back seat cushion. Once secure, he ducked under the Bimini and took the passenger seat.

She tried not to stare at the way his borrowed wet shirt molded to his chest. Failed miserably. Her mouth went dry. With a quick swallow, she gave the boat a little juice, eased their position a few feet further from shore. "Now what?"

"Slip up as close as you can to the tip of that outcropping without showing us to anyone on the other side. Then we wait."

"Again, I'm thinking this isn't such a good idea. How long?"

"A few minutes to maybe fifteen. Even with the entire Monroe Sheriff's Department looking for him, I can't imagine Arnie being too far away."

"So the signal just stops?" She let the boat's idle move them in the direction Trent requested.

He nodded. "Hopefully he'll believe it's a malfunction and will want to do a simple swing around the area to see if he can spot us."

"And we'll be over here instead of over there where he believes we are." This *really* didn't sound good at all. More like dangerous and stupid, all mixed together. "He has a gun. Maybe two. We have a couple of bats."

"We also have the element of surprise."

"What good is that going to do us?"

"Once he rounds that point, power up and aim straight for him."

What? "Why?"

"Because his instinct will be to run." Trent scanned the horizon. The rain had eased to a light drizzle. "I want to see where he heads."

"That's insane."

"Maybe." He lowered the Bimini and secured it on the sides and back. That preparation didn't bode well either.

The coolness of light rain tickled her bare arms. "You're expecting me to chase him."

"Possibly."

They sat silent for a few minutes. An hour. Time passed so slowly, twisting her gut, she couldn't tell how long they waited.

In the misty drizzle the low thrum of a slow moving boat tightened her hands on the wheel. *Oh boy.* They couldn't yet see whoever it was, but the vessel idled just on the other side of the thick stand of mangroves, its powerful engine vibrating right through her skin.

Trent's gaze flicked to hers then he stood to grip the bar running above the console. "Ready?"

No. One hand gripped the wheel. The other flexed on the throttle.

What if that other boat only hosted an innocent party out for a rainy afternoon ride on the water?

Whoever they are, they're about to get more than they bargained for in less than thirty seconds. Again her fingers flexed.

The other boat swept wide and slow around the point of mangroves. In that instance her gaze locked with Arnie's and her breath caught in her chest.

"Now." Trent's voice, low and demanding, skittered across her suddenly chilled skin.

She sucked in a strangled gulp of air and shoved the throttle forward. Her boat sprang ahead, its bow lifting from the water. Arnie's mouth hung open for a fraction of a second. He fumbled at his controls but then his big boat made a graceful arc through the water away from them.

"Go." Trent's feet and hands braced, all of his attention focused on the man they chased.

And they *were* chasing him. Arnie's sleek boat – bigger, with more power – pulled away. But her boat was smaller, more maneuverable in the shallower waters. Both of them tore across Blackwater Sound towards Key

Largo.

Although the Sound was an open expanse, Arnie wouldn't be able to pull far enough away from them to hide. He had one of two choices. Head north towards Biscayne Bay, through Blackwater and the two Sounds after this one, or maneuver his way east over to Pennekamp then hit the Atlantic. There he'd lose them. Her little boat didn't have the power or speed to keep up with him in the open waters of the ocean.

If she were Arnie, she'd hit the Atlantic.

A slight adjustment and she was on the inside of Arnie's projected path towards The Cut, a man-made channel that would take him to the eastern side of Key Largo and the Atlantic. Trent slid a sideways look at her.

A calculated risk, but wasn't that what he wanted? Her to take risks?

What they would do once she beat Arnie to The Cut, she had no idea. Nor did she really think Trent had a plan beyond frustrating Arnie. The other man wouldn't lead them anywhere except on a wild chase. But chasing him, that gave her a sense of control.

Maybe that was all this was about, that psychological shift.

As long as Arnie didn't start shooting at them.

She shoved the throttle further forward. Adrenaline shot through her, quickened her heartbeat, her breathing. Her boat responded and they edged closer to the channel.

A few sailboats and two catamarans sat anchored in the cove like area created by a thick stand of mangroves.

In between the boats a fancy dinghy, one with a stand-up console, puttered around with only a dark-haired driver on board.

Minutes passed like seconds. Jillian's hair streamed behind her, tangling in a wind that stung her cheeks and notched the rush of power filling her. They were going to beat Arnie to The Cut.

She shifted the wheel a slight amount and aimed to block the other man's entrance to the channel. On his boat, Arnie stood behind his wheel, legs braced apart, chin tucked to his chest. From the short distance between their boats she could see the maniacal grin spread across his mouth. He twisted the wheel, shoved the throttle forward, and his bow lifted further from the water. The hull of his huge vessel bore down on them.

Now what?

Chapter Twenty-Three

"JILLIAN!" TRENT SHOVED AWAY from where he stood, intent on grabbing her boat's wheel. Arnie Phelps, in his powerful boat, aimed straight at them on the open water of the Sound. *Not happening this afternoon, not any afternoon.*

"Got it." Jillian wrenched the wheel to the right, whipping them in a tight arc away from the rush of the other man's boat.

Trent grabbed the top railing as the other vessel went by in a whoosh of speed. A wall of water hit the side of their boat, rocked them and knocked Trent flat on his ass on the bottom of Jillian's boat.

He pushed himself upright, wobbled to his feet, and wrapped one hand around the railing near the console. Jillian had gotten them out of the way. *That's what matters.* He rolled his shoulders, twisted his head side to side. What were a few more bruises added to his already extensive collection?

He scanned the area in front of them. Arnie had made the channel entrance. The bow of his big boat dipped lower as he eased his speed.

With a quick sideways glance at Jillian, Trent nodded

and she swung their boat to follow the other one through the channel. *God, she was tough.* Held firm and didn't fall apart. *How much more could any man ask for in a woman?* Impressive as well as beautiful. Stubborn and independent.

No knight on a white horse for Jillian Rose. No, she would ride *beside* her knight, charging forward next to him. Into battle. Protecting those she loved.

Even as Jillian slowed their speed, their little boat bounced as she steered them into Arnie's wake. Still holding the rail, Trent pulled his gaze away from her to scan the area as they slipped underneath the Overseas Highway Bridge.

"That's coral." He waved a hand towards the greyish, razor sharp sides of the channel.

One hand on the wheel and the other on the throttle, she nodded. "There's a coral cap over the island. This area is usually just called The Cut. Splits Key Largo in two."

"Prime real estate." He examined the area as they passed through. Large houses rose on either side, many with protected notches cut into the coral walls for yachts and other ocean going craft.

"Can be." Jillian throttled further back as she edged closer to the southern side of the channel. Ahead of them Arnie barely missed a larger boat heading west. "What do we do once we hit Largo Sound?"

"Which way would he head to get to the Atlantic?"

"North or south. Regardless of direction, he'll have to navigate his way through mangroves to get to open water. South would be easier."

"And Dane's property is towards the south end of Largo Sound."

"Arnie's too big to play chicken with, Trent."

"Really?" For a moment he took his gaze off Arnie's boat and aimed a grin in her direction. Her hair, wind whipped and wild, framed her face. Narrowed in concentration, her gaze shifted between her console, the channel and the boat in front of them. "*You* were doing a damn good job of playing chicken back there."

"Thought you wanted me to take more risks." Without looking at him she made an adjustment to their heading.

A deep laugh rumbled his chest. Beautiful, focused and sarcastic. What a combination.

He was afraid she'd hooked him. Line and sinker.

The smell of char-grilled meat filtered in on the strong, damp breeze. Someone at one of the houses they passed barbequed a late lunch or an early dinner. Simple pleasures. How many years had it been since he'd made time for anything remotely like an afternoon barbeque?

With friends. People he cared about.

That same breeze lifted the ends of Jillian's hair, whisked several strands into her face. She tucked them back behind her ear. Met his gaze.

Her eyes widened and for that single moment he was mesmerized.

"Jillian —"

She blinked, lifted her head. "We're close to the end of The Cut."

Right. Business first. Barbeques, maybe never.

But *maybe* could change, become a possibility. His fingers tightened on the metal railing.

DC was cold this time of year and there was a field office in Miami. Not much more than an hour's drive north of Key Largo.

Focus, Sawyer.

After a gentle curve to the right, Arnie tossed a look over his shoulder then sped up, angling for the point where the channel dumped into Largo Sound. They followed his lead, their speed increasing in increments the closer they got to the end of The Cut.

Arnie blasted out onto the open expanse of the Sound, angling south just as Jillian predicted. As they made the opening themselves, clouds parted above them. Silver light coated the water's surface, sparkling across the bow of their boat.

Good sign or not, Trent didn't know, but at this point he had to make a decision.

Out here on the Sound, with the wind blowing and their engine revving, he leaned close to Jillian so he wouldn't have to yell to be heard. "Chase him, but let him get a distance away from us. Once he hits the mangroves and can't see us when he looks back, veer off."

She nodded. "So he's not aware of whether or not we're still with him."

"Right."

"And then?"

"We go find Dane and your sister."

✧ ✧ ✧

JILLIAN, SITTING IN HER captain's seat with her hands loose on the wheel, held her boat at a nearly motionless idle. Close to thirty minutes had passed since they let Arnie slip away and the man hadn't returned to Largo Sound. She and Trent had made a slow tour of the southern end of the Sound.

Waiting.

So far, so good. No Arnie.

Trent lowered the binoculars she kept in the boat, pursed his mouth for a moment. That intensity to his blue eyes looked good on him.

She averted her gaze to stare at the egrets roosting in the mangroves, the birds' white feathers stark against the deep green of the trees. *Trent will leave. Life will go on, even with my heart broken.*

It's already breaking. She shoved that thought aside and rescanned the area.

The heaviest of the clouds had retreated to line the horizon. Large patches of clear sky reflected off the water, intensifying the blue and green colors, while the heavy breeze brought the sea's brininess to tickle her nose. *Sunset should be spectacular.*

We'll make it to sundown. She hoped.

"I think we're good to go." Trent set the binoculars on the seat behind him. With his legs braced apart and his hands splayed at his hips, he smiled at her. Light glinted off his eyes, made them dance in the late afternoon.

Her heart thudded hard against her chest.

It's already broken.

This no-strings thing wasn't working so well for her. Neither was pretending she didn't care.

She swallowed once. "Directly to Dane's?"

Without the binoculars pressed to his eyes, he scanned the area once more. "Yes."

Sudden queasiness churned in her stomach. Snapping the throttle into gear, she set off at a slow pace while Trent continued to study the area. *God, I hope we're not heading into an ambush.*

Or leading one directly to Hayden.

✧ ✧ ✧

"WHAT ARE YOU DOING HERE?" Hayden's words hit Jillian like a slap across her face.

"Looking for you." In spite of her sister's tone, relief at finding her flooded Jillian's system, weakening her knees. She stiffened her legs, forced herself forward across the threshold, and took a quick glance around the foyer area of a large, partially finished house. Outside, a stiff late afternoon breeze rattled the shutters.

"I told you this morning to stay out of this, Sis." Hayden stood at the center of the entryway, one arm around her middle and the fingers of her other hand threaded through her tawny hair to hold it back from her pale face. Her green cat eyes wide with a mixture of anger and fear, she pressed her lips together.

"And I told you I can't."

From behind Jillian, Trent closed the door. He touched the small of her back as he moved in to stand at her side. "Where's Dane?"

Hayden's gaze flitted between the two of them. "He's not here right now. You two shouldn't be, either."

"He left you here alone?" Jillian kept her gaze on her sister.

"Only for a little while. We needed supplies and after seeing you earlier, he thought it best if I stay here. Out of sight."

"Probably for the best." Trent nodded and held out his hand. "I'm Trent Sawyer —"

"I know who you are." Hayden ignored his hand. "Dane told me about Arnie stealing the Oasis and blowing her up in Blackwater."

"You know Arnold Phelps?" Trent's voice low and measured, he curled the fingers of his outstretched hand, lowered his arm. "Do you also know where I can find him?"

Hayden studied his face for a few moments. Jillian studied her sister. The anger that seemed right on the surface barely hid the anxiety riding Hayden's eyes, leaving them dark and vulnerable.

Oh, Sis. Let me help.

"No, I don't know where Arnie is. That man's dangerous. But Dane should be back soon. Maybe then I'll be able to offer you something more than water." Hayden let go of her hair then shrugged one shoulder in a nonchalant move that fell flat. With a sigh, she led them through a cement floored hallway and further into the house.

In what might, one day, be a kitchen, Hayden waved

them to a makeshift table in the center of the room. On one wall, large plated glass windows formed a nook and overlooked the small lagoon where they'd tied their boat.

Hayden pulled three bottles of water from a cooler sitting on a plank topped counter. With the bottles in her hands, she stopped and stared out the windows. "Who hit you, Jilly?"

Jillian's hand went to her bruised cheek. "Trent believes it was Eric."

"Oh." Hayden's face paled further. Then she shook her head and handed them each a bottle. She perched on the edge of one of the white, plastic chairs scattered around the room. "I really didn't want you involved, Jilly."

"Then why did you send her that kilo?" Trent twisted the top from his bottle and took a long swig.

"Because if anything happened to me, she'd have the evidence of who was responsible."

"You sent it to her blind. Then the DEA showed up."

"The DEA? Oh no."

"They're holding your father."

Hayden's gaze flew to Jillian's. "Dad? But he has nothing to do with any of this."

Jillian wiped at the condensation coating her plastic water bottle. "I wish you didn't."

"Jilly, I don't. I was in the wrong place, at the wrong time."

"Dane is here." Trent set his bottle next to the cooler and headed towards the back door that opened onto the span of dirt leading to the dock.

"Don't –" Hayden jumped up. Her seat tumbled back, rattling against the cement floor.

Trent's hand on the door knob, he threw a quick glance back over his shoulder. "Dane has already seen our boat, I need to get out there."

Hayden started forward.

"No. You two stay here." Trent headed out the back door. The screen slapped shut without a single bounce.

To keep Hayden from following, Jillian wrapped her fingers around her sister's elbow. Hayden's shoulders drooped and her eyes glistened.

That depth of despair ate at Jillian.

I'm supposed to keep you safe. Always. How the hell did this get so messed up?

On a muffled sigh, she pulled Hayden into an embrace with her sister's hands tucked between them. After a few seconds, Hayden slipped her arms around Jillian's waist and rested her head on her shoulder.

They stood that way for several moments.

"Why didn't you tell me what was going on?" With one hand rubbing small circles on her sister's back, Jillian smoothed Hayden's hair back and pressed her lips against her forehead.

"I was scared. Still am." Hayden's words whispered between them. "I thought I could take time to figure it out on Jazz' boat. Then when they blew it up, I *knew* they would hurt you, too."

"Sis–"

"And he did." She straightened and touched the edge

of the bruise on Jillian's cheek. "You're all I have left, Jilly. I can't let anything else happen to you."

"Hey." Jillian ignored the moisture stinging her eyes and gave a small shake of her head. "I'm supposed to take care of you, not the other way around."

"Sometimes you should let someone else do the caring. I've been nothing but a burden. I'm trying to stop that."

"You know, technically, we still have Mom and Dad." Jillian brushed several more strands of Hayden's curls away from her face.

A small smile flitted over Hayden's mouth. "Right. Talk about a burden."

Jillian hugged her sister. Coming so close to losing her, the pain of that tightened her stomach. Her throat.

"The DEA really has Dad?"

"He tried to steal the package. They were there when he did that."

The back screen door slicked open. Trent entered. He caught Jillian's gaze but she couldn't read his closed expression. Dane followed with a plastic grocery bag tight in his hand and his face just as shuttered as Trent's. Hayden wiped at her eyes with the back of her forefingers before turning to face the men.

Neither Dane nor Hayden glanced at each other.

Jillian glared at Dane, although not sure how mad she was at him since he'd obviously kept her sister safe. But he had to have known how worried Jillian would be, knowing her sister was alive but in danger.

Unless....

She touched her sister's arm. "Does Dane know you left me a note?"

Dane's startled then narrowed gaze went to Hayden's whose own gaze flicked to Dane's then to the floor.

There's my answer.

How many more secrets are there?

"THESE ROSE WOMEN." Trent let his humorless chuckle break the silence. He shifted his glance between the two sisters huddled together in Dane's unfinished kitchen and Dane himself who stood with the screen door to his back. "Was their grandmother this way? Thinking she knew best and not listening to anyone else?"

Disturbed construction dust floated in the air, backlit by the afternoon sunlight filtering in through the multi-paned windows facing the lagoon as the silence stretched again. Trent raised an eyebrow.

Finally, Dane nodded. He wiped a hand over the several days' worth of dark whiskers along his jaw. "I'd like to say Rosey was worse, but lately I'm wondering about that."

Hayden's chin lifted, her green eyes shot daggers at Dane. "You didn't have to help me."

"No I didn't." Dane moved farther into the room. He set the bag of groceries on the makeshift plywood counter. Opening the ice chest, he emptied the contents of his bag into the chest. He straightened then faced them with his back to the counter and his legs braced apart. "I'd offer you something besides water, but you're not staying."

"Such hospitality." Trent mirrored the man's stance and set his splayed hands at his hips.

Dane didn't have a gun either, by choice or not, Trent wasn't sure, but he wouldn't want to face the man in a fight. They'd both end up hurt.

A sudden buzz hit Trent's inner ear.

The back screen slicked open. He and Dane spun to face the threat.

The buzz abruptly stopped. Trent went still.

A dark-haired man, with sunglasses over his eyes and a ball cap pushed back and high on his forehead, stood at the open door with a Colt 1911 .45 caliber pistol pointed at Jillian's chest.

Nice weapon. Trent's eyes narrowed. If the stranger pulled the trigger, he'd put a serious hole in her. *Not going to happen.* Trent flexed his fingers.

"Look at what I have found." A barely discernable accent laced the depths of the stranger's smoky voice.

A niggle of recognition prickled along Trent's skin. "Who are you?"

The man smiled, the look cold and hard. He took another step into the house. The screen door slicked closed behind him. "I knew you in particular, Mr. FBI, would be an issue."

"Wade Landry." Trent let his hands dangle at his side. He noted Dane did the same. "Youngest prince of Cadeau. Felicity's brother."

Chapter Twenty-Four

TRENT ROLLED ONTO the balls of his feet as he studied the prince. Landry's grim smile widened to a sardonic grin.

The gun aimed at Jillian was an issue.

Dane's kitchen, although large, lacked defensible space. While Trent and Dane could rush the prince, that left both Jillian and Hayden vulnerable as targets.

Trent mentally raced through the information he'd gleaned on the Landry family earlier at the hotel. The two princes were dark where Felicity had been blonde. Different mothers. Tight family ties. In addition, the two Cadeau princes had received extensive military training. Wade excelled.

Talk the situation down. Avoid hand to hand combat. Trent wiped the back of his hand over his mouth. "What do you want with us?"

Landry pulled off his sunglasses and tucked them in a shirt pocket. His eyes resembled black holes, devoid of light. "Answers."

"To what?"

"To *why* my sister was killed."

"Felicity Chambers." Jillian tilted her head to one

side and crossed her arms over her stomach. "Eric's ex-wife."

Tent threw her a sideways glance. She seemed to completely ignore the gun aimed at her. He admired the audacity even as his heart constricted. *No sudden moves, sweetheart.*

Landry's mouth turned downward but he nodded once then directed his attention to Hayden. "You are the current girlfriend. The one everyone believes to also be dead."

Hayden's throat visibly working, she lifted her chin.

"Why would anyone here know *why* Felicity died?" Trent pulled the prince's attention back. "The police say she had an accident. That she fell down the stairs."

From the corner of his eye he noted Dane's subtle shift in position, a partial blocking of Hayden, a partial bunching of muscles much like a cat preparing to strike.

"No. Not an accident." Landry's gaze touched on each person before resting a moment longer on Dane. Landry's lips twitched before he focused again on Hayden. "You were there, when she died."

With moisture shining in her eyes and her gaze locked on the prince's, Hayden nodded.

"What?" Jillian's head jerked towards her sister.

"Don't." Trent kept his voice low as he touched Jillian's arm.

Her honey eyes darkened to amber, she threw him a quick glance then focused on her sister. "That's why you were so upset that night. You *were* at Felicity's?"

"I was in the study with Felicity when —"

"Back up." Jillian, arms now crossed over her chest and a frown marring her forehead, faced her sister. "What were you doing there in the first place?"

Hayden's mouth tightened.

The gun still pointed in Jillian's general direction, Landry leaned against the kitchen door frame and motioned for Hayden to continue.

Dane's gaze flicked between the women and the prince, same as Trent's.

Doesn't either one of them care about the damn gun pointed at them?

Hayden puffed out a deep breath. "Felicity had called. She wanted to talk."

"Why?" Jillian glanced at Trent. "About what?"

Hayden wet her lips. "Eric."

Bingo.

Landry lifted his head. With his eyes dark and focused on Hayden, his mouth tightened.

Trent slid a glance towards the weapon in Landry firm grip. "If all you're looking for is information, we'd be happy to help, considering we're curious, too. Why don't you put that away and we can all sit down and talk."

The prince's mouth twitched again. "Why don't I stand here, like this, and she continues to answer my questions?"

"It's a little intimidating to have that pointed at us when we've done nothing to you. If she develops amnesia all of a sudden, the rest of us are at risk."

"I feel the need of added incentive."

"Why?" Hayden blinked several times then reached a hand towards her sister. "I'll tell you what you want to know."

Jillian took her hand.

"Hayden." Dane's voice low, he held her gaze.

"Felicity was his sister." She pressed her lips together then sighed. "I'd feel the same if something had happened to mine."

Jillian squeezed her sister's hand then shot Trent a look under her lashes. He narrowed his gaze. *Why the hell not? Let's all ignore the gun and commiserate with each other.*

Crap.

Dane's wary expression matched what he suspected was mirrored his own face. This could actually work, depending on too many damn uncontrollable factors. As a stalling tactic, however, it could buy enough time to figure out a real plan of action. Trent gave Dane a subtle nod.

Besides, he had his own suspicions about what happened the night the princess died. Suspicions about Hayden's possible involvement and hope Jillian's sister had been nothing more than an innocent bystander caught in a web not of her making.

Guess we'll all find out together.

"Please continue." The tip of the Landry's weapon lowered a small fraction.

"Eric had been acting strange. More than preoccupied. Obsessed, really. I didn't know why." Hayden sniffed. "He told me it was my imagination."

"He's such a jerk." Jillian wrapped her sister close

while both Hayden's hands gripped her sister's arm.

Beyond a flicked glance between the two women, Landry didn't react to them moving together.

So far so good.

"When Felicity asked me to come after midnight, I went."

Trent raised an eyebrow. "Why so late?"

"She didn't want to risk anyone seeing me there."

"You didn't think that odd?" Trent shifted a few inches, positioning his body at more of a right angle between the prince and the women.

Hayden shrugged, glanced at Trent, then back to the prince. "I wanted answers."

The corner of Landry's mouth twitched again. "Something I understand."

"I parked in the back like she asked. I did wonder if she was setting me up although I couldn't figure out for what."

"Taking the fall for the smuggling Eric's involved in?" Trent rolled his shoulders.

"I didn't know about the smuggling when I got there." Hayden glanced between them all.

"The precursor." Landry frowned, his chin dipping lower. "That smuggling ring is another part of the reason I am here. To find where the weak link is in our production. To find who is stealing from our country."

Trent glanced at Dane then back to the prince. "Let us help you."

"You cannot." Landry waved the gun towards Hayden. "Continue."

"I think we *can* help." Trent ignored the prince's snarl. Risky, but a calculated risk. "Once she finishes telling her story, I believe we'll find we're after the same two people. Eric Chambers and Arnold Phelps."

A small twitch beat along Landry's jaw. "Why do you want these two men, Mr. FBI?"

"Personal score to settle with them both."

"Something else I understand. But this one needs to finish her story. I don't yet have all of my answers."

Humor the man. One step at a time.

Trent met Jillian's worried gaze over her sister's head. Hayden's eyes stayed focused on Landry, although her fingers clenched and unclenched on Jillian's arm.

Trent nodded once. "So Felicity caught Eric stealing the precursor? Or was she involved?"

"No, she wasn't involved. She said he'd been using the connections he'd made during their marriage. She was explaining all of this when Eric showed up at the house. She shoved some papers at me before she pushed me into a closet."

"Where are those papers now?" Trent shot a glance at Dane. Those papers might be what Chambers really wanted.

Hayden threw a quick look at her sister. "I had a spare set of keys tucked into my duffel, so I had access to Rosey's. I taped those papers to the underside of the bottom drawer under the bar." Hayden pressed her lips together for a quick moment. "They're kind of like a journal of sorts, implicating Eric. I've read over the pages, but there's a lot there I don't understand."

"What happened to my sister?" Landry's voice tight, he lowered the gun several more inches.

"I could hear her arguing with Eric then they moved out of the room. Once it got quiet, I snuck out and followed." Hayden swallowed hard and blinked back the moisture trembling on her lower eyelashes. "I was hiding in an alcove on an upper landing when I heard Felicity fall down the stairs."

The prince made a noise, low in his throat. More of a growl.

Been there. Done that. Right now, Trent didn't envy Landry's feelings.

Of course, there was the gun. Made Trent suspicious of the prince's motives.

Landry scanned all the people in the room before settling again on the women. He lowered the gun even more. "You didn't *see* Chambers push her?"

"No. But I *heard* Arnie ask him *why.* Eric said – he said she was a liability. That liabilities had to be dealt with. That's when I knew, if he ever found out I was there, I'd also be a liability. Somehow I got down those back stairs and out to my car. I was so *relieved* I'd left it unlocked. I thought I'd gotten away. I was heading home. But then he called." Hayden's voice hitched. "I let it ring and ring. The voicemail picked up and …."

"Did he threaten you on the voicemail?" Trent narrowed his eyes. That would be too easy. "We can use that against him, if he did."

Silent, Landry's dark eyes absorbed everything.

Hayden shook her head, the movement quick and

jerky. "It wasn't any kind of direct threat. He said ... he was sorry he'd missed me. Sorry I had to rush off. That he hoped I was feeling all right and that we really needed to get together so he could make sure I didn't spread any nasty germs to my sister."

The blood in Trent's veins chilled. "He threatened Jillian."

Hayden blinked several times as tears spilled over her lashes. Jillian brushed the tips of her fingers over her sister's cheek.

"So –" With her eyes closed for a moment, Hayden turned her cheek into Jillian's palm and covered Jillian's hand with her own. "I thought if I stayed away from you, if I didn't go to the police, you'd be okay."

Anger boiled hot in Trent's gut. Chambers would pay for all of this. "How did you end up with Arnie's picture on your cell?"

"You found my phone?"

"Shamus and Ted did."

"In those papers I left at Rosey's, Felicity had the addresses of several warehouses near Biscayne Bay."

"Does Chambers own them or simply manage them?"

"I don't know for sure. But when we docked the Symphony at Biscayne Bay, it was like the opportunity fell in my lap. The warehouses were there. We were there. When I got to the first warehouse, though, there was Arnie. When he left, I went in. I took three of those packages."

"Three?" Jillian and Dane's voice fused into a chorus

of outraged disbelief.

Trent resisted shaking his head. Of course she took *three*.

Although Jillian kept her arm around her sister's shoulders, she pulled a few inches away to stare at her.

"One was mailed to your sister." Trent wiped a hand over his mouth. The prince now aimed his gun at the floor a few feet in front of the women rather than at any one in particular. Trent's respect for negotiating skills ratcheted several degrees. "One package was left in the safe. The third?"

"The safe at your house?" Dane aimed his hot glare at Hayden. "Did you leave it there when you left Jilly *that note?*"

Hayden wrapped her arms around her middle and gripped both her elbows. She nodded but didn't glance at Dane "I didn't think Jilly would actually get into the safe."

Dane set his hands on his hips. "I have the *third* package stashed."

"Here?" Landry's chin lifted a fraction. His eyes closed for a brief moment but they snapped open before Trent moved more than a foot. The prince shook his head. "I mean no harm to any of you."

"Then why the gun?" Dane, his jaw tight, rolled up on the balls of his feet.

"Insurance." Landry aimed the weapon at Dane's head. The prince's nostrils flared and his chin lifted all the while keeping his gaze locked on Dane's. After several tense moments, the prince lowered the gun, flipped the safety, and tucked it in his waistband.

Trent expelled the breath caught in his throat.

"Thank you, Miss Rose." Landry's gaze flicked between the two women before he focused on Dane. "Could I see the package?"

Trent met Dane's eyes, nodded once. The other man left the room as Trent turned back to Hayden. "Arnie followed you back to the boat? That photo you managed to get shows him on board."

"Somehow Arnie knew about the Symphony. He was there when I got back, so I didn't go onboard. I hid behind the tall planters against the shower building and took that photo."

"I told Eric you went with Jazz." Jillian pressed the back of her free hand to her mouth.

"You didn't know not to tell him." Hayden touched her sister's shoulder. "After I snapped that shot, he jumped off into a dinghy. Then the boat exploded."

"Heading to that warehouse saved your life." Trent leaned against the counter, crossed his arms. Stupid or not, that need to know had kept her alive. So far, at least.

"All those people on board. Jazz —" Tears flowed freely down Hayden's cheeks.

Dane reentered the room. With one look at Hayden, he stopped and his suspicious gaze hit every other person in the room. On a grunt, he tossed an unopened package to the prince before he pulled Hayden away from Jillian and into a tight hug.

Landry, with a knife from his back pocket, cut a small slit in the package then raised it to his nose. His mouth tight, he nodded.

"One question." Trent frowned at Landry. "How'd you know to come here?"

"Your friend Arnold isn't the only one who can plant a tracking device."

Trent exchanged a quick glance with Jillian before he shook his head at the prince. "That's your sailboat moored in the cove near Rosey's."

"Yes." Landry inclined his chin.

"We need to turn all this over to someone. Who do we call?" Jillian's gaze hit each one of them. "Ted, Shamus? Or those two DEA agents?"

"None of them." Landry folded the knife and slipped it into his back pocket. "Chambers killed Felicity, as I had suspected. It is my duty to take care of this piece of shit."

Trent's gut tightened. He crossed his arms over his chest. "We can't stand aside and let you kill him."

"Why not? You killed the one who took your sister's life, yet you would deny me that vengeance?"

Trent worked his jaw.

How'd Landry gain that piece of information? Not exactly secret, not for public consumption, either.

"There isn't a day I regret not saving Cassie. But taking that murdering SOB's life didn't bring her back." Nor had it brought the satisfaction Trent thought it would. Instead, the empty hole inside had only gotten deeper, more hollow. He spared another glance for Jillian. That complete acceptance in her eyes as her gaze held his loosened the knot in his gut. He refocused on the prince. "Let us help take Chambers down. Capture him and Phelps. We can make sure they pay. That they both stay locked up for a long, long time."

"With what Hayden knows, along with what she grabbed, the DEA will have a solid case against them both." Dane, an arm around Hayden's shoulders, moved so he and Trent bracketed the women.

Hayden raised her watery gaze to Dane's. "Eric thinks he's smarter than all of you, that I'm a brainless bimbo."

"So let's show him you're not." With the back of his hand, Dane touched her cheek.

"This is no longer your fight." Landry crossed both arms over his chest. He stood with his legs spread shoulder width apart.

"That's where you're wrong." Trent mirrored the prince's stance. With his chin lifted, he held the other man's gaze. Chambers had hurt Jillian. He continued to threaten her. That wasn't something Trent would let stand.

For a long, silent moment Landry studied Trent. "As long as you understand I will not hesitate to kill Chambers if the need arises."

Trent nodded once. That was one thing he understood better than anyone.

Vengeance.

Chapter Twenty-Five

CHILLED, JILLIAN RUBBED HER HANDS TOGETHER. The calendar might say February, but the temperature rarely dipped this far. Or maybe her nerves made her cold. Almost closing time at Rosey's and so far things had unraveled as they'd expected them to unwind.

Business had slowed in the past hour and now the last of the stragglers settled their tabs and paid Trent who stood positioned behind the counter. Appreciative of the fact her employees had run the afternoon shift without her, and wanting them out of harm's way, she'd sent them home earlier. Only she and Trent remained for close-down.

Eric sat in the far corner, his back to the railing, nursing his second beer of the evening.

No sign of Arnie.

The papers Felicity had died for, that Hayden had hidden, now lay tucked on top of both kilos of precursor in Rosey's safe. Papers implicating Eric, but not his connection in Cadeau.

Jillian rubbed her arms. They couldn't close the windows, couldn't close out the chilly breeze. Not yet. They needed those windows open.

Red lights twinkled on the dark water, reflected from strands of small lights one of her employees had strung earlier, in honor of the upcoming holiday.

Valentine's Day.

A day for lovers. Trent would be gone by then, back to his life somewhere else without her. *He'd be alive, though.* And she'd be alone. Without a Valentine.

Unless she asked him to stay. And he said yes.

What if he says no?

Wade Landry could have killed any of them earlier. Had that actually been his intent.

Trent gone. Dead. That thought added to her chill. But if he went back to his life without her letting him know how she felt, that she *loved* him, he'd be just as gone from her life as if he'd died.

... you have the heart of an adventurer, Jilly. Did she? Or was she a coward who wouldn't reach for what she wanted?

Her bottom lip between her teeth, her gaze wandered around Rosey's.

Still no sign of Arnie.

Hayden, Dane and Wade had hidden on Wade's sailboat but should now be somewhere close by, on the water, keeping tabs on what happened here.

Watching. Waiting.

Jillian caught Trent's eye and made a face. He grinned back.

Business as usual.

The man in his element. Structured adventure. Controlling what could be controlled, calculating the risks.

Rolling with the rest.

The last few hours stretched her nerves to their limit.

Did she have the guts to let go enough to grab hold of him?

To tell him she loved him?

If they made it through this … to see dawn.

With a deep breath, she wiped down several of the empty tables and made her way toward the edge of the room.

"Closing time, Eric." She forced a smile to her stiff lips. "Time to settle your tab."

"Did you know there were only five bodies recovered from the Symphony? Not six, like there should have been."

Jillian went still.

Eric nodded. He focused on the half empty beer glass in his hand, swirled it as he stared. "Your sister is alive, Jillian."

Her mouth went dry.

"But then, you know that." Eric met her gaze. The side of his mouth lifted in a rueful half smile. "When were you going to tell me?"

"I wasn't." She straightened, shifted so Trent had a direct line of sight. They were the only three left in the place, the point they believed Eric would make his move.

Disappointment they were right twisted her stomach.

Eric glanced at Trent, set his gaze back on her. "Why not? I love your sister. She loves me."

"Really?" Jillian let a shade of derisiveness color her voice.

He shrugged one shoulder. "I *am* the one she called."

"What?" She feigned surprise and sat hard on a chair at his table, careful to not block Trent's view. "When?"

"Earlier this evening." Eric shrugged. "She's meeting me here, as soon as you close down."

Jillian's heart stuttered. They wanted this, what they'd planned and set in motion, yet her hands trembled at the reality. She closed her eyes for a brief moment then stared at the man across the table. "Why, Eric? What's she so afraid of? Who wants her dead?"

He pressed his lips together before shoving his glasses back up his nose. "I'm afraid that would be me."

In the time it took her to blink, Eric pointed a lethal looking gun aimed directly at her heart.

Oh, shit. Expecting a weapon and staring down the barrel weren't the same thing at all. Unlike the sense she'd had off Wade earlier, she *knew* Eric wouldn't hesitate to use the gun. Her breathing shallow, she swallowed hard around the lump stuck *dead* center of her throat.

Eric laughed, the sound sick amidst the gentle lapping of water against the pylons underneath Rosey's. "Mr. Sawyer, why don't you come from behind the bar and join us?"

"I don't think so." Trent, with one elbow on the bar and his other hand out of sight, smiled.

"Do you really want me to shoot her?"

"You won't. Not yet. That's not the game plan."

Jillian sent Trent a quick, narrowed look. That was *their* game plan. No one had given Eric the rules. And he was obviously psychotic. Bad combination, even when they expected it.

"You task me, Sawyer. You really do. I know the only possible weapon you have is Jillian's ever present baseball bat. I'm not getting close enough for you to use that." Eric stood and waved the gun at Jillian. "Up."

She slid another glance at Trent but stood and wrapped her arms under her breasts. While she trusted him, he'd better know what he was doing or he'd get an earful when this was over.

"What do you want from us?" Trent addressed Eric but sent her an easy smile.

Sense of adventure be damned.

"Hayden took something that doesn't belong to her." Eric's words snapped her attention back to him.

"That package of precursor? That's yours?" Her gaze on him, she tilted her head and frowned. "You were here. You know the DEA took that."

"Your sister took more than the precursor."

Jillian let her eyes widen. "*You* were the one who got her involved in this? Why?"

"Hayden involved herself when she decided to help Felicity. She compounded that when she snuck into my warehouse. Now I want what Felicity gave her, what Felicity stole from me."

"I don't have anything else."

Trent's head angled slightly to the right and with his hand still under the bar, his chin lowered. "What is it you're looking for, Chambers?"

"Papers." Eric's gaze darted around the area. "I've

been sitting here for the last hour wondering where she could have hidden them. I don't have any answers, but I'm thinking one of you do."

Again Jillian shook her head. She took a half step backwards. "Maybe Hayden has them and is bringing them with her."

"Maybe." Eric's mouth lifted in a sly smile. "And maybe it's a trap. Which is why I'm here now rather than later."

"Where's Arnie?" A layer of disdain coated Trent's voice.

Eric's smile dimmed a little. "Who?"

"Why play coy now?" Trent shrugged then leaned back from the counter. The fingers of his free hand curled around the edge. "We know Phelps broke into Jillian's house, chased us down. Blew up both the Oasis and the Symphony. On your orders?"

Eric's mouth twitched. His chin lifted and he narrowed his eyes. "What difference does it make to you?"

"While you've been trying to figure out where Hayden could've hid your papers, I've been wondering about the whole set-up." Trent shrugged one shoulder. "About the Oasis. About your connections. The way I see it, your henchmen steal local boats, head out and meet the ship carrying the *official* load of precursor, sneak onboard and take what you see as your share then fade into the dawn. With all the stolen boats, why haven't the locals caught on to the thievery?"

Trent's good. Even without all the pieces of the puzzle.

Behind his glasses, Eric's eyes practically glowed.

"We *borrowed* those boats from people who wouldn't miss them for a few hours or even a few days."

"So finding Trent onboard the Oasis really messed things up?"

"Who knew that damn boat belonged to some ass from the FBI?" Disgust lined Eric's voice. "But that issue and all the resulting problems will be dealt with as soon as Hayden gets here."

"Who's helping you on the Cadeau side?"

Jillian frowned. "That would have to be what's in those papers he keeps going on about. Is it someone who works for the royal family? Or someone who works for Blackthorne?"

"None of that matters. Once Hayden arrives and we have the beautiful reunion scene between the sisters, I'll get those papers."

"And then?"

"Phelps will burn this place down with the three of you inside. End of problem."

"That's what you thought when you shoved Felicity down the stairs." Hayden's voice carried from the water side of the railing behind Eric.

Right on time. Trent vaulted over the bar at the same moment Chambers spun around with a snarl.

Trent tossed the bat to Jillian then rushed Chambers and knocked the man to the floor. The gun slid across the wood planks. Straddling Chambers, he punched him in the mouth. The asshole's head snapped back, hit the floor and he went slack.

God that felt good.

Trent stood to glance over the railing where Wade Landry gripped the stud to keep the rowboat they'd borrowed from rocking while Dane and Hayden tied their ropes to the pier. Once secure, the three climbed over the railing and through the wide window. They spread out around the man lying unconscious on the wooden planked floor.

Jillian pressed her foot on top of Eric's shoulder, her bat primed and ready. Trent almost wished Chambers would come to so she could take that swing.

She more than deserved the opportunity.

"Arnie's still out there somewhere. Still a problem." Trent scooped up Chamber's gun and slipped it in his waist band at the small of his back. Now back in his comfort zone, he knelt beside the unconscious man. "Anyone have handcuffs? Rope? Something to tie this moron's hands?"

"That won't be necessary." Quiet for such a big man, Arnie slipped in through the open doorway. In one hand he held a large glass jar full of clear liquid, in the other a gun pointed at Jillian. He set the glass container on a nearby table.

A thick wick stuck out of the jar's lid. *Phelps will burn this place down. End of problem.*

Trent, his hands out with palms forward, slowly eased himself into a standing position. Beside him, Dane had rolled onto the balls of his feet.

Arnie pulled a lighter from his pants pocket. Lit the wick. He moved away from the table, further into the room, and smiled as he swept his gun arm in an arc indicating them all. "Move away from Chambers."

A growl low in his throat, Landry pulled his own gun, aimed at Arnie. "You can shoot whomever you wish, but *you* will also be dead."

"Not if I shoot you first."

The prince's mouth lifted in a feral half smile. With his gaze locked on Arnie's, he lowered his chin. "Try it."

Hayden's scream rent the air. She went down hard, the thud shaking the floor. Eric, sitting with his legs stretched out and her in his lap, held one arm around her waist, the other at her throat.

"I'll break her neck if any of you heroes so much as move an inch." He scooted backwards, away from Trent.

Hayden, her eyes wide, whimpered at the same time she dug the nails of both hands into his arm.

"You always were a wildcat." Eric tightened his grip on her neck. "You know I won't hesitate to kill you. Here and now. Then I'll have Phelps shoot your sister."

"No." Hayden squeaked the word out.

Trent's heart stilled in his chest.

Not Jillian.

"He wants to kill us all anyway." Jillian hefted the bat. "What do we have to lose by fighting?"

"Not a damn thing." *As long as you keep yourself safe.*

"I was hoping you'd say that." Jillian's gaze on him, the corner of her mouth lifted in a grim smile. She swung fast and low, connecting with Chambers' side.

In the shock of the hit, Eric loosened his hold on Hayden. She twisted in his lap, dug her fingers into his face. Dane barreled forward, rushing towards them.

A shot pierced the air. Dane went down. Hayden screamed again as she scrambled away from Eric towards Dane.

Trent snatched the gun from the small of his back. He took aim at Arnie and fired. The big man's mouth dropped open. He clutched his chest. In almost slow motion Arnie lifted his gun arm. Trent cross-stepped forward, fired again. The force knocked Arnie onto his back.

Trent caught Jillian's gaze. She was okay. *More than okay.* The vise around his chest loosened as a scant smile lifted the corners of her mouth. She hefted her bat then scrambled towards her sister.

Hayden knelt next to Dane, pressing pink, blood soaked napkins against his side. So far he remained conscious.

Landry squatted in front of Chambers with the tip of his gun pressed to the man's chest. Trent hesitated. The prince's voice low, he said things to Chambers no one else could hear.

The coward's death wouldn't bring Felicity back, but Landry had his own peace to make with that unwelcome fact.

Trent flicked another glace at Jillian. She had her cell to her ear, calling the cavalry.

He knelt on one knee, checked Arnie's vitals. Pulse faint, but steady. Phelps would probably survive. Trent snatched the man's weapon. Rising, he pivoted towards the others and tucked that gun at the small of his back near the other one.

"Shamus has an ambulance coming?" He crouched at Dane's side, opposite of Hayden.

"Yes." Jillian slipped her cell into her front jeans pocket. "He's on his way, also."

"Stop Landry." Dane, his skin pale and breathing sketchy, jerked his chin towards the prince. "We both know he shouldn't go down that road."

Trent squeezed Dane's arm then shifted to look up at Jillian. Her eyes wide and worried, she knelt next to Trent. With her bat on the ground, she laid her free hand on his forearm.

"Thank you." Jillian pressed a warm kiss along his jaw. "Stop Wade, if you can."

Something inside his chest twisted, tumbled, and fell. But he held her gaze and rubbed his knuckles over her cheek.

He *loved* this prickly, courageous woman.

There has to be a way to make this work.

First though, this mess needed to be wrapped. He pushed to his feet and moved to where Landry crouched next to Chambers.

"Landry." Trent cuffed the man's stiff shoulder.

"Why shouldn't I shoot him? Right here. Right now." Landry's voice, low and vibrating, scraped across the small space between him and Chambers. "He has no remorse. Deserves no mercy."

With his glasses crushed on the floor next to him, Chambers' unfocused gaze darted between them. He rubbed the backside of his hand over his nose.

"It's not him that concerns me." Trent gripped

Landry's shoulder. "Don't do this. Turn him in. Let him rot in prison."

A sudden, loud buzz echoed in Trent's ears. *No.* He met Chamber's manic gaze.

The buzzing continued. Grew louder.

Chambers shoved forward, knocking Landry's gun hand.

The gun went off and the bullet smashed the bottom portion of Arnie's glass jar. A pungent, oily stench filled the area as liquid poured across the table and onto the wooden planked floor. For a moment silence replaced the buzz in Trent's ears. Then a loud whoosh filled the air as the spreading liquid hit the lit wick and hot flames shot up from the oil spilled across the table and floor.

Chambers scrambled to his feet. Trent grabbed for him, but the man evaded and rushed toward the wide, open window. There, Chambers pulled his body halfway through the opening.

Asshole isn't getting away that damn easy. Trent launched forward, wrapped his arms around Chambers' legs, yanked him out of the window then lay sprawled across the wooden floor planks with Chambers underneath.

On an oath, Chambers bucked him upwards, twisted and jerked one of the guns from Trent's waistband before scurrying backwards until his back hit the short wall underneath the window.

Trent rolled into a crouch, his fingertips pressed to the wood planks of the floor. The crackle of the fire behind him punctuated the thickening smoke.

Chambers swung the weapon between the women,

Landry and Trent.

"Come on, Eric." Trent hunched his shoulders. *We need to get the hell out of here.* Still crouched with his fingertips to the floor, he raised onto the balls of his feet. He couldn't reach for the other gun, couldn't make any sudden moves, or he'd set Chambers off. So he kept his head up, his gaze on the man. "Put the gun down, Eric. Otherwise that fire's going to trap us all."

"I'm not going to be arrested." Chambers shook his head. He settled his aim on Trent.

"Yes, you are." Jillian's voice strong, she stood next to Dane and her sister with her bat braced in front of her. "And we're all getting out of here before this place burns down around us."

"Think again." Chambers, his arm lifting another fraction, aimed the weapon at Trent's head. "Say goodbye to your boyfriend."

A gunshot rang out from behind Trent.

Eric, half his face gone, crumbled to the ground.

Landry, his gun still pointed at Chambers, held his other hand out to Trent.

Trent took the offered hand and pulled himself upright. "Thanks."

"Don't mention it." The prince's dark eyes empty, he shrugged then bent to take the weapon from Chambers' limp hand before checking his wrist for vitals. Landry shook his head and stared at the dead man. "Maybe it is better this way."

Maybe it was. Trent spun around. The fire had licked up the far wall and ignited the stuff covering the ceiling.

In the few moments it took him to gauge the situation, strands of blazing, fake dried grass fell to smolder on the wooden planks. A crackling blaze blocked their escape through the open doorway.

"Let's go, people." Trent ignored the blood seeping through the linen napkins pressed to Dane's side. *No time to deal with that. Not right now.* Between him and Landry, they pulled Dane to his feet and balanced him with his arms over their shoulders. "Through the window. Let's go."

Hayden climbed over the side, into the rowboat. She steadied the boat while, with Jillian's help, they lowered Dane into the boat.

Trent met Landry's gaze. They couldn't let Arnie burn to death, even if that's what they both preferred.

Landry nodded once before they hurried to where the big man lay close to the burning wall. Heat scorched Trent's back and smoke burned his lungs. Between the two of them, they drug Arnie's prone body to the window. With Jillian's aid, they manhandled him over the sill.

Once the unconscious man and the prince were safely in the rowboat with Dane and Hayden, Trent motioned to Jillian. "Over the side, sweetheart."

"Not without you." Her chin lifted. She offered her hand.

As brave as any soldier he'd ever known, his lady stayed by his side.

My lady. My warrior.

"Where else did you think I was going?" He held her

gaze for a heartbeat then wrapped his hand around her fingers and squeezed. "Let's get the hell out of here."

✧ ✧ ✧

DAWN BROKE ON A DISMAL, grey morning. Fire trucks and other emergency equipment filled the parking lot adjacent to what had once been Rosey's Place. Personnel trudged through standing puddles of water from rain that had fallen an hour earlier. Too late to save the bar and grill, but enough to drench them all.

Jillian tucked a scraggly strand of hair behind her ear. She edged closer to Trent. He tightened his arm around her and gripped the fireman's blanket snug around them both. They leaned against the front push-bar of one of the patrol vehicles, taking in the hustle of activity around them. Chunks of charred wood floated nearby, all that was left of the pier, rocking gently in the disturbed water.

So much destruction, so little left.

No one had protested when Hayden had climbed into the ambulance with Dane. A nasty gunshot wound, he was still in surgery. Hayden would be there when he came out, she wasn't going anywhere.

Wade Landry had been whisked away by the State Department, along with Arnie. The locals hadn't liked the jurisdiction power play, but after being slapped down, they licked their wounds with a lot of muttering about cowboys playing lone ranger.

Now that dawn arrived, divers would soon head down to recover Eric's body.

Jillian shivered.

Under the blanket, Trent tightened his hold. He rubbed the palm of his hand down her arm.

"What are you going to do now?" Her gaze locked on the debris lapping against the shoreline, she tried to ignore the way the vise around her chest squeezed the air from her lungs.

"Now as in this morning?" He stared out at the water. "Or now as in the next few days?"

One corner of her mouth lifted. Neither, but she'd go along with him for now. *God, where's my courage when I need it?* "As in this isn't really over, is it? Even though Eric's dead and once Arnie recovers, he'll be in prison somewhere. For a long time."

"Your sister is safe. I have an answer for Ben on why the Oasis was blown up. Why wouldn't this be over?"

"Because we have no idea who helped Eric on the Cadeau side."

Trent shrugged. "Not my investigation any longer."

"Like that's going to stop you?" From the corner of her eye, she saw his lips twitch.

"Careful. You've done pretty well with the investigating part of this yourself. Maybe you're starting to like my sucky job."

"It's a loose end. Don't you want the answer?"

"Yeah, I would. But it's not my loose end any longer. It's Landry's. The DEA's." He shook his head. "It's out of my hands now."

"You're just going to let it go?"

"I didn't say that, now did I?"

She ran the tip of her tongue over her lips. "Biding

your time again?"

"Patience is a virtue, *darlin'*." He shrugged the shoulder pressed to hers. "Actually, Agent Simmons has already been notified. They have a few leads in Cadeau but will have to deal with International protocol and red tape. They'll get the guy. Probably before your dad is released."

"My dad." A small prickle of shame wound through her. "I'd sort of forgotten about him."

"I'm sure he'll give you an earful once he's out."

No doubt.

"I've been thinking." Trent rubbed a hand down her arm. "Last time I checked the weather in DC it was snowing. Freezing cold while it's warm and balmy down here. There's a field office in Miami. If I still have a job I thought I'd ask for a transfer."

"Really?" Her heart stopped. *Breathe, Jilly. Breathe.*

"I'd kind of like to see you in a bikini this summer."

"You've seen me in considerably *less* than that."

"Yeah, but I'm a guy and there's something about untying those little pieces of string."

Is he talking about continuing their pseudo, mutual lust, relationship, or exploring something deeper? She wet her suddenly dry lips.

He rubbed his cheek over her hair. "I wondered if you might want some help rebuilding Rosey's. I'm pretty good with a hammer. I could help rebuild your dream."

"Rosey's was never my dream." That clenched vise around her chest tightened in slow, painful increments. *I better grab what courage there is before it completely deserts me.* "I have a better idea."

"Really?"

With the heat of his gaze on her bowed head, she re-wet her lips and rushed the words before she lost her nerve. "What if we build a new dream? One for us both?"

Air, as in a shocked gasp, escaped Trent's mouth.

Nothing ventured. Definitely nothing gained.

I should've kept my mouth shut. She pressed her lips together.

"Jilly, we've known each other less than a week" His shadowed eyes unreadable, he stared at the water. His voice lowered to almost a whisper. "Both our lives are in limbo. Neither of us know where we'll be tomorrow or what the future will bring."

Courage, Jilly. Remember? Her foot already lodged in her mouth, what did she have to lose? She tilted her head and rubbed her cheek on his shoulder. "Quit playing devil's advocate."

A shudder scudded through his body, echoed through hers.

Dammit. Whatever's coming can't be good. She swallowed around the sudden lump in her throat. Pressed her lips together. Hard.

He continued to stare at the water. "There are things about me you don't understand."

"Explain them to me."

His eyes closed and his chin. A deep seated sigh raised then lowered his chest. "The Task Force I'm part of, the one headed by Ben Garrett, is comprised of men and woman with *extra* abilities. Abilities that set us apart from normal law enforcement."

"What kind of abilities?" She joined him in staring at the water.

"The kind that make – *made* – me an excellent Hunter. The Task Force is a covert group of psychics culled from different agencies."

"A group of psychic law enforcement officers?" No wonder he didn't blink at Rosey's presence. Jillian pursed her lips. "Sounds like a fun group."

"You have no idea."

"So you're psychic, what does that matter in the long run?"

"*Was* psychic, Jilly." He angled his head, gazed at the remnants of Rosey's Place. "I'm broken. Lots of theories. Ben's favorite is blowback from the shooting. That the bastard himself was psychic and when I took him out, he took part of me out. Maybe it'll come back. Maybe it won't."

"Trent."

"I'm *broken*."

"Not in any way that matters, Trent. Not to me."

"Jilly –"

"I *love* you." *Oh, God. I can't take that back.* "I love *you*. All of you. Even the broken pieces."

Silence stretched. He opened his mouth, closed it. Pulled her tight against him. "I love you, too."

That coiled knot inside loosened. *He loves me.* "Then live a little, *darlin'*. Take one of your calculated risks. On me."

A slow smile lifted the corners of his mouth. "There's no one I'd rather take a risk with, Jilly."

Yes.

"But as a cautious betting man, I have an innate need to hedge my bets."

Cautious? Since when? She pulled a slight bit away so she could see his face. "How are you going to do that?"

Those dark shadows deepened the blue of his eyes, spoke silent volumes of promise. Her breath caught as he ran the tip of his index finger over her lips. "Marry me, Jilly."

"Marry you?" She blinked and the loosened vise around her chest fell completely away.

"I'd be a fool to let you get away. You're strong and brave." He shrugged that shoulder again. "You don't need me to rescue you, you rescue yourself. And while you're at it, you managed to rescue me. From myself."

"I don't know what to say."

"We don't have to do anything right away. We can take our time, as long as you want. As long as I know you're mine. And I'm yours. Say yes."

She closed her eyes and pressed her hand over his. Then she kissed his palm. "Yes."

Trent tugged her into his embrace, wrapped her tight in his arms. The fireman's blanket slid off their shoulders. Behind them, in the east, the sun broke free of the lowering clouds. Brilliant dawn colors tinted the water around the charred remains of Rosey's.

A faint tinkle of glass against glass echoed in the distance.

"I think your grandmother approves." Trent kissed the side of her mouth, the tip of her nose. He rested his forehead against hers. "I love you, Jilly Rose."

"And I love you, Trent Sawyer."

To stay up to date with Pamela and to learn more about her upcoming releases, sign up for her newsletter:

http://eepurl.com/bbOUjv

If you enjoyed DARKWATER ECHOES and would like to see more stories in the PSI Sentinel series, please consider leaving a review for this book with your favorite ebook seller.

Every review is appreciated.

You can also visit her at the following places on the web:

www.PamelaMoran.com

facebook.com/pamelamoranauthor

goodreads.com/PamelaMoran

pinterest.com/pamelamoran

Twitter: Pam_Moran

Available 2017:

DARKWATER TIDES
PSI Sentinels, Darkwater Guardians (Book 2)

DANE PATRICK SLICED the last thin strip of prosciutto in half. He resisted the strong urge to flip his knife and stab it into the heavy maple chopping block.

Rosey's Crew, Caterers Extraordinaire.

Except this evening the kitchen portion of that crew consisted of himself and Hayden Rose, catering a fancy spring fundraiser aimed at the elite of Key Largo.

His fingers tightened on the knife handle before he loosened his grip and set the utensil aside. With a glance at the simple black watch on his right wrist, he drummed his fingers along the edge of the green, white veined, marble counter.

Three more hours. Then escape.

From outside a steady drone of sounds filtered in through the arched doorway to his right. Laughter mixed with the low murmur of voices in conversation, the soft mix of live jazz.

Damn.

He pulled at the collar of his stiffly starched, short sleeved, button down white shirt. What he'd give, *right now*, to be out there playing with the band. Lost in music. Instead of trapped in this oversized kitchen trying to ignore the mere presence of the one woman who bothered the hell out of him.

Hayden.

How long does it take to grab a container of peppercorns from the damn pantry?

Dane shoved away from the counter, ignored the ache in his side from the gunshot wound he'd suffered two months previous. His mouth tight, he angled his head to each side, lifted his chin, and rotated his shoulders, but the movements did nothing to ease the tension riding his body.

Damn Hayden Rose.

He wiped a hand over his mouth, spun towards the double doors of the Butler's Pantry.

I'll find that damn pepper myself. Get on with the next food assignment. Stay busy. Then get the hell out of here.

Away from Hayden. Away from temptation.

In that order.

Before he had time to change his mind, he strode across the long kitchen towards the pantry then yanked open the double doors. Hayden, her green cat eyes wide and locked on his, stood behind the butcher's block in the center of the spacious pantry. A dark haired woman, a few inches shorter, held a hand over Hayden's mouth and a gun to her temple.

Dane's chest constricted for half a breath.

Crap. Double fuck.

Hayden's tawny curls, pulled back at her nape, left the paleness of her normally tanned face evident in the harsh glare of the overhead light. *Hang in there, Sweetheart.*

His nose twitched at the sharp bite of scattered peppercorns. A thick arc of the stuff trailed across the wooden block. Only moving his eyes the barest amount, he did a quick scan. No knives in here. Nothing to counter the woman's gun.

"What's going on here?" His stance wide, he raised his hands, palms forward, and gestured with his chin towards the weapon. "That's not a toy."

"Really? Who do you think you are? Sherlock Holmes?" The stranger's dark, feral eyes flashed with impatience, and maybe a hint of uncertainty.

"At your service." He dipped his chin a fraction.

"Funny man." The woman's wide mouth curved downward. She dug her thumb and fingers into Hayden's cheeks. "Your boyfriend, pretty lady?"

Still full of fear, Hayden's eyes narrowed.

"See, that's what you and I need to talk about." The woman, dressed in a white shirt and black pants, same as he and Hayden, leaned closer to Hayden's ear. "Boyfriends."

Available now:

GAVIN'S WOMAN
(PSI Sentinels, A Darkwater Novella)

Gavin Dunbar, liaison between the PSI and the government, is a low-level psychic himself. A man of the present who believes the future is too nebulous, too fluid – that it can't be trusted. His reasons are mired deep in a past he has no desire to examine. After all, in his world, having a soul-mate doesn't equate to happily-ever-after.

Tragedy has brought Calea Fontaine to a crossroads and has her reassessing her future without the man she loves. A seer from a long line of seers, Calea knows, firsthand, that while Fate might try to guide a person along a path, Free Will has a way of trumping Destiny.

Or does it?

Along the storm ravaged Oregon coast, a predator stalks Calea with an obsession born of a dark ache, an overwhelming need to control and possess at any cost. The only obstacle standing in his way is Gavin Dunbar's own obsession.

STOLEN SPIRIT
(PSI Sentinels, Book One)

Hearing his dead ex-girlfriend's voice in an empty room is enough to make a man question his sanity. Worse is when that ex insists she shouldn't have died. Broken cop Jake Carrigan has no interest in delving into a past full of heartache and regrets. But he can't deny she still matters, even if she's simply a voice in his head.

Hannah Dixon is having a hard time believing she's dead. How can she be when she feels so much inside? She can see Jake, can talk to him, but she can't touch him. And right now, touching Jake is all she wants.

Jake's probe into Hannah's death stirs up a sinister psychic link, something dark that will stop at nothing to keep its secrets. To protect her own heart, Hannah left Jake once. Can she leave him again to protect his life?

BLIND SIGHT
(PSI Sentinels, Book Two)

Death plagues Gabe Nicholetti's dreams, but he can't save the people in his visions. The most he can do is bring their killers to justice. But this time, this victim makes it all personal.

Rily Carrigan is a dead woman, or she will be in a matter of days as her past rushes forward to shatter her carefully constructed world. But Rily doesn't believe fate is absolute. How is she going to convince the man who's seen too many die that it's possible to save her life?

Just outside a small, Oregon town, something malevolent lurks, waiting to seize what was once promised then stolen. Together, Gabe and Rily need to find a way to deny fate and keep Rily live.

ELSIE'S SECRET

(A PSI Sentinel Novella)

A PSI agent, Sebastian Alexander has secrets that once came between him and the woman he still loves. Finding her prowling around where she doesn't belong turns his simple reconnaissance into a rescue mission threatening to blow everything apart. Is he willing to risk his secrets to save her life?

Elsie Quartermaine has one goal. Save her nephew from a sadistic kidnapper. Sebastian is the one man who can help her. But divulging her secret puts more than her life in jeopardy. Can she trust Sebastian with her nephew's life? Her own? What about her heart?

As dawn creeps over the horizon, can they find enough trust in each other to stay alive?

To stay up to date with Pamela and to learn more about her upcoming releases, sign up for her newsletter:

eepurl.com/bbOUjv